New York Times and **USA Today** Bestselling Author

Diane Capri

"Full of thrills and tension, but smart and human, too. Kim Otto is a great, great character. I love her."
Lee Child, *#1 World Wide Bestselling Author of Jack Reacher Thrillers*

"[A] welcome surprise… [W]orks from the first page to 'The End'."
Larry King

"Swift pacing and ongoing suspense are always present… [L]ikable protagonist who uses her political connections for a good cause…Readers should eagerly anticipate the next [book]."
Top Pick, Romantic Times

"…offers tense legal drama with courtroom overtones, twisty plot, and loads of Florida atmosphere. Recommended."
Library Journal

"[A] fast-paced legal thriller…energetic prose…an appealing heroine…clever and capable supporting cast…[that will] keep readers waiting for the next [book]."
Publishers Weekly

"Expertise shines on every page."
Margaret Maron, Edgar, Anthony, Agatha and Macavity Award-Winning MWA Grand Master

ALSO BY DIANE CAPRI

The Hunt for Jack Reacher Series

(in publication order with Lee Child source books in parentheses)

Don't Know Jack (The Killing Floor)

Jack in a Box (*novella*)

Jack and Kill (*novella*)

Get Back Jack (Bad Luck & Trouble)

Jack in the Green (*novella*)

Jack and Joe (The Enemy)

Deep Cover Jack (Persuader)

Jack the Reaper (The Hard Way)

Black Jack (Running Blind/The Visitor)

Ten Two Jack (The Midnight Line)

Jack of Spades (Past Tense)

Prepper Jack (Die Trying)

Full Metal Jack (The Affair)

Jack Frost (61 Hours)

Jack of Hearts • (Worth Dying For)

Straight Jack • (A Wanted Man)

Jack Knife • (Never Go Back)

The Jess Kimball Thrillers Series

Fatal Distraction

Fatal Demand

Fatal Error

Fatal Fall

Fatal Game

Fatal Bond

Fatal Enemy (*novella*)

Fatal Edge (*novella*)

Fatal Past (*novella*)

Fatal Dawn

CAST OF CHARACTERS

Michael Flint
Kathryn (Katie) Scarlett
Alonzo Drake
Sebastian (Baz) Shaw
Felix Crane
Laura Oakwood
Selma Oakwood Prieto
Bette Maxwell
Madeline (Maddy) Scarlett

and
Carlos Gaspar

For the readers who have supported me and enjoyed my books and asked for more.

I couldn't do this without you.

Thank you.

"Nothing stays secret forever. Save time. Call me first."

—*Michael Flint*

CHAPTER ONE

MICHAEL FLINT SHIVERED IN the damp morning chill. He was a long way from Houston, the place he called home these days. He hadn't planned to be here in London long enough to need a coat.

Get in, get out, and no one gets hurt. That was his goal.

Flint watched and waited while each element fell according to plan.

He had a great view. Mayfair was one of the most exclusive areas of London, and the neo-Georgian houses that surrounded Grosvenor Square reeked of very old money used to full advantage.

The verdant park in the center of the square reflected the British climate that ensured no plant went unwatered for long.

Bronze statues of Eisenhower and Reagan stood rigidly proud in the corners. They were an unlikely sight in this most British of spots, but the affluent district had long been popular with Americans, which explained Flint's presence here.

At 8:20 a.m., a postman appeared at the end of the street, precisely on time, as he had every day this week. He worked his way from door to door, pushing bundles of mail through ornate brass letterboxes.

Flint was dressed in black jeans, black leather jacket, and supple black leather gloves that fit like a second skin. He balanced easily on the deserted gantry platform halfway up the tower crane.

The construction crew working on the north side of Grosvenor Square would arrive in forty minutes. An American crew would have been on the job hours ago, but construction times were strictly limited here to the hours wealthy residents found acceptable.

Plenty of time to get what he came for if the postman followed his routine.

Flint scanned the large garden square seventy feet below once more. Frost crusted the grass inside the park, which was uncharacteristically empty of people. Otherwise, he saw nothing out of the ordinary.

He shivered and hunched deeper into his jacket. He'd been waiting only an hour, but the damp cold compressed his body from all sides like he was standing naked in a meat locker.

He felt as stiff as the statues in the park. By the time the air had warmed enough for the usual crowds to enjoy being outdoors, he'd be long gone.

He had a clear sight line to the home, thirty-five yards away, of James Ashton, the ostensible owner of a priceless painting.

The painting wasn't rightfully his.

Ashton's uncle, Reginald Taylor, had inherited it from his father. But in 1940, the Nazis had stolen it from a French woman.

A month ago, the same French woman had turned to Flint after her other attempts to find it had failed. She wanted her painting back and Flint's job was to get it.

Normally, his persuasive powers were formidable, but experience proved they rarely worked on the dead. And Reginald Taylor was very dead.

Which was what had led Flint here. To James Ashton, Taylor's heir.

He was also Taylor's murderer.

When Flint tracked Taylor down, he'd found that Ashton had killed his rich relative in Taylor's New York apartment some time ago and left him stuffed in the freezer.

Because Taylor was something of a recluse, his death hadn't been discovered until Flint had reported the murder anonymously.

Ashton was now running from the law, holed up in his London penthouse with a savage little Welsh Corgi and a professional around-the-clock security detail.

Ashton hadn't once stepped outside the luxury apartment since he slid inside, cloaked by darkness, last week.

Flint had watched the place for seven days before a plan had emerged.

Not a perfect solution, but a workable one.

Flint adjusted his earpiece. He heard only the expected silence from inside the residence.

Ashton and his companions didn't routinely gather in the common rooms until after nine o'clock.

Flint raised his binoculars to check the sensitive listening device he had propelled with an illegal air pistol from his position atop a tourist bus two days ago. He confirmed that the device remained glued to the top-floor window.

He checked his pockets.

He felt the remote control and the small crowbar resting against his sides where he'd placed them.

The pistol snugged into his belt at the flat center of his back looked lethal enough at a glance, which was all the inspection time he planned to allow. The puny thing was one of the few remaining legal weapons in Britain only because it had no stopping power.

Ashton might not recognize the gun as worthless, but his security detail would if they got a close enough look.

Flint picked up a crossbow fitted with a serrated dart designed to embed itself into wood. The dart was secured to high-strength wire. He'd secured the wire to the tower crane.

A leggy, lithe brunette crossed the square, chattering away on her cell phone.

Two nights ago, Flint had followed her to a bar, where she bent his ear for an hour. She was broke and only too happy to carry his message for the right price.

He checked his watch.

Exactly 8:28.

He'd paid the right price, and she was right on time. He'd promised her a generous bonus when she completed the job, and her eyes lit up like sparklers. He nodded as if she could see his approval from that distance.

She crossed the road, made her way between rows of security barriers, and entered the large concrete building that occupied the entire western edge of the square. The American embassy.

The message she carried was simple. He'd instructed her to say that Ashton would be surrendering himself into custody. She would also mention that the authorities might have to turn a blind eye to the manner in which Ashton actually surrendered.

Flint had supplied her with enough details to interest law enforcement on both sides of the Atlantic.

But she would reveal those details only after Ashton signed the necessary documents—which Flint carried in his pocket—relinquishing all legal claims to the French woman's painting.

Flint's gaze returned to the postman, who had now reached Ashton's residence.

He climbed the steps.

He pushed a bundle of mail and a small yellow envelope through Ashton's letterbox.

The postman descended the stairs and moved on toward the next house.

Flint moved his tongue over his teeth and pulled the remote from his pocket. He counted slowly to ten, giving the postman time to move a safe distance away and the security detail time to retrieve the envelope.

At precisely 8:45 a.m., Flint pushed the button on the remote.

He imagined the yellow package expanding exactly as it had during his tests.

The edges of the package would burst. An almost invisible dust would spray out, covering everyone within a ten-foot radius.

Only it wasn't just dust.

It was *Mucuna pruriens*, an itching powder so incredibly powerful that the plant from which it was derived was known as the Devil Bean in Nigeria.

There was enough powder to disable the security detail for the length of time Flint would need. Longer if they tried to wash the powder off with water.

Flint fired the crossbow at the solid wood center of Ashton's rooftop garden.

The dart landed squarely as aimed, taking the long wire to its destination.

He tested the wire with his full weight, and the dart held. Flint clipped himself on and zip-lined straight to the flat rooftop.

He pulled the crowbar from his jacket and pried open the door that led from the roof to the interior of the penthouse. He headed straight for the stairs, pulling the pistol from his belt as he ran.

He'd estimated sixty seconds to find Ashton, collect his signature, and then convince him to walk down five flights of stairs, across six hundred feet of the most expensive real estate in London, step onto American soil, and capitulate.

No problem, right?

Flint reached the top floor of the penthouse apartment.

The floor plans he'd studied showed the kitchen at the base of the rooftop stairs. The remaining two thousand square feet on the top floor was an open floor plan with breathtaking views of Mayfair.

The spiral staircase in the center led down to bedrooms on the floor below.

Flint barely noticed the stunning views as he passed down through the sixth floor and entered the master suite directly below, on the fifth floor.

He stopped outside the massive door to the master suite for a quick breath. He raised the gun to shooting position. He silently pushed the door open and stepped inside.

A quick scan of the enormous bedroom revealed an exceptionally high king-size bed against one wall. Sheets mussed. Pillows tossed.

Except for a snoring, short-legged Welsh Corgi, the bed was empty.

The house had no exits, secret or otherwise, that Flint had failed to monitor, so Ashton was somewhere inside the house. Hopefully alone.

Because the air pistol would not fool anyone for long.

Flint scanned the bedroom walls until he located the nearly invisible panel that could have been a doorway.

He padded quickly to the panel and pushed. It opened silently to a modern bathroom, massive even by his Texas standards.

He glanced back at the Corgi. Still sleeping. Some watchdog.

In the center of the dark granite tile was a matching marble bath large enough to accommodate four adults.

On Flint's right the same marble lined a similar-sized shower with curved glass.

On his left were a bank of blindingly bright gilt cabinetry, mirrors, countertops, sinks, and golden faucets fit for King Louis XIV.

Straight ahead, opposite the swinging panel door, was a hinged, six-foot steamed-up glass panel that led to a sauna.

Flint headed across the marble floor, rapped on the glass, and stood back, poised to shoot.

Ashton pulled the glass door inward and stepped through the steam. His well-muscled body was naked and glistening with sweat.

"James Ashton, I presume." Flint leveled the air pistol directly at the shorter man's heart, as if the gun's payload might actually cause more than a bad bruise if his aim landed even a millimeter off target.

Ashton's dark eyes narrowed. He pulled his arm from behind his back.

Flint instantly recognized the weapon Ashton held in his hand because he owned one himself.

Glock 19 Gen4. Utilitarian, tough, reliable. Comfortable grip, controllable recoil, easily concealed. Used by law enforcement because of its stopping power.

A perfect choice for a man anticipating precisely this situation.

"Drop it," Flint said, as if he could back up the threat with the puny air pistol.

His life and history lacked many things.

He'd never known stability or human warmth or a conventional existence of any kind.

He counted on danger first, unpredictability second.

He accepted everything exactly as it came.

He felt no shock, no surprise, no disbelief.

His entire life had trained him for moments precisely like this. Ashton was a problem in need of an immediate and practical solution.

Nothing more.

Nothing less.

Flint's brain registered the micromovement of Ashton's right index finger beginning to apply pressure on the trigger.

He knew where the first bullet would be aimed.

Ashton smirked.

Flint dropped onto his left side as Ashton fired.

He twisted away as he hit the floor.

He heard the shot and felt the air move past the empty space where his right shoulder had been a split second before. Glass exploded and filled the room with reflecting shards like a kaleidoscope.

Ashton's eyes widened in surprise. He'd expected the first shot to do the job.

His combat skills were rudimentary. He'd practiced a specific plan, probably on a range somewhere, with a tutor. He was unable to react to the unexpected.

The Corgi began barking from the bedroom.

Ashton twisted his body, moved his right arm stiffly, and aimed the Glock toward Flint again.

Flint ducked behind the marble bath in the center of the room.

As Ashton aimed and fired, he moved in the opposite direction, shooting on the run.

The Corgi's barking intensified.

Ashton's second shot hit the marble. A boulder-sized chunk blasted off and landed four inches from Flint's leg. Chips slashed his face. He felt the blood trickle down his cheek.

Ashton reached the open panel door. He grabbed a pair of sweatpants from the hook with his left hand and struggled to don them as he moved into the bedroom, firing again and again into the bathroom where Flint crouched behind the marble tub.

The Corgi was frantic now. His barking was almost as deafening as the gunshots bouncing inside the tiled bathroom.

Ashton fired again until the Glock's fifteen-round clip was done, tossed the gun aside, and dashed through the bedroom door into the corridor.

Flint scrambled to follow after he registered the empty weapon's clang on the floor. He was two steps toward the bedroom when he turned and went back for the Glock.

A man like Ashton would keep his gun close while he slept.

Flint ran to the bedside table. He rummaged around in the drawers while the Corgi's snarling, snapping barks continued.

He found two more fifteen-round magazines.

He slapped one of them into place and dropped the second into his pocket before he rushed out in hot pursuit.

CHAPTER TWO

FLINT SPRINTED DOWN THE corridor, following Ashton's only possible route toward the elevator. He reached the elevator after the doors had closed and the car was already descending.

He shoved the Glock into his waistband and dashed down the emergency stairs to the ground floor.

He pulled the door open.

Two armed security guards stomped and shouted in the entranceway, covered in *Mucuna pruriens* powder, cursing and scratching their arms raw.

Flint glanced at the elevator, which was still descending.

He ducked behind the door and ran down two more flights to the basement level, where the staircase ended. He opened the fire door and stepped into a parking garage.

The elevator had been called back upstairs. Ashton must have exited into the garage.

Flint looked around for Ashton's head bobbing above the vehicles. He spied a valet stand on the opposite side of the elevator door.

A powerful engine roared to life. Flint watched as a glistening black Ferrari with Ashton at the wheel raced up the ramp and out to the street.

Flint surveyed the closest vehicles and the keys on the valet stand. He grabbed a key marked "Suzuki" and inserted it into the only Suzuki motorcycle near the stand.

Seconds later, Flint raced up and out of the garage, following Ashton's Ferrari along the small street behind Grosvenor Square.

He couldn't see the Ferrari, but he could hear it straight ahead before it turned south along Park Lane.

Flint ignored all distractions and concentrated on the Ferrari.

Ashton drove wildly, dangerously, looping around Hyde Park Corner to get away.

Flint leaned forward over the Suzuki and accelerated flat out behind, but it was no match for the powerful sports car.

Flint had come too far to give up now. He whipped his head around looking for an opening. It was still early. Still cold. Not many pedestrians and tourists along the sidewalks.

He found his chance. A wide pedestrian walkway, almost empty.

Flint pointed the Suzuki and opened the throttle around Wellington Arch.

A young woman pushing a baby stroller yelled and shook her fist.

Flint saw the Ferrari ahead, speeding up Constitution Hill toward Buckingham Palace. Flint gained ground on the long, straight road.

He glanced up to see deep red traffic lights at the top of the hill and a line of vehicles waiting for the green.

Ashton moved into the empty oncoming travel lane and sped around the stopped vehicles and through the red light.

Horns blasted in protest.

Flint's Suzuki followed right behind, almost on the Ferrari's bumper.

Ashton turned across the plaza toward the Victoria Memorial.

Pedestrians, bicycles, and vehicles moved out of his way, horns blasting, fists shaking, voices raised to outrage levels.

An old man hobbled into the car's path. Maybe he was blind or deaf or even suffering from dementia, but unlike the others, he didn't hustle out of the way.

The Ferrari bore down on the man, almost right on top of him before Ashton jerked the wheel to the left to avoid running the old fellow down.

The Ferrari spun dangerously and stalled. Angry onlookers surrounded the car, yelling.

Flint stopped the Suzuki and dismounted.

He pulled the Glock from his waist.

People stepped aside when they saw the gun.

Flint approached the Ferrari. He tapped the window with the Glock. Ashton looked up, wild-eyed and disheveled.

"Get out," Flint said.

Ashton nodded. Flint backed up to allow him to open the door.

Ashton started the Ferrari and floored the accelerator.

The wheels were still cocked hard left.

Flint jumped out of the way.

The wheels spun, pushing the Ferrari sideways. Ashton couldn't correct. He slammed into the steps of the memorial.

Flint dashed toward the Ferrari but before he reached the car, Ashton leapt out, still barefoot and wearing only sweatpants.

Flint chased him down and jumped onto his back, propelling them both into the kidney-shaped pool surrounding the memorial.

Dazed, but not defeated, Ashton swung a looping right.

Flint blocked with his left elbow, deflecting the weak arm, and countered with a hard right uppercut.

Ashton's jaw snapped shut. His head whipped back. His eyes closed, and he slumped forward.

Flint's blood boiled, but he had come too far to kill the bastard without getting what he needed first.

He pushed Ashton up against the low wall and held him there with his forearm while he steadied his breathing.

Then he reached down and scooped a handful of the icy water, and threw it in Ashton's face.

Again. And again.

Until Ashton looked up and glared at him.

"What the hell do you want, man?" Ashton whined, blinking and shaking the rivulets off his cheeks. "I don't even *know* you."

"Drop the gun!"

Flint looked behind him. Five men wearing bright red ceremonial uniforms were pointing very unceremonial assault rifles at him.

The man in the middle motioned toward the ground with the barrel of his gun. "Queen's Guard! Drop the weapon!"

The crowd had grown larger. There was a sea of men, women, and children along with a few dogs standing well back from the memorial.

Sirens approached from a distance. Flint saw blue flashing lights rounding the corner and heading his way.

He raised his arm slowly and placed the Glock on the edge of the stone wall. He turned to face the guard, both hands in the air, palms out. He donned his best smile, the somewhat friendly one.

"I'm an American citizen. I—"

He felt Ashton thrashing around in the water.

He turned back as Ashton reached the stone wall and grabbed the Glock.

Flint lunged out of the way a split second before one of the guards fired three times in rapid succession.

Each shot hit Ashton squarely in the torso and punched him back like a rag doll. He collapsed into the shallow pool as his blood pumped briefly and turned the water around his body sickly red.

The guards trained their weapons on Flint. He didn't move.

With Ashton dead, Flint's mission was stalled but not over. He'd find another Reginald Taylor heir and get the required signatures before the deadline. He always did, and this time would be no exception.

But first he'd need to avoid the criminal consequences of their screaming car chase across London, a task that would undoubtedly involve a lot more than the embassy turning a blind eye.

He'd be lucky if he spent only one night in the cells, but he'd spent plenty of time in worse places.

CHAPTER THREE

THE TRIP TO PADDINGTON Green Police Station was routine. All presumed terrorists were processed in the typically blue-and-gray Harrow Road facility.

Sixteen cells were located belowground for high-security prisoners held for questioning in a separate custody suite. Flint had been there before.

He was no terrorist, but the Queen's Guard would naturally have assumed otherwise.

He didn't fault them. He'd have made the same choice.

The long list of crimes he had committed today alone justified the assumption.

If they ran a routine background check, the situation would become infinitely more difficult.

Simply possessing the Glock was enough to make them lock him away somewhere. Ashton would have to be explained, too.

As Scarlett had told him when they were young miscreants long ago, cops judge you by the creeps you're arrested with, whether or not the dudes are worse than you.

Flint's first hour in the interrogation room passed slowly.

The chairs were uncomfortable, the room was too hot, and no one offered him coffee or anything else.

He wasn't charged immediately, which was a good sign. He had a better chance of quick release if no formal charges were made.

Once paperwork entered the system, it took on a life of its own and would need to be dealt with.

Shortly after his arrival, the Metropolitan Police began their tedious processes and one of the young officers read him his rights.

After the formal reading, Flint remained silent. The officer said, "You want a lawyer or not?"

Flint pretended to consider the question for a few seconds. A quick response would cause additional problems. "I think things will go faster if we skip lawyers, don't you?"

"Suit yourself." The young officer turned and left the room.

Flint had made the lawyer mistake before. Lawyers delayed and complicated these situations beyond all reason. He was better off on his own.

Scarlett knew whom to call if he didn't check in with her before close of business today. He could rely on her to follow through.

After another hour, the investigating officer entered. This one was older and more experienced. He introduced himself as Deputy Inspector Gates.

Flint didn't alter his relaxed posture. Gates sat on the chair across the table, rested his forearms on the metal, and folded his hands.

"We're investigating your situation, Mr. Flint, and we have a few questions for you." His Cockney accent was thick and his tone firm.

Flint didn't engage in role-play. "I have the right to make a phone call."

"You can do that after you answer my questions." Gates was a heavy man and the room was uncomfortably warm. Sweat trickled down the sides of his face.

"I'll hear your questions after I make my phone call."

Gates frowned and wiped the sweat away. "You were offered a lawyer and you refused."

"I don't want to call a lawyer, obviously."

"No one else can possibly help you right now, Mr. Flint." Grant's patience was already in short supply. Predictably.

"That's my decision to make, isn't it?" Flint's tone remained calm and steady.

"We've run a background check. We found your passport, but no further information about you. Nothing but a brick wall. Why is that, Mr. Flint? What are you hiding?" Gates wiped his brow with his palm and rubbed sweat onto his pants.

Flint said nothing.

The back and forth continued like that for a while. Gates varied his techniques, but Flint never varied his nonresponses.

In the end, Flint stonewalled until Gates recognized the stalemate. He'd left Gates no choice but to lock him in the cell and leave him there.

Flint lay on the cot and covered his eyes with his arm. A nap was a good idea.

He wasn't worried. He had plans for the weekend.

Scarlett would make the phone call and he'd be back at the hotel before midnight.

CHAPTER FOUR

FLINT EMERGED FROM THE luxuriously hot shower, toweled off, and slid into the white terry-cloth robe hanging on the back of the door. At long last, he'd been extracted from custody and returned to the hotel paid for by the French woman who owned the expensive painting.

His contact at the American embassy should have deployed after six hours of radio silence. The guy was as reliable as an old dog and he owed Flint big time. Flint's release had never been in question, but the delay was longer than expected.

His date was not pleased.

Ginger had waited as long as she could, but the narrow window of time they'd planned to spend sightseeing in London had been consumed by his hours in custody.

She'd left him a note by the hotel's phone before she caught her flight to Barcelona.

See you next time. xoxo G.

He crumpled the paper and dropped it into the trash.

He punched the speaker on his ringing cell phone.

"This is Michael Flint." His voice sounded hoarse in his own ears. Caused by the dampness in the cells overnight, probably. He cleared his throat and ran splayed fingers through his wet black hair.

"Mr. Flint," said a woman's voice he didn't recognize, "please hold for Mr. Sebastian Shaw."

Flint recognized the name. Shaw was a wealthy Texan, the kind who made his money the old-fashioned way—his daddy gave it to him. But he was clever enough. He'd built the original millions into an invitation to the billion-dollar club at least twenty years ago.

The photos Flint had seen in the newspapers suggested that Shaw lived a pampered country-club life. Slim, well dressed, with expensively darkened hair that otherwise would have been white by now. Plastic surgeons were likely responsible for the youthful face. Shaw was probably about sixty, give or take a few years.

"Fine," Flint said. Nothing more.

He skipped the usual questions, such as how Shaw had acquired his name and his private cell number. Shaw was the kind of man who had access to anything and anyone, anytime.

He also skipped the useless questions, such as why Shaw was calling him. The call could only be about one thing—business. They didn't travel in the same social circles. Not even close.

Flint looked at the phone's screen and identified the caller's origin. Houston, Texas. It was early evening there, the middle of the business day for a man like Sebastian Shaw.

Flint walked into the hotel suite's sitting room and placed the phone on the table where room service had laid out his meal. A crystal balloon glass filled with deep red wine twinkling in the lamplight waited beside his steak. So tempting.

After he'd been holding the open phone line for five minutes, his stomach growled again. He hadn't eaten for the past thirty hours. He lifted the silver cover off the plate and smelled his expensive food, which was going cold.

He didn't care if Sebastian Shaw was one of the two richest men in Texas. Flint's body was hungry and his bank account wasn't.

He'd give Shaw another thirty seconds. After that, the guy could call back tomorrow. Or never. Flint didn't care.

A man like Shaw was bound to be nothing but trouble anyway. Flint had a job to finish, and he'd had plenty of trouble already.

Almost as if he'd sensed Flint's limited patience, a brusque voice invaded the room through the phone's speaker exactly two seconds before the expiration of his thirty-second deadline.

"Flint, this is Baz Shaw. I need to meet with you tomorrow morning. My office."

A Sunday-morning meeting?

Flint was scheduled to fly back to Houston today. He could meet late tomorrow morning.

But his experience said giving in to any man right at the outset was always the wrong way to go.

Clients called only when they seriously needed him. He was always the last resort. He held all the trump cards, which was exactly the way he liked it.

"Unfortunately, Mr. Shaw, I'm not available tomorrow."

Which was technically true.

He'd already promised the French woman an in-person report on the status of her painting.

After that, he'd planned a working dinner spent searching for Reginald Taylor's remaining heirs. The most likely heir to be in possession of the painting now lived in Scotland.

He wanted the current case wrapped up before he moved on to the next, and his thirty-four-hour stint at Paddington Green had put him behind schedule.

"The matter is urgent," Shaw said, with no urgency in his tone at all.

The hell with this. Flint picked up his wineglass and sipped. "I can recommend someone."

"You are the one I want." Shaw's deep voice remained steady, but Flint heard the force behind his words all the same.

Shaw was used to getting what he wanted.

The clash of wills was inevitable. Might as well have it right at the start.

Assuming this was the start of something.

Which he hadn't agreed to yet.

He accepted work on his own terms or not at all. "Mr. Shaw, my dinner is getting cold."

"I'm disappointed," Shaw replied, as if he were a complete stranger to the condition, which he probably was. "I used my connections to get you released tonight because Katie Scarlett assured me you were the only man for the job. Was she wrong?"

His connections? Scarlett? What the hell had she told him?

Flint swiped an open palm across his face. Saying no to Shaw was easy.

Refusing Scarlett had been impossible ever since she'd wrestled him to the ground when they were kids.

She was the first human being who had ever cared about him. They'd been through a lot of tough times since then. He'd do anything for her, even when she didn't make it easy.

He'd owe her forever.

She was the closest thing to family he'd ever had.

Simple as that.

He set the wineglass down, squared his shoulders, and bowed to the inevitable as graciously as possible. "How can I help you, Mr. Shaw?"

"Tomorrow morning. Ten o'clock. My office." Shaw's voice and manner remained unchanged, as if he hadn't just coerced Flint to cooperate. He disconnected.

Flint shook his head. The man was a demanding, cold bastard, for sure.

Flint worked with difficult wealthy clients all the time. They were the only ones who could afford his fees.

But Flint could already tell this guy was going to be a special kind of trouble.

He glanced at the digital clock on the bedside table. Running out of time.

He uncovered the steak, cut off a healthy chunk, and popped it into his mouth before he pressed the "1" button on his speed dial.

She'd occupied that position since his first cell phone, mainly because she was the only person in his life who'd been with him that long.

"Scarlett Investigations. This is Kathryn Scarlett speaking." She paused a moment, probably checking the caller ID. "Sorry, Flint. Give my apologies to Ginger for ruining your weekend. Shaw insisted that you were the only man for the job. And he's one of my two best clients. Pays me more than half a million a year. What else could I do?"

Flint chewed and swallowed the first bite of steak while she talked. Even cold, the steak was something special.

He offered token resistance because she expected it. "So you don't care if I turn him down then?"

From long experience, he knew she'd start talking and keep at it until he capitulated. Which gave him time to wolf down the steak.

"Turn him down? Why would you do that? Shaw's a jerk, but his check always clears. I'm not running a charity here, Flint. It's fine for *you* to work whenever you damned well please, but *I've* got bills to pay and a kid to support." She barely paused for breath.

Flint hadn't seen Scarlett in a couple of months at least. He imagined her behind her desk, readers perched on her nose magnifying eyes to the size of quarters, wild black hair, doing five other things simultaneously as she talked into the speaker.

"Besides, he's right. This isn't a routine heir-hunting job. If it were, I'd have already done it myself. This woman is more than simply hard to find. She's a ghost. Hasn't been seen or heard from in at least two decades. I've already exhausted all the usual resources. Who else am I gonna call, huh?"

Flint had finished about half his steak and a few bites of everything else. Another couple of open-ended questions and he'd have filled his belly. "Who's the woman and why is Shaw looking for her?"

"So this one is right up your alley. Her name was Laura Oakwood, last records we found. Who knows what she's calling herself these days. Shaw's gotta find her so he can buy Juan Garcia Field. You know it's the largest independently owned land grant field in rural Texas? Shaw won't pay your usual fee. He knows you usually take half. But half is way too much money on this one. He'll pay ten percent."

She waited half a moment to allow objections and he grunted to get her moving again.

"Anyway, Shaw says he's had a first option on that field for years. And if he can get Laura Oakwood to sign over her mineral rights before the option expires, he can buy the field and, I don't know, make even more billions, I guess. Who cares? We've been looking for Laura Oakwood for weeks. No luck. Anyway, we know she's not dead, which would solve the problem. Or at least we can't confirm her death, and believe me, we've tried. And Shaw's option expires in less than, um, sixty-nine hours. We've got until eleven o'clock Tuesday morning, Houston time. You're our last hope."

"*Our last hope?* Come on, Scarlett. Cut the drama." Flint scowled, pushed the empty plate away, and picked up the wineglass. "What happens if Shaw misses his deadline?"

"Don't even think about it." Her tone was stern. She never took crap from anyone, especially Flint. Hadn't since they were kids standing back-to-back in the school yard and wasn't likely to start now.

No wonder she wasn't married. Who in the world would put up with her every day?

He was as close to her as anybody except her kid, and even he needed time away simply to keep the peace.

Of course, she'd say the same about him.

"Shaw can't get an extension on the option, if that's what you're asking."

"Why not?" Flint glanced at his watch. Time to go. He dropped the robe onto the plush gray carpet and dressed while she talked.

"Because Felix Crane holds the backup option and he's already put the money in escrow. As soon as Shaw's option expires, the prize is Crane's. End of story. Everybody knows they hate each other." She paused for a quick breath. "Crane's a client, too, and he's no teddy bear either."

Felix Crane was another name Flint recognized.

A mean son of a bitch, by all accounts, just like Shaw.

They were well matched in every respect.

Crane's background and his net worth were similar to Shaw's, give or take an oil glut or shortage or two.

Their rivalry was legendary.

Biblical, even.

Just like she said.

"Standing between warring giants isn't a healthy way to live, Scarlett. Those guys have the morals of a ravenous lion. Either one will eat you alive without even thinking about it." He picked up his watch, slid his wallet into his jacket.

"You got that right. I don't know what started their blood feud, but I've been in the same room with those two and I can tell you, the experience is not pleasant." She stopped to draw another quick breath.

She'd been a competitive swimmer once. She could hold a lot of oxygen in those lungs. "If Shaw doesn't come up with Oakwood's signature on that consent form before the final bell, he loses. There's no way he'll allow that to happen. *No way.* He'll do whatever it takes. *Whatever.* You understand?"

"We'll figure it out. Someone knows where she is. Nobody simply disappears. Not remotely possible." Flint tossed the rest of his things into a bag and glanced around the suite to be sure he'd left nothing of value. "Send me everything you've got so far on the Oakwood woman. I'll read it on the plane."

"Already done. I don't want to talk about this stuff on an open line, but I sent my summaries in encrypted files to your secure server this morning so you'd have the info before Shaw called. Didn't you read them? You finished that French woman's painting job yesterday, didn't you? What the hell have you been doing since then, anyway?" His jaw tensed.

"Not much, thanks to you."

"Yeah, yeah," she said, blowing off his complaint.

Flint hated to owe anybody anything. Owing Shaw a favor was so far from ideal the distance might exceed a round-trip ride to Mars.

"Send me everything you have on Crane, Shaw, and whatever you can dig up on this so-called blood feud, too. I'll take a look." He kept his voice even. "I've gotta catch a plane."

Five minutes later he was on his way to Heathrow.

The French woman would have to wait.

CHAPTER FIVE

AFTER MORE THAN TEN hours of uneventful flight time, the Boeing 787-8 Dreamliner landed in Houston.

He'd read Scarlett's materials until he had a clear understanding of the Oakwood case file.

The situation was odd for an heir hunter like Scarlett.

Most unlocated heirs weren't actually missing at all. Maybe they'd moved without a forwarding address, or changed names, or skipped out on a bad debt, or even died in a different city from the one they'd lived in before.

With a bit of time and diligent searching, those people could be located and Scarlett was nothing if not tenacious. She was good at the job.

But the Oakwood woman's situation was completely different. Oakwood had actually vanished, and Scarlett had developed a solid theory to explain her disappearance.

If Scarlett's theory was true, then she'd been right to bring him into the case.

She'd never find Oakwood on her own before Tuesday's deadline.

He'd read through Scarlett's notes twice, and then he slept in the first-class cabin bed for the rest of the flight. When the captain announced their initial descent into George Bush Intercontinental Airport, Flint used the toilet and shaved in the minuscule sink.

He was the third passenger to deplane.

Inside the terminal, ten feet from the security checkpoint, two well-dressed, bulky white men stood together, feet braced apart, hands clasped in front.

Both wore sunglasses. One was bald and a bit taller than the other.

Flint's jaw clenched and his eyes narrowed. Private security, no doubt. Had to be. These guys were too ugly to be anything else.

Law enforcement and three-letter agencies were more diverse these days, too.

Shaw must have sent the two escorts for insurance, worried that Flint wouldn't show up. Which was more than insulting.

He didn't feel like being escorted anywhere at the moment. He'd promised to meet with Shaw, but he would do the meeting and everything else on his own terms. The sooner Shaw figured that out, the better.

Flint glanced across the terminal. He timed his steps to merge into the crowd of passengers flowing past after disembarking from another gate.

Fifty feet along the corridor, he looked back. Shaw's men followed, as expected.

Suspicion confirmed. They were here for him.

Flint strode the long hallways toward the escalator to ground level, careful to stay inside the herd. He peeled off at his usual exit and hustled outside.

Houston's springlike air warmed his skin after London's damp had chilled deep into his bones. He resisted the urge to stretch like a cat in the sunshine.

He'd called a car service from the plane. The SUV he'd ordered waited at the curb along with Alonzo Drake, the best driver on the planet.

Flint climbed into the black Lincoln Navigator and closed the rear passenger door behind him. He met Drake's eyes in the rearview mirror. "Let's go. Now."

Drake replied, "You got it."

The limo pulled away seconds before Shaw's security detail emerged from the building.

Flint looked back to see the two exit the terminal. He observed the way they moved. They weren't quick. The one with hair favored his right leg, the way an aging athlete does, as if old injuries remained painful.

They stopped moving and stood together on the sidewalk. One had a cell phone to his ear, probably calling to report mission failure.

Flint smiled.

The victory was temporary.

Shaw's men would camp out at his house until he showed up, but that was okay. They'd chosen to collect him at the crowded airport because it served their purposes, not his.

He would handle them in his own neighborhood, where he'd be free of surveillance and witnesses.

Flint settled into the backseat for the thirty-minute drive to Houston's downtown historic district. The morning sky promised a warm day and plenty of sunshine.

Drake lowered the privacy partition between the seats and met Flint's gaze in the rearview mirror. "Since you don't have the painting, I'm guessing things didn't go so well in London."

Flint shrugged. "I didn't expect to bring it back with me. But you're right. I didn't get what I went after."

Drake grinned. "How's the amazing Ginger?"

"I didn't see her."

Flint's relationship with Ginger was casual. They liked each other well enough, but he wasn't the love of her life. Which was fine with him.

"Want me to drop you at Market Square Park?" Drake's phone was ringing.

"Perfect." He'd walk home, as was his habit. He enjoyed the exercise.

Drake raised the soundproof partition and answered his phone. The conversation lasted for the rest of the drive. He pulled the limo over to the curb in the middle of the block.

The park was crowded with people enjoying the perfect weather.

Flint waited for a stream of cyclists to pass before he grabbed his bag and stepped out. He was on the move before the Navigator rolled away behind him.

Flint traveled quickly through the early morning crowd, dodging vehicles and pedestrians.

When he stopped for a traffic light before crossing the street, he caught a whiff of cigar smoke ahead of the middle-aged man who approached from his left and stood beside him.

He was dressed casually, but his blazer and polo shirt were both silk, and his khakis were equally expensive.

"You're Michael Flint, aren't you?" His voice was gravelly, like he'd spent years drinking bourbon along with smoking cigars like the one he held between his fingers. He extended his right hand. "I'm Felix Crane."

They shook hands. Crane's grip was firm, his handshake strong, businesslike.

The traffic light changed. Flint stepped off the curb and Crane walked with him.

"Can I buy you a cup of coffee?" Crane spoke around the short cigar clamped between his teeth.

Flint kept moving. "I'm afraid I've got another appointment."

"With Baz Shaw." Crane nodded. "I was hoping to talk with you first."

"About what?" Flint glanced toward Crane, who easily kept up with Flint's rapid pace.

The guy was in good shape for a man of his age and obviously bad lifestyle habits.

"Laura Oakwood. Baz wants you to find her. That would be a mistake."

Flint slowed. He didn't want Crane to follow him home and the only alternative was to handle him now. "Why?"

"Stealing from desperate women is not what you're about. Or so people say." Crane puffed the cigar and blew a perfect smoke ring. "Hear me out. At the very least, you'll know more about Shaw's motives than you do now."

Flint stopped and faced him. "And what is it that you want from me, Mr. Crane?"

Crane's mouth lifted and his eyes crinkled at the corners, but the effect was more sneer than smile, as if he'd won the first round of their match.

Which he had.

He clapped Flint's bicep with an open palm. "Let's get that coffee. I won't keep you long."

Crane probably would have preferred an Irish coffee or something stronger in a local bar, but Flint gestured toward an outdoor café half a block down the street. "We can grab a cup there."

The café was busy with the Sunday-morning breakfast crowd. They found a table near the back still cluttered with the last patron's dishes. Yellow congealed eggs mixed unappetizingly with ketchup on the plates.

A harried waitress picked up the mess. "What can I get you this morning?"

"Black coffee," Crane said.

Flint held up two fingers. The waitress nodded and hurried away. He waited.

"I've checked you out. Your background is as shadowed as your life, isn't it? Orphaned as an infant. Parents unknown. No siblings. Raised yourself. Marines. Then Secret Service or CIA or deep-cover FBI for a while, some say. Privately self-employed now." Crane rested his forearms on the table, the smoldering cigar still clinched between the stubby first and middle fingers of his left hand.

Crane's nails were well manicured. Maybe he'd been a wildcatter once, but those days were long behind him. "Word is, you're the go-to guy when the situation calls for brains as well as brawn. You find people when everybody else has tried and failed and given up. You take a hefty fee for the job, too."

Flint did not reply, but he secretly acknowledged the results of Crane's background check.

Not completely true but close enough to his cover story to be unsettling.

He made a mental note to bury those files even deeper.

"Laura Oakwood is the kind of woman who should be simple to find. But she's not," Crane said, narrowing his eyes against the smoke's updraft as he puffed again. "We figured she was dead. Turns out there's no evidence of that, either."

"So I've been told." Flint wondered how much Crane actually knew about Laura Oakwood, and how he'd acquired his information.

Crane blew out a long stream of smoke. "Pretty clear that she doesn't want to be found."

Flint ran through a quick review of Scarlett's solid work.

In early efforts to find Oakwood, she had begun with the standard checklist of searches for unlocated heirs. National Missing and Unidentified Persons System, tax rolls, property title searches, census, and other public records had all turned up nothing.

The next level—private databases, social media, and skip-tracing methods—also came back empty.

Oakwood had very little family history to check. Scarlett came up empty there, too.

Scarlett's team took to the field. They performed basic private investigation work—last known address, knocking on doors, talking to neighbors and merchants in Oakwood's old neighborhood.

No one had seen or heard from her in twenty-eight years.

Or so they claimed.

An heir hunter less skilled than Scarlett would have concluded that Oakwood was, indeed, dead. It seemed the only possible answer.

Except that normal dead people eventually leave a paper trail.

Laura Oakwood's paper trail, such as it was, ended when she was eighteen and living in Wolf Bend, Texas.

At that point in her investigation, Scarlett had tried another approach. She'd turned farther back in Oakwood's personal history, to the last few months before Oakwood left home.

Which eventually led Scarlett to believe that Laura had participated in a convenience store robbery where two people were murdered, and then she'd vanished.

That was when Scarlett had hit the wall and turned to Flint as a last resort.

Scarlett hated to admit defeat—particularly to Flint.

"Ms. Oakwood's apparent desire for privacy doesn't seem to bother Mr. Shaw. He thinks she'd like to know about her inheritance because everyone would want to know they were entitled to fifty million dollars." Flint paused and leveled his gaze at Crane. "While there might be people on the planet who feel otherwise, I suspect Mr. Shaw is right, don't you?"

Crane's bushy gray eyebrows knitted together over the bridge of his substantial nose. His eyes narrowed. "You don't know Baz Shaw, do you?"

Flint cocked his head. "I don't know you either."

"Fair enough." Crane paused while the waitress poured coffee into two thick white mugs from a black plastic carafe. She left the pot on the table and scurried off.

Crane took up the conversation again. "Baz and I grew up together in West Texas. Known him all my life. My daddy knew his daddy and our granddaddies knew each other before that. Point is, I know everything there is to know about Baz Shaw. You don't."

"Point taken. He'd likely say the same about you." Flint sat back from the table, legs crossed, hands loosely clasped in his lap. "How is that relevant?"

"He wants to cheat Oakwood out of her rights in the Juan Garcia Field. Don't seem right to me." Crane nodded once, firmly, as if he was satisfied with his answer. "Whatever Baz offered to pay you, I'll double your fee not to do the job."

"Pay me to do nothing?" Flint raised his eyebrows. "Sounds like government work, doesn't it?"

Crane guffawed, which turned into a hack and then into a coughing fit.

He swigged the coffee to calm himself.

When he regained control of his breathing, he said, "Truth is, Baz and I are planning to bury the hatchet."

"That so?"

"We've been fighting for so long, we don't remember what started us off. We've agreed. This deal will be the end. Best man wins." Crane picked up the coffee and swigged the last of it before refilling his cup. "We're all in. Whoever gets Juan Garcia Field gets everything."

"What does that mean, exactly?"

"Garcia's too big. Too much potential. Added to current holdings, the man who gets Garcia will own everything else sooner or later and bury the other man anyway." He shrugged and took another draw on the cigar. "Inevitable."

"So you're just going to stop fighting each other? After all these years? Glasnost? Total transparency? End of the war? Winner takes the spoils?" Flint arched his eyebrows.

"Yep. We'll meet up and have a ceremonial handshake and that'll be that." Crane grinned and puffed. His eyes crinkled behind the smoke. "Last man standing. Winner take all. Nothing more to fight about. We're too old."

Flint nodded as if he believed the story.

It could have been true.

But it probably wasn't.

Old warhorses like Shaw and Crane didn't simply quit one day because they finally realized their war was destroying them both. Not in Flint's experience.

"Well, I appreciate the heads up, Mr. Crane."

"What I know, though, is that I can't trust Baz Shaw to keep his word. If he wins, he'll just keep fighting, trying to bury me. I win, I'll have enough to walk away." Crane's steady gaze never wavered.

He pointed the two fingers holding his stogie toward Flint. "You can win either way. Take my offer, you get paid whether Baz finds Laura Oakwood or not. He can't find Oakwood without you. Garcia Field will come to me. All you have to do is let his deadline expire."

"It's an interesting proposition. But no. Thanks for the coffee." Flint stood. He retrieved his bag from the floor. "I'll be in touch."

Crane had asked Flint not to do the Oakwood job and he had refused.

Which meant Crane had no alternative but to stop him from succeeding.

Or at least he'd try.

Flint didn't look back, but his instinct said Crane wouldn't follow. Chasing people down the streets of Houston wasn't Crane's style.

Flint was now half an hour behind schedule. He picked up the pace and walked around pedestrian traffic toward his address.

His residential neighborhood was popular. Sundays meant kids playing outside, dads washing cars, moms gardening. He waved to a few neighbors he recognized but didn't stop to chat.

As he rounded the corner of Baker Street, his earlier guess about the bulky white guys from the airport was confirmed.

Shaw's security detail was camped out in a dark brown sedan parked at the curb in front of his cozy bungalow.

CHAPTER SIX

FLINT WAS DUE IN Shaw's office in less than an hour and he had things to do first.

Although it would be faster, he couldn't simply let these guys do their jobs and escort him to the meeting. Flint had said he'd meet with Shaw, and he would. He didn't need watchdogs.

Flint took the cases he wanted, when he wanted, and handled them as he chose. Sebastian Shaw might be one of Scarlett's best clients, but he was nothing special to Flint. First chance he got, he would have that discussion with Scarlett. He'd do this job for her, as a favor or because she'd hound him until he consented. But after this, no more. The last thing he needed was to be in the middle of a war between Felix Crane and Sebastian Shaw, and it seemed there was no way to avoid the conflict on this case.

He scanned the activity on his block. Too many people were outside enjoying the weather. Too many witnesses. He'd ask these guys nicely to go away. But if they refused, things could get ugly. He didn't want to take them down on the front lawn. Nor did he want these jokers inside his home.

The best option was the alley behind his garage. He'd give them a chance to walk away, but if things developed as expected, he could leave them in the back for the garbage collector.

But his angle of approach was wrong. He was behind the sedan. He wanted the two goons to see him, follow him.

He turned right at Simon Street and hustled west along the abandoned alley to the opposite end of the block. He turned left and headed east along the sidewalk toward his house facing the sedan parked at the curb.

He walked purposefully. He didn't hurry. He gave them plenty of opportunity to notice him. He was five steps away from the vehicle before the driver nodded in Flint's direction and said something to his partner.

Flint closed the distance. He stopped on the sidewalk and tapped on the passenger's window with his door key protruding between his fingers from inside his closed fist. A key made a good weapon if it came to that.

The sedan's window slid down. The passenger spoke first. "Michael Flint?"

"Who's asking?" Flint stepped back for a better view inside.

Close up, the goon in the passenger seat looked like he'd lost a dozen fights against a top-ranked heavyweight. His eyelids drooped and a chunk of his right ear was missing below scruffy brown hair. The ragged cartilage suggested the ear had been torn off a while back by a pit bull's teeth.

The driver's knobby head was shaved and his full cheeks were pockmarked with acne scars. Both of them would scare small children in the daylight, but Flint had seen worse.

"Let's go inside." The knobby-headed guy opened the driver's door and stepped onto the pavement. "We need to talk about Laura Oakwood."

"Sorry. I'm running late." Flint backed up another step to the sidewalk. "Another time, maybe." He walked along the sidewalk to his concrete driveway and turned left, leading them toward the back of his property. He heard the driver's door click shut and then the passenger door open and close.

Heavy boot steps hit the concrete behind him.

When Flint reached his garage, he kept going around the side and toward the stockade fence that separated his backyard from the alley.

Both men followed.

"Hold up!" Baldy shouted. "We just want to talk." Flint passed through the gate into the alley.

He dropped his bag to one side and stood behind the open stockade gate until the two goons came close enough. Through a crack in the boards, Flint saw that Baldy held a Taser in his right hand. His partner likely held another.

Sure. Just talk. With two Taser X26c units charged up and ready to fire. Talking was the last thing they had planned.

Flint wondered why Shaw would send these two his way. It didn't make sense. But he had no time to work it through. He'd deal with Shaw later. He was in the crystal-sharp zone where everything seemed to move slowly and time felt without end.

Earless walked through the stockade fence gate first and looked the wrong way, to the right, eastward down the alley.

Baldy came right behind him. Halfway across the threshold, Baldy turned his head to look left.

Flint leaned on the stockade gate and shoved. Hard.

The gate swung fast with Flint's entire weight behind it and smashed Baldy's face and flattened his bulbous nose. Blood spurted everywhere. He howled like an outraged bull. He dropped the Taser and raised both hands to his pulped flesh.

The noise drew his partner's attention. Earless turned quickly, pivoting on his left foot, slightly off balance. He seemed to have momentarily forgotten the Taser in his hand.

Flint stepped farther into the alley, away from the stockade gate, for room to move.

Both goons advanced toward him, emboldened by weapons and outrage. Baldy's busted nose forced him to breathe through his mouth as blood ran down his face and dribbled from his chin onto his shirt.

Flint let them come at him, to get momentum established. And then he moved, too, just as fast as they were moving. Force and bulk set to collide and explode.

Flint threw a left hook at Baldy and caught him hard on the ear and his head snapped sideways.

Flint was already throwing a right uppercut that landed solidly under the second guy's chin. His head went up and back and he lost his grip on his Taser. The weapon dropped and bounced on the pavement.

Both goons wobbled and stumbled backward, leaving their chests unprotected.

Flint pounded home a hard right to Baldy's solar plexus. Baldy's eyes widened, his mouth formed an O, he doubled up and crouched and held his knees.

Before Earless had a chance to react, Flint carried through and delivered the same blow to his solar plexus. He folded up the same way and fell on his side on the ground near Baldy.

Flint retrieved the first Taser. He pressed the trigger, aiming fifty thousand volts at twenty-six watts for five seconds straight at Baldy's bare neck. The Taser performed perfectly as it was designed to do. Instant loss of neuromuscular control. Baldy flopped to the ground and twitched like a fish with uncontrollable contractions of his muscle tissue.

Flint turned the Taser on Earless and touched his exposed skin with the live device, stunning him. Flint quickly located the second Taser, aimed, and fired the maximum charge at the already-stunned Earless.

The fight lasted not more than twenty seconds, start to finish. Both men were coiled unconscious in fetal positions on the asphalt. Flint was barely breathing hard.

He stood over the two for a couple of moments. He checked pulses. Not dead, but they wouldn't be coming after him again anytime soon. Now that his adrenaline had slowed to a manageable level, he wondered again why they'd come after him in the first place. It was one of the first questions he planned to ask Shaw.

Flint stepped back and pulled out his smartphone, snapped photos of both men, and returned the phone to his pocket. He tossed the spent Tasers into the bushes behind the house next door, stepped inside the stockade fence, and pulled the gate closed. He locked the gate securely.

When they regained consciousness, disoriented, sore, and bleeding, it would be a while before they found their way back to the sedan.

He'd be long gone.

But he expected to meet them again. They didn't seem the type to give up after the first round. Next time, they'd be better prepared.

CHAPTER SEVEN

REVIEWING SCARLETT'S SUMMARY FILES on the plane from London last night had suggested a few leads. He'd begun work on the first before he landed in Houston.

After dealing with Crane and the two goons, he didn't have time to pursue the leads any further before the meeting with Shaw. Inside his house, he took a quick shower and dressed in clean work clothes: jeans, boots, shirt, and leather jacket. He collected cash, credit cards, and disposable cell phones from the safe behind the flat-screen TV.

He hesitated before grabbing his Glock and slipping it into his pocket. Patted down to confirm his passport and personal phone. He didn't plan to leave the country, but he rarely left the house without his passport. Life, he'd learned long ago, was unpredictable.

He glanced at the clock. Drake would be waiting at the park in ten minutes. He let himself out the front door, fired up one of the burner cell phones, and made the call as he hurried toward the Navigator. His source picked up immediately.

"What did you find out?"

"You were right," his source said without preamble. "A girl. August 16. Six pounds, four ounces."

Which meant Laura Oakwood had given birth to an heir. Did she keep the child?

His source said, "The baby's father is listed on the birth certificate as Rosalio Prieto."

He nodded. Laura Oakwood and her high school sweetheart became parents just six weeks before she disappeared. Rosalio Prieto was the second lead he planned to follow as soon as possible.

"Don't suppose there's any cord blood or anything else for DNA?"

"Back then? In rural Texas?"

"Right." He ran a palm over his head and cupped his neck. "Anything else noteworthy?"

"Eyes brown. Hair black. Daughter's name is Selma Oakwood Prieto."

"Selma? Wonder where that came from?" He waited for the traffic light. Drake was already parked at the curb across the street.

"Do you want me to find out?"

"Please." He was a few steps ahead of Shaw and Crane and his goons on the baby's existence. He wanted to stay that way. "Can you alter or wipe the records?"

"They're old records. Not electronic. You'll have the originals by courier within the hour. No copies exist."

"Excellent work." The traffic light changed and he stepped into the crosswalk, moving swiftly. After a couple of beats, he drew in a quick breath. "Anything unusual about the baby?"

"Unusual?"

He didn't have time for chitchat. "Birthmarks? Six toes? Eyes different colors? Anything I can use to identify her twenty-seven years later?"

"Nothing like that, no." His source paused. "But her newborn screening test was positive for low normal hemoglobin. The parents were advised to retest at six weeks. There's no record of that retesting in the hospital files. If she gave the baby up for adoption, the follow-up could have happened somewhere else."

"What does low normal hemoglobin mean? For the baby. I know what hemoglobin is. Red blood cells."

"I'm not a doctor. Do you want me to find out?"

"As soon as possible. I'll call you again when I can." He pressed the button to end the call. He'd reached the Navigator and stepped inside. While Drake drove the few blocks to Shaw Tower, Flint dismantled the burner phone and threw bits out the window onto the busy streets.

He processed the new information he'd learned since he landed and filed it away in his head. Crane could have tracked his flight data from London. But more likely he was watching Scarlett and monitoring her calls. Which was how he'd found Flint this morning after Drake dropped him at the park. Shaw and his goons might be monitoring, too. Shaw was the client. He had a right to know everything, anyway. But not until Flint decided to tell him.

Normally, he'd have called Scarlett with the information about the baby at this point. This was her case they were working, and they were on a tight deadline.

He gave his head a quick shake. They both had plenty to do. This baby angle could be another dead end anyway. He would tell her when, and if, the lead turned into something useful.

CHAPTER EIGHT

SEBASTIAN SHAW TOWER, THE tallest skyscraper in Texas, rose like an obelisk from the pavement near the center of downtown Houston.

It was a monument to the man.

A marvel of modern engineering, the shining reflective bronze-glass building appeared to be twisting its way from the center of the earth into the stratosphere like oil gushing to the sky.

Flint recalled clearly when Shaw had purchased an entire city block and demolished the historic buildings over protests and a public outcry. Not that he let that stop him, of course. Shaw had even successfully insisted that the FAA reroute air traffic to accommodate his whims.

Shaw was a man used to getting everything he wanted, every time. Which was too damn bad, because Flint was nobody's sycophant. Never had been, never would be. The sooner Shaw figured that out, the better.

After a nauseatingly fast elevator ride to the penthouse eighty stories from the lobby, Flint stepped into the sky high above Houston and glimpsed Shaw's breathtaking view of the city.

Scarlett waited, arms folded, frowning. She wore a black suit with a short skirt and her hair was cinched tame by a wide silver barrette.

Red lipstick emphasized her tight-lipped disapproval. "You're late," she said, as she walked away, red spike heels tapping on the granite floors.

"Nice to see you, too." He shoved his hands in his pockets and hustled behind her. "Go ahead and lead the way. I'll catch up." His sarcasm didn't faze her, or slow her stride. Situation normal.

The penthouse office suite, maybe twenty-five thousand square feet of it, seemed to be devoted to Shaw alone. Aside from the required structure around the central elevator bank, the massive space contained no walls. The effect was like standing on a platform suspended in the air.

Artfully placed furniture pods revealed the intended use of smaller areas at a glance. Flint's sight line included three groups of office furniture with desks, several seating areas with and without big-screen TVs, a lounge with a bar, and a dining room that might originally have been located in a European palace.

Art was limited to items that could stand alone on the floor or rest on flat surfaces. Only the views adorned the floor-to-ceiling glass walls.

Scarlett kept walking. She didn't speak and neither did he. Eventually they arrived at a monstrous desk and credenza flanked by low chairs and tables. Behind the desk, leaning back in an oversize green leather chair, sat the unmistakable master of all he surveyed. He looked exactly like the five glossy publicity photos Flint had seen in his quick internet search. Which probably meant the man was perpetually posing. Good to know.

Shaw's body was fit and his mind sharp, by all accounts. He must have been a real lady-killer in his youth because even now he was long on movie-star good looks. He wore the luxury surrounding him as comfortably as an old bathrobe.

"Baz Shaw, this is Michael Flint," Scarlett said.

The men shook hands and exchanged nods. Scarlett sat in one of the client chairs and Flint took another. Shaw walked over to an elaborate bar cart as he talked.

"Laura Oakwood. Missing twenty-seven years. Hell, she could be dead. Probably is." Shaw poured Scotch into crystal whiskey glasses

He handed one to Flint, one to Scarlett, and raised the third in a silent toast. It was 10:20 in the morning, too early for Scotch. But they drank anyway.

Shaw leaned against the desk, facing Flint. "What makes you think you can locate her when no one else has?"

"I can find anybody, dead or alive." Flint didn't boast. Simply stated the facts.

Shaw's lips parted to reveal wide teeth, too white for a sixty-year-old smoker. Not a smile because his eyelids relaxed and his gaze held steady. "What about Jimmy Hoffa?"

"Nobody can disappear forever." Flint lifted his Scotch, sipped, and rested his hand across his knee. "Are you hiring me to find Jimmy Hoffa?"

Shaw threw back his head and laughed. He opened a small box on top of his desk and pulled out a cigar. He offered the box to Flint and to Scarlett. While they prepared to smoke, Shaw puffed to get his draw going.

"I'm sure you've read the files. Katie can answer your questions, if you have any." He took a quick look at his watch. "About forty-nine hours left now. Every resource I have is at your disposal. Whatever you need, let Katie know and she will make sure it happens."

Flint grinned. This job might be fun. It wasn't often Scarlett took orders from him. In fact, he couldn't remember a single instance since she'd held him facedown in the dirt all those years ago. She saw the grin and scowled at him.

"Where will you start?" Shaw asked, still puffing the cigar, which seemed unwilling to draw properly.

"According to the summary in the file materials Scarlett sent to me, Laura Oakwood was almost nineteen years old when she participated in a convenience store robbery. Her boyfriend, Rosalio Prieto, was a year older. He was shot and killed by the store clerk, and a customer also died. The clerk was wounded." Flint steepled his fingers and narrowed his eyes. "The clerk's story was that the boyfriend shot first and wounded the clerk. He says he then shot the boyfriend and killed him in self-defense. He says he wounded Oakwood, too. Then the clerk fell behind the counter and passed out. At that point, he says, Oakwood shot and killed the customer before she grabbed the cash and ran."

"That's what we think now. And it's almost what the clerk told the local cops at the time, yes." Scarlett paused and inhaled the way she did when she'd been stretching the truth. "But the clerk didn't know the second gunman was female."

Flint raised one eyebrow. "So the summary you sent me varies from the police reports, then?" He'd acquired the forensic reports from his source after reading Scarlett's summary, but he hadn't bothered to acquire the police reports since they weren't computerized and Scarlett had already summarized the case for him.

"That's right. These police reports are brief and sketchy and not particularly helpful for our purposes, but I'll send them to you if you want them. Based on our investigation, the store clerk's error seems to have been the mistake that allowed Oakwood plenty of time to get away. Although she probably would have escaped anyway, given how long it took to identify the dead gunman as her boyfriend."

"Which means Oakwood had a strong motive for hiding back then," Flint said, and nodded. "Makes her exponentially more difficult to find. No wonder your routine searches turned up nothing."

"Going back to Wolf Bend, getting the local police to identify the boyfriend, and chasing his records down through to the robbery where he died was a breakthrough of sorts for the Oakwood case." Scarlett resettled in her chair. "The store clerk's statement to the police was that during the robbery, both gunmen were wearing ski caps with masks over their heads and faces. The second gunman was tall but not skinny, and the way she was dressed—jeans and a sweatshirt—the clerk thought she was a man. Oakwood was calm and controlled at all times, he said. Two guns were recovered at the scene, but she took the third gun with her and it was never found. Oakwood took the cash with her, too. About thirty thousand dollars. Of course, it was a while before the cops arrived out at that location, so she was long gone by the time they showed up. Forensics eventually backed up the store clerk's story. There was no reason to question his identification."

Flint knew how these things tended to play out in small towns back then, when law enforcement had limited resources. Record keeping was usually the last thing on the to-do list. Equipment was old, too. Which all added up to everything Scarlett said was totally plausible. "But the mistaken identity of the second gunman sent the local police down the wrong path?"

Shaw listened and sipped without adding anything. Maybe he'd learned to wait out Scarlett's long-winded answers, too. Or maybe she'd already told him all of this and he was simply watching for Flint's reaction.

"That's right," Scarlett said. "Initially, first responders thought there was only one gunman and he was dead at the scene, so they were in no particular hurry to identify him."

"Lack of imagination," Shaw said, frowning. "Like with the 9/11 attacks. Locals didn't imagine there would be a different answer."

Scarlett nodded and warmed to her story. "The female victim was identified right away, but she wasn't a suspect. She was a local woman, a customer. When the clerk regained consciousness after surgery two days later, his eyewitness account of a second male suspect caused the local cops to start looking for a second man. They rousted a few deadbeats, showed the dead gunman's photo around a few hangouts. Stuff like that. No luck. Then they caught a break. It took them a few days to identify the first gunman as Rosalio Prieto using his fingerprints to check criminal records databases. In those records, they found a male known associate who could have been the second gunman."

For Shaw's benefit, she explained, "Known associates are tracked by law enforcement because criminals tend to stick together and travel in the same packs. It's a way to locate criminals who often have no fixed addresses. The locals put out a BOLO. Two weeks after the robbery, the man turned up dead of a drug overdose in another town. At that point, they thought both gunmen were dead. The robbery case wasn't technically closed because of the missing gun and money, but they stopped actively investigating."

Flint rolled the cigar between his thumb and fingers, feeling the smooth Cuban tobacco. "So you're thinking Oakwood didn't know that the locals had bungled the case? She believed she'd been identified and was the subject of a manhunt? That's why she ran and why she's still in hiding?"

"Exactly." Scarlett hadn't touched the booze or the cigar. Not because she didn't appreciate both. She was focused on the case with the same laser intensity she applied to everything. "There's no statute of limitations on murder. Ballistics prove the second gunman killed that woman in the convenience store. And the second gunman's criminally responsible for the boyfriend's death, too. If the cops found out Oakwood was the second gunman, even after all these years they'd issue a warrant for her arrest. The first time she popped up on anybody's radar, be it a passport or a parking ticket, she'd be arrested, tried, and convicted in a hot second. She'd no doubt get the death penalty, too." She arched her eyebrows and gave him a flat stare. "We do execute women in Texas, you know."

Flint considered the logic as he puffed the cigar. After a few moments, he said, "If we go with that theory, then you're thinking our Bonnie and Clyde probably had an escape plan in place before the robbery, and she simply followed through on that plan after things went south. Makes sense."

Flint paused and nodded, although that theory didn't seem likely to him. What happened to the baby? Assuming the young parents kept the child, where was she while her parents were liberating the cash from the convenience store? "Do we have any closed-circuit camera footage? It would help me to see how Oakwood carries herself, how she moves. She'll have changed a great deal since then, but body movements and speech habits are hard to mask."

"This store was a relic, Flint. Located at the corner of back and beyond." Scarlett shook her head. "Place was on a well-traveled truck route, though. Fair amount of cash changed hands there over the course of a week. And they'd had robberies before. Even so, no surveillance cameras as far as we know."

"How do you know you're right about Oakwood being the second gunman?" The moment the words were out of his mouth, he wished he could take them back. Scarlett was laying out her theories for Shaw's benefit. She needed Flint to support her, not shoot holes in her evidence.

For the first time, she looked defensive. Her chin rose in the way he recognized that meant she'd made up her mind and she wouldn't back down, no matter what. "The clerk said he wounded the second gunman and the location of the blood evidence shows there were two women in the store, not one. Oakwood disappeared without a trace, maybe that very night. What other reason could there be for her to run away and keep hiding all these years?" Scarlett took a deep breath. "But you're right that I can't prove it. Not until we find her. We won't know for sure until then."

"Let me be clear." Shaw returned to his chair and gazed across the desk toward Flint as if Flint had passed the first test or something. "Even if Katie's theories are a thousand percent right, I'm not interested in bringing Laura Oakwood to justice. The robbery case was over long ago, and wherever she is, she can stay there as far as I'm concerned. All I want is to find her and buy her mineral rights. I need her signature on the papers. That's it. We're not threatening her. Exactly the opposite—when she signs, she'll be a wealthy woman. She should want to help us. Understood?"

Flint nodded again, but he didn't promise. He believed Scarlett was right on all counts because the theory made sense. Oakwood had killed a bystander in the course of committing an armed robbery. Flint didn't see himself as any kind of cop, and hunting murderers was not his job. But leaving Oakwood free and making her richer than the entire GDP of some third-world countries didn't sit well with him, either. No time to figure that out now. He'd cross that Rubicon when he came to it.

Flint shrugged. "There was a lot of blood at the scene and not all of it belonged to the clerk, the customer, or the dead robber?"

"That's right," Scarlett said. "A newer forensic blood analysis technique is how we figured out the escaped killer was a woman, not a man. That was our first break in the Oakwood case."

Flint nodded. The blood analysis was how he'd learned about the baby, too. Maybe Scarlett already knew, which made him feel better about not telling her. "But I found no DNA reports on Oakwood in the files. Do we have any?"

Shaw's eyes narrowed and then his mouth tilted in what might have been a grin or a smirk or something in between. "We have unidentified blood from the scene, which we believe belongs to her. We've tested it. There is nothing in the databases from Oakwood to use for a definitive match, of course. But when she's located, we should be able to confirm the blood was hers. Katie, please see that he receives those DNA reports. What else do you need right now to get started?"

"Here's what I don't need." Flint lifted his right ankle and rested it on his left knee, relaxed, as if he hadn't been attacked in that alley less than an hour ago. "I work alone. Nobody needs to look over my shoulder. If I want help, I'll ask for it."

Shaw's rugged face closed like a cloud had crossed his features. "Who is following you?" His tone was belligerent, probably faked.

Flint pulled out his phone and located the snaps of the two goons he'd left in the alley.

Shaw looked at the photos and shook his head. "I don't know those guys. Sorry." Shaw handed the phone to Scarlett.

"I'll find out who they are." She studied the shots, pressed a couple of buttons to send the photos somewhere, and returned Flint's phone.

"Did you pull any ID off them?" He shrugged. "Why?"

"They don't look all that great in these pictures, so I can't be sure. But I think they're a couple of freelance land men I dealt with from Oklahoma a few years ago. They find the owners of unclaimed mineral rights and get a cut of the deal. In this case, it would be a substantial amount of money. Millions. So they'd be highly motivated to succeed, let's put it that way." Scarlett looked Flint directly in the eye. "In the Oklahoma case, the rights owner ended up in the hospital, as I recall. These guys don't ask nicely."

Legitimate land men were often hired for such work. To determine mineral rights ownership, find the owners, and negotiate leases with them on behalf of the oil companies. Usually, they worked for a slice of the royalty pie. It was lucrative work. But these two weren't like any real land men Flint had ever met.

"Tell me about it." Flint's shoulder complained again, remembering the hard blow he'd delivered, using the gate, to the gnaw-eared guy. The Juan Garcia Field seemed like a project a little too complicated for a freelancer, too. These two guys definitely had the vibe of hired muscle. Mercenaries, probably.

Flint leveled a steady gaze toward Shaw. "If you didn't hire these knuckle-draggers, then who did?"

"Felix Crane, most likely. He's the only one in line with a claim to Juan Garcia Field if I can't exercise my option." Shaw shrugged and swigged his Scotch. "Who else would it be?"

Crane. So the entire time he was chatting Flint up at the café this morning, his plan B was to disable him from a job only he could do.

Which meant that Crane was not only devious but dangerous as well.

Good to know.

Flint stood. "Is there anything else before I head out?"

Scarlett looked up from her chair. "Head where? Nobody knows where Laura Oakwood is."

"If this job was easy, you wouldn't need high-priced talent like me, would you?" Flint walked away, savoring Scarlett's scowl, while Baz Shaw laughed.

After he'd put twenty feet of distance between them, Flint turned back and grinned at her. "Are you coming? We've got work to do."

CHAPTER NINE

WAITING FOR THE ELEVATOR, Scarlett never relaxed. Shaw had her wound tighter than usual, and Flint wondered why.

He smiled. "Maddy called me. She invited me to her birthday party on Saturday." Maddy was Scarlett's daughter. She was turning six and Flint found everything about her delightfully amusing. She was a handful for her mother, though, which wasn't too surprising. As his foster mom used to say, the apple never falls far from the tree.

"She's very excited about the party, but she's insisting that you need to be there." Scarlett's frown eased a bit and her lips turned up slightly at the corners. "I told her you wouldn't miss it unless you were absolutely unable to show up."

Flint nodded. "That's what I told her, too." He didn't mention why Maddy was so keen to have him at the party. Scarlett wouldn't be happy about the present she'd requested. He didn't have time to peel her off the ceiling right at the moment either.

Scarlett cocked her head. "I sent you those DNA blood reports, but I haven't had a chance to look at them all. I've been too busy with everything else. We haven't known about the whole robbery thing for very long, and the police reports are worse than useless. Somebody didn't like filling out the paperwork back then, I guess."

The elevator arrived and they stepped inside. The moment the doors sucked closed, the elevator car seemed to drop from the sky in a free fall that left his stomach on the eightieth floor.

When they landed with a soft bounce at the bottom, Flint replied, "That's what I figured."

"DNA doesn't seem important until we find Oakwood and have something to match it to." She scowled again, wrinkling her face in the way he'd seen thousands of times before. Which meant nothing but trouble coming his way. "What did I miss?"

Maddy could scrunch her face into that same scowl and for the same reasons, but the look was a lot cuter on a five-year-old.

He waited until they'd left the building to answer. He glanced around for Crane's mercenaries. They'd had time to follow by now, but he saw no sign of them.

He lowered his voice. "Looks like Oakwood could have been a new mom. Blood analysis shows she'd either recently miscarried or delivered, probably within four to six weeks of the robbery."

Scarlett's scowl turned meaner. In Flint's experience, after she'd screwed up, she was more impossible than ever. She hated to make mistakes. And not reading deep into those blood reports was a major misstep. She was usually much more thorough.

Drake waited inside the black Lincoln Navigator at the curb out front. Flint opened the door and Scarlett slipped into the backseat. Flint slid in beside her and pressed a button to lock the soundproof privacy screen into place. He flipped the control switch that added frequency interference to the cabin.

Scarlett arched both eyebrows and pursed her mouth, but she didn't object to his extra precautions. Too bad she hadn't been taking those steps all along. Crane and Shaw were two powerful men who would stop at nothing to get what they wanted. Flint expected them to monitor everything she did, even sleeping at night. After his experiences this morning alone, putting a few extra barriers in their way seemed prudent.

After Drake merged into the flow of traffic, Flint said quietly, "You didn't know about the blood evidence. So you haven't checked for live births or abortions in the area hospitals within, say, four to twelve weeks prior to the robbery, have you?"

He didn't believe the abortion angle, and Scarlett shouldn't either.

Rosalio Prieto, named for his grandfather, was by all accounts a religious young man. He wouldn't have agreed to an abortion.

Laura could have had the abortion without telling him, but Flint already knew she hadn't.

"Easy enough to find out." Scarlett picked up the thread.

They'd worked together many times before. She could often guess how his mind worked. But not always.

She said, "The only people who might believe that convenience store was worth robbing were people who already knew a lot about the business and its customers. So Oakwood or the boyfriend was a local. Or they knew someone who was local. There can only be a couple of hospitals within twenty-five miles of that store."

"Couldn't have been that many babies born, or not born, out there during the relevant time frame, either. You should be able to isolate the hospital pretty quickly. Grab the info and then wipe the records to buy us a few more hours once Crane and Shaw or those two land men figure out what we're doing." Flint rubbed the back of his neck with his hand. His muscles were feeling stiff. "And while you're at it, identify those two guys. Get me full background checks on them."

"Mind your manners." Her tone was sharp and her scowl even more fierce. "I don't work for you, regardless of what Shaw said back there."

"Or I could quit. Leave you to do this yourself, now that I've pointed you in the right direction." His tone was harsher than he'd intended, but she'd already caused him a lot of grief today, whether she knew it or not.

She grinned. But she didn't argue. No reason to.

He breathed deeply.

Unlike anyone else, sometimes Scarlett got on his last nerve. It was a rare talent she'd displayed that first day at the state-funded boarding school they'd both been dumped into.

She'd developed the talent over the years and wielded it as deftly as a surgeon's scalpel.

Scarlett always knew when to thrust and when to parry.

Sisters were like that, he'd been told.

But she wasn't really his bossy big sister. She just acted like it whenever he let her get away with the game.

Under different circumstances, he would have told her about Oakwood's baby. They'd worked together before and usually shared intel. She was trustworthy. Reliable. Working on a short timeline like this would have been easier with her team to help.

But she was being used. Shaw and Crane were keeping close tabs on her. Safer to assume the two goons were watching her, too. Anticipating her moves. And his.

They thought watching her would reveal everything Flint discovered before he chose to report back. So far, they'd been right.

Time for a change.

To stay ahead of the problems, he couldn't trust her as he usually did.

As long as Scarlett was easier to find, easier to anticipate, and giving them new information whether she realized it or not, they'd follow her and not him.

Which might just give him the breathing room he needed to function effectively.

He'd rather tell her. He wished he could. But Flint expected trouble at every turn and he was usually not disappointed.

No one knew him better than Scarlett. When she found out about the baby, she'd be pissed, but she'd understand why he made that choice.

Not that she'd forgive him for it.

She'd make him pay, which was only fair.

"Finding the hospital and records on the abortion, or the baby if there was one, is pure grunt work. My staff can take care of it." Having won their little contest of wills, Scarlett backed off. She had good instincts. "We'll identify those two land men. What else?"

"You know how I work."

His methods were unorthodox, but that was exactly why he succeeded where others failed.

He'd tried to analyze his success a few times. Mainly, it came down to using his talents in a way that was unique to him.

Not really instinct but choices based on ingrained experience.

Whatever words he used to describe how he worked, they'd been inadequate to persuade the relentlessly methodical Scarlett, so he didn't even try to replow that old ground.

"The fly-by-the-seat-of-your-pants method, you mean?" She scowled, annoyed again. "We don't have time for that."

He shrugged. "Tell you what, you use your methods and if you find Oakwood first, I don't get paid. How's that?"

"I can't fail here, Flint." She drew and held a long breath and folded her hands in her lap. She lowered her voice. "I've chosen Shaw instead of Crane. Which means I've lost one of my two biggest clients already. I've got to keep the other one. I have to keep my business alive and food on the table. I'm on Team Shaw now. And so are you. There's no going back."

"No matter what?" The question was a ritual test of her determination.

She raised her chin. "No matter what."

He pinched his lower lip between two fingers. Briefly, he reconsidered his decision not to tell her about the baby. No. Not yet.

Then he nodded. "Okay, then."

The Navigator had traveled five miles through traffic and approached the offices of Scarlett Investigations. Drake parked at the front curb.

Flint and Scarlett climbed out and entered a much less ostentatious building than Shaw Tower. The low-rise brick structure had been constructed in the nineteenth century and housed only one tenant.

Flint followed Scarlett into a conference room where multiple video screens, filled with images from Laura Oakwood's past, lined one wall. She pulled up an old road map of the area surrounding the convenience store Oakwood had robbed back in late September. At the time, the store was called Mildred's Corner.

Scarlett had said the intersection was nothing much back then, and she didn't exaggerate.

One lonely stretch of Texas blacktop crossed another without so much as a yield sign to mark the occasion. At least sixty miles from any real town in any direction. A few shacks dotted the dusty pastures along the roads.

Yes, only a knowledgeable felon would expect to find anything worth stealing at Mildred's Corner convenience store.

Scarlett pointed toward the ugly building. "The big attraction back then must have been that tall rusty awning over the pumps that kept the sun off as long-haul truckers filled up with diesel."

"The faded sign promising 'Cold Drinks' inside didn't hurt either." But Flint was familiar with the area along that particular stretch of nothing, and Scarlett was, too.

Long after the Mildred's Corner robbery, they'd met and spent eight years together in Bette Maxwell's boarding school and foster home only ten miles north of that store.

The Lazy M Ranch.

He'd been eight when he arrived. Scarlett was ten and already the unchallenged queen of the place.

He'd given no thought to Bette Maxwell since he'd left there fifteen years ago.

Back then, the land around her old ranch was dry and barren and the sun had burned his scalp mercilessly every day. He ran a palm over his head as if he could still feel the peeling skin.

Scarlett's fast search for hospitals within thirty miles showed three medical centers, but two had opened later. Only one facility had served the community back then.

Flint had done the same research earlier.

"Do you know anyone who works at Central Branch Hospital?" Flint lowered his voice as if he might be overheard.

Scarlett swept her premises for listening devices and employed the latest privacy technology, which was fine. Her business demanded no less.

But she usually recorded everything that happened within these walls, and that wasn't okay.

No computer system in the world was hackproof. The entire US government couldn't prevent hacking, even at the Pentagon.

Men like Crane and Shaw could buy the best hackers in the world, if they needed to. The two goons would probably try to beat the information out of her instead.

Either way, for Flint, silence was a better choice until he ran this one down himself.

"Our question needs to be answered quickly, and we don't have time to follow all the rules. We need a favor." He didn't say not to ask Shaw, but the command was implied.

Scarlett folded her index finger and tapped her knuckle against her lip. Her gaze focused on the screens in front of her.

Finally, she looked at Flint. "Maybe. Let me deal with it. We'll find out. What else?"

Another screen showed the crime scene and newspaper photos of Mildred's Corner before and after the robbery. The police records were reasonably thorough for the time and place, Flint supposed.

He'd seen the photos already. He'd noted the location of the bodies and the blood at the scene.

The clerk had lied about what happened in at least one particular incident.

The customer's body, a woman slightly younger than the clerk, was found behind the counter. She wasn't simply a bystander.

What was she doing back there?

But those lies might be irrelevant. He'd added them to his short list of leads. Leads he wouldn't discuss here and now.

Another screen displayed a photo montage of Laura Oakwood and Rosalio Prieto. Those had been in the files, too.

A pretty young cheerleader. A handsome football player. Driver's license and high school yearbook photos. They looked like a wholesome slice of Americana.

Another lie.

Flint looked away from the screens.

The original medical file would be delivered to Drake before Flint returned to the Navigator. There were no copies of the file.

Still, Scarlett would find out, somehow, that there'd been a baby born to Laura Oakwood at Central Branch Hospital six weeks before the robbery.

If she didn't figure it out for herself, then Flint would tell her.

If the lead panned out, she'd need to know.

The important thing was what Crane and Shaw would do with the knowledge once they acquired it.

The baby-or-no-baby task would keep those watching Scarlett occupied and out of his way for a few hours.

He glanced at the clock.

"Where would a young woman fugitive without much money run to from that place, and how would she get away?" He slouched against the wall to watch her work through the problem.

"Back then?"

"Right."

"It was a lot easier to get lost inside the US back then. No cell phones we could trace. Not much electronic anything, really. Easier to change her name, her appearance, and hide in plain sight. She'd have had to leave No-Man's-Land, Texas, but it was totally doable." Scarlett rested both hands on her hips, thinking.

"You've found heirs no one else could locate inside the country before." Flint shook his head. That answer didn't feel right to him. "Shaw and Crane would have used their influence to find her inside the US. Could she hide from those two, even if she was in witness protection? Which she's not, by the way. I checked."

"Not likely. I've got a team on the US angle already. We'll keep looking. But let's say she left the country." Scarlett cocked her head, looking at the maps. "Mexico was the logical choice. Our Bonnie's would-be Clyde, Rosalio Prieto, was the son of first-generation Mexican immigrants. He'd have been familiar with the country, fluent in Spanish. Mexico is close. The border is porous as hell, and it was worse back then. We've got two teams down there already."

Flint waited a bit longer.

Mexico was the obvious answer.

But it felt wrong.

Too easy.

Oakwood had avoided detection for a long time now. She deserved more credit.

What he knew about her was limited. But she'd proven she was brave, smart, cautious, and clever.

She wouldn't have made a dumb mistake like running south all the way through Texas for the Mexican border, especially while lugging a baby, when she thought law enforcement was in hot pursuit.

And even if she'd done a dumb thing like that, he was more likely to succeed by assuming otherwise.

He'd yet to fail by overestimating his quarry, but he'd made the mistake of underestimating once before.

Absently, he rubbed the long scar on his chest, evidence of what that particular mistake had cost him. It was a lesson he didn't intend to repeat.

"I guess Canada was an option. Long way to travel and she probably believed there was a manhunt going on for her at the time." Scarlett's tone became thoughtful. "She'd have had no way of knowing about the mix-up with the second gunman. Or the delay in identifying Prieto. She'd have been running full out, and running from here to Canada wouldn't have been easy."

She paused and then nodded again like she'd made up her mind. "US or Mexico makes the most sense."

"Agreed," Flint nodded.

Maybe for a single woman, Mexico might have made sense.

Flint leaned deeper against the wall.

But Oakwood was a new mother.

Assuming she kept the baby, which he was betting she had, the baby would grow up.

For starters, an Anglo child would have attracted undue attention at school or in any village south of the border. Oakwood would have considered all that, but Flint didn't say any of it.

He said, "In Mexico, she'd be found. Arrested."

"But not extradited." Scarlett's eyebrows knitted above her nose. "Because she'd be subject to the death penalty in Texas for her part in the robbery, and Mexico wouldn't send her back to that possibility."

Scarlett had always been stubborn once she latched onto something, and Flint could see she'd made up her mind about Mexico. "Texas could have waived the death penalty to get her back."

He said, "Not a chance in Hell."

"So she escapes to Mexico and she's gone forever." Scarlett's voice slowed as she walked through her thoughts. "Explains why no one has been able to find her."

"So far." Flint grinned. "No one's found her *so far.*"

Scarlett paused, drew a deep breath into her lungs, and held it a second before she exhaled. "Mexico is a huge country. We've got barely two days to get this done. We've got to narrow our search."

"I have some ideas. Stay on both the US and Mexico options. Most likely answers are usually the right ones." He pushed away from the wall. "But find out about the kid first. We might get lucky. The hospital should have a footprint, at least. There could be blood for DNA comparison once we find her, too, if we need to prove identity."

Flint walked toward the exit. "I'll call you in a couple of hours."

"Where are you going?"

Briefly, he reconsidered telling Scarlett the rest of what he'd learned from the blood reports and the hospital files.

No. Crane and Shaw were listening.

And even if Shaw wasn't listening, she'd report to him because he was her client.

Besides, she'd pull the reports again and figure it out for herself soon enough.

"I'll call you. Get me the police reports. And find out about the kid." He left the building.

The Navigator was waiting at the curb.

Crane's land men were waiting at the Navigator.

The two he'd left on the ground in his alley, up and on the hunt again now, too.

Drake was nowhere to be seen.

CHAPTER TEN

MAYBE EARLESS AND BALDY looked slightly worse in the sunlight after the alley fight, but they weren't all that handsome to begin with.

The extent of lingering damage, if any, was hard to quantify. Their gray suits were rumpled and dirt-stained. The Taser leads would have left marks on their fat necks, but from eight feet away Flint couldn't see the vampire bites.

Flint glanced around quickly. Few pedestrians sauntered along the sidewalk and vehicle traffic was light.

Scarlett Investigations was located in a quiet section of Houston, where Scarlett's business was known to law enforcement and allowed to operate under the radar.

Her clients, some of them less than savory, came and went without attracting undue attention in this neighborhood.

Police rarely bothered to circle the block. Surveillance was limited to Scarlett's systems.

In short, Flint was on his own, but things could be interrupted without warning at any moment. Far from ideal.

He continued his steady stride toward the Navigator. "Step aside, gentlemen."

He'd bested these two twice and he could do it again. They were slow learners.

For their first two encounters, he'd mistakenly assumed they were Shaw's men.

Now that he knew they weren't, his options had expanded.

"Right this way, Flint." Baldy reached for the limo door and pulled it open like a well-paid doorman.

They must have overpowered Drake somehow because he would never have allowed them anywhere near his Lincoln and remain vertical.

Flint's steady approach placed him fifteen feet from the Navigator.

Baldy made a sweeping gesture with his open palm.

Earless spoke. "After you."

His voice was higher than Flint remembered. Squeaky, almost.

Flint narrowed his eyes behind his sunglasses. Both of them were way too old to be sporting that much acne on their puffy faces. Which probably meant steroids. Both were abusers. Maybe for a long time.

A lucky break. Flint ran through the options in his head while he pressed forward without a millisecond's hesitation.

Flint scanned the area. No matter how quiet things were on the street right now, it didn't seem prudent to take them out here on the sidewalk in front of Scarlett's office in broad daylight.

And if he did get rid of them now, Crane would only find new mercenaries to take their places. Better ones, presumably.

At least he recognized these two. Might as well work with what he had. For now.

"Where's my driver?"

Earless pointed an elbow toward the back of the Navigator. "Taking a nap."

"We got off on the wrong foot, I'm afraid," Flint said and stopped walking two feet beyond arm's reach. He shook his head in mock apology.

Earless breathed easier. Baldy's shoulder tension relaxed slightly.

"I talked to Crane. You're land men and he's your boss, right?" It was a guess. But since Shaw had disavowed them, Crane became the most logical puppet master by default.

Earless cleared his throat. He folded his hands in front of his ample abdomen. "Crane's our client."

Flint shrugged, suggesting clients and bosses were one and the same, necessary evils the world over.

"There's plenty of money here, Flint, and not much time. We should work together." Baldy's tone was high and whiny, like a teenager cajoling his parents for the car keys. "Make sure we keep Oakwood away from Shaw until the time runs out. Crane pays when he says he will. No need to get greedy. We're willing to share if you are."

"So you've found Oakwood, then?" Flint narrowed his gaze behind the sunglasses. "Got her hidden somewhere?"

"Yes." Baldy's gaze darted to Earless for the briefest of moments, which told Flint all he needed to know.

"To do my job, I'd need to find where you've hidden her. Then grab her away from you. Then get her to sign everything over to Shaw," Flint said. "That about it?"

Earless smiled like a hungry hyena. "You could try to do that, sure."

"Or I can agree to help you out, lay low, and get paid anyway? You'd give me a third of your fee, right?"

They exchanged glances.

Flint pressed his lips together as if he were seriously considering the offer. Finally, he nodded. Once. Decisively. "Yours could be a better plan, given the time constraints. But I don't do business with people I don't know."

"Fair enough." Earless pulled out a brown glossy business card and handed it to Flint. Shiny gold print formed a bold logo. "SW." A smaller cursive font declared, "Share the Wealth, Inc."

Flint flipped the card over and read two names and two phone numbers on the back.

"Which one of you is Dwayne Paxton?"

Earless said, "That would be me."

"Marcel Trevor over here," Baldy said.

Flint nodded and slipped the card into his pocket, careful not to disturb the fingerprints until they could be lifted and run through the databases.

These two looked like ex-cons. They'd be in some criminal database somewhere—and probably not for loitering around limos on Sunday afternoon.

Flint noticed a line of steady traffic from the church down the street. A gaggle of high school boys with a basketball were approaching from the south, horsing around.

"We're starting to attract attention here. Tell you what. I've got plenty of work to do and you've got the Oakwood problem solved. I don't need to tangle with you guys." Flint nodded again.

He put a friendly expression on his face and shrugged. "I'll stay out of your way. You've beat me to the prize and you'll give me a third of your fee. Seems fair. I get paid for doing nothing. Your client offered me the same deal, so he's okay with the arrangement. There's no problem as far as I'm concerned."

Flint cocked his head. He'd never give anybody a third of his fee. The idea was laughable.

These two wouldn't give him thirty-three percent either.

All he was trying to do right now was get away clean.

"Fair enough." Trevor slammed the limo door closed and stood away from the Navigator on the sidewalk.

"Works for us," Paxton said.

"Okay. But don't tell Crane. Or Shaw. Or anyone else. We need to make it look like I'm still on the job. I'll go through a few motions. Places you've already been. Stuff you've already done," Flint said reasonably. "Otherwise, Shaw will just hire someone else to replace me, right? You'll have to go through all of this again."

Flint slipped his hands into his pockets and moved toward the back of the Navigator. He glanced into the back window.

Drake lay flat on his back, eyes closed, still breathing.

Several lines of traffic had come up now, as if more people were leaving some sort of event farther south.

Flint opened the hatch, checked Drake's pulse, which was strong, patted his pockets, and located the spare remote access system fob.

"You know how to reach me," Flint said to Paxton and Trevor as he slammed the hatch and waved. He walked between passing vehicles, around the left side of the Navigator, and opened the driver's door. "I've got your numbers now. I'll stay out of your way."

Paxton said, "We'll call you to check in from time to time."

"Perfect." Flint slid into the driver's seat and locked the doors.

The powerful engine fired up immediately when he pushed the start button. He waved again and pulled the Navigator away from the curb, headed west.

When he glanced into the rearview mirror, Paxton and Trevor were gone.

They'd been watching Scarlett, and they'd probably return to their task. They expected her to report to Shaw, and those reports would keep them up to date on Flint's progress.

They hadn't found Oakwood. They expected him to. But they planned to prevent Oakwood from signing her rights over to Shaw once Flint found her.

They weren't geniuses. They were experts at self-enrichment. It was the right play.

They'd already tried to find Oakwood and failed.

If Flint found her and cut them out, they'd lose out completely. Not acceptable.

If they followed Flint and pushed him aside once he found Oakwood, they would win.

He was feeling better about keeping the info about the baby from Scarlett. He'd keep Scarlett in the dark as he needed to during the rest of the hunt.

But she'd be spitting mad when she found out.

There would be consequences. He winced.

Remember to wear your body armor when you tell her. He rubbed the scar she'd left on his chest all those years ago.

CHAPTER ELEVEN

DRAKE WOKE UP A few minutes into the drive to Mildred's Corner. He sat straight up in the back of the Navigator, one hand held to the side of his neck.

"What the hell is going on here?"

"Welcome back to the land of the living. I'm driving you to the closest ER to get your thick jarhead examined."

Drake, the proud Marine, glared. "Like hell you are, leatherneck."

Flint grinned and pulled over at a gas station to fill up while Drake climbed out of the back. He stretched cramped limbs and walked around the pavement before making his way to the men's room.

Flint grabbed a package from the car. His source had delivered the hospital records as promised.

He opened the envelope and reviewed the pages. He slid the records inside, closed the envelope, and tossed it into the backseat.

By the time Drake returned, Flint had paid cash for the gas, stocked up on road food, and resettled himself behind the wheel. Drake moved into the front passenger seat. His eyes were concealed behind reflective sunglasses that snugged close to his face. He swigged a cold soda.

"How exactly did those two guys manage to lay you out?" Flint rolled the Navigator out of the driveway and onto the blacktop. Speed leveled out at eighty and he set the cruise control. "You forgot everything you learned in combat training?"

"Funny," Drake snarled, and popped a few Tylenol capsules from a bottle he found in the glove compartment then gulped the soda chaser. "Nothing wrong with me that busting their fat heads won't fix."

"Good plan. Happy to help." Flint laughed.

He'd known Drake a long time. Trusted him. They'd served together in the Marines and worked together frequently. Like Flint, Drake didn't make idle threats he couldn't deliver.

"But it'll have to wait. We've got something else to do first."

"Like what? And where the hell are we going, anyway?" Drake drained the last of the cola and dropped the empty can into the foot well.

"My original plan was to fly in your helo. As good as you are, even you can't pilot a Sikorsky while you're unconscious." Flint grinned. "So we're driving to West Texas."

"Are you kidding me? What the hell for?" Drake kneaded his forehead as if he could force the chemically induced headache away.

Flint's grin widened. "Man, you're grumpy when you first wake up. No wonder you live alone."

"Yeah, well, what's your excuse? Ginger won't have you?" Drake laid his head back against the headrest.

After Flint left the city behind, the drive from Houston north and west to Mildred's Corner was pretty much the way he remembered it. A strange sense of déjà vu settled over him.

He'd been two days past his eighteenth birthday when he left Bette Maxwell's boarding school and foster home to join Uncle Sam and see the world.

He was a scrappy kid feeling a burning need to fight without landing in prison, which Bette said was surely coming. Flint believed her.

Uncle Sam provided a better opportunity, he'd been certain, because Uncle Sam had offered Scarlett the same opportunity two years earlier for similar reasons. Neither of them had ever looked back.

Flint stared at the dreary landscape surrounding the Navigator.

Maybe there'd been a bit of gentrification out here, but some things never changed.

Like dirt and dried weeds as far as the eye could see. Like long, flat stretches of blacktop, shimmering in the heat, that seemed to lead to the end of the harsh, flat earth until the road fell off the edge into nothingness.

Exactly as depressing as he remembered it.

Now and then he met an oncoming vehicle. Usually a farm truck or a tractor that had pulled out from a dusty driveway, suggesting that acres of empty ranch land still lay beyond the road on either side. He'd seen a few head of cattle and an occasional scrawny horse or two, heads down, mowing the weeds. Nothing else for miles.

The drive seemed endless, as if the Navigator were standing still. But the speedometer said the car was cruising at eighty miles per hour and steadily covering the pavement.

Before they reached the dead center of the state, Flint turned north on the road that connected nothing to nowhere—only God knew why anyone had bothered to build it.

Fifty miles farther on, the crossroads at Mildred's Corner popped up from the flat land. Back then, it must have seemed like a rusty oasis. The original building and everything else about Mildred, except for her name, were long gone.

A modern truck stop combo, probably about ten years old, occupied the spot now. Big rigs were parked on one side in an orderly fashion. On the other side, pickup trucks, dusty vans, and SUVs filled the vertical parking slots.

A sign pointed to car wash bays and air hoses around back. Newer diesel and gas pumps stood proudly under cover, but the high metal awning that deflected the throbbing heat was painted white more regularly than Mildred's old one had been.

Even on a Sunday, the place was busy.

Customers milled about the pumps and streamed steadily in and out of the convenience store. The store's windows were plastered with flyers that promised sandwiches, snacks, and cigarettes inside. Neon signs announced cold beer, distilled spirits, triple-X-rated adult DVDs for rent, and several types of lottery tickets.

Mildred's Corner was still the only one-stop shop between distant points on the Texas map. The kind of place you'd have to know about before you'd believe it existed. Just like Scarlett had said.

Which meant Laura Oakwood must have known Mildred's convenience store was here. She and Rosalio had known what kind of customers Mildred's served, and when, and why.

They'd have known about the cash, too. How much Mildred collected every week. Where the cash was hidden inside the building. How Mildred carted the brown deposit bags off to the bank twice a week, Mondays and Fridays. Every week without fail.

Oakwood and Rosalio would have known the best times to rob the place and how long it would take to get a cop out here, too.

And how to get away clean.

Flint chewed on the inside of his lip.

He identified only three possible reasons Oakwood could have known those things.

Either she had worked here at Mildred's, shopped here, or knew someone who did.

Would any of the three options be of much help to Flint after all these years? Probably not.

But he had to get a fresh angle or he'd fail just like all the others before him.

Failure was never an option. The idea that Oakwood could hide from him was simply unacceptable.

He could find anyone, anywhere, anytime.

He'd never failed and he didn't plan to start now.

What he needed was to soak up Laura Oakwood's life like a white carpet soaking up spilled red wine. He'd internalize everything. He'd figure it out.

Flint slowed the Navigator as they approached the driveway, and Drake lifted his head. "What's up?"

"We're here." Flint pulled off the road and found an empty parking slot near the back corner on the east side of the building.

"Okay, I'll bite." Drake turned his gaze slowly from side to side, looking at the truck stop and the acres of nothing that surrounded it. "Where the hell are we?"

"The scene of the crime, my friend. Where else would we be?"

Flint slid the transmission into park, pushed the stop button, and stepped out of the vehicle. Fuel and idling diesel engines assaulted his senses like a blaring wall of oil stench.

He ducked his head back into the SUV. "Go inside and check around. See if you can find any old-timers. Somebody who remembers an armed robbery here years ago. Two people were killed."

"What do you want to know?"

"Anything about a woman involved in the robbery. Her name is Laura Oakwood. Still at large."

"You really expect me to find anybody who knows anything after all this time?"

"Not really." Flint pulled his head out of the SUV. "But maybe you'll get lucky."

Flint had come here to get the feel of the place. He didn't plan to find anything much that might help to locate Oakwood. Twenty-seven years was a long time.

He pushed the door closed behind him and walked toward the rows of idling diesels.

The noise outside was deafening.

He wondered whether gunshots from inside the building could have been heard out here the night of the robbery. Was it possible that there were truckers here when the robbery went down?

The files he'd read didn't name any witnesses on the outside of the building. From what Scarlett said about its quality, the police report, once he finally got it, wouldn't name any either.

He counted sixteen big rigs. Tractors hooked to various trailers hauling products across Texas. Two were car haulers, a couple were open trailers full of produce, and the rest were closed containers and tanks transporting bulk liquids. A few of the tractors had license plates on the front where he could see them. He noted Missouri, Colorado, and California.

Truckers were a friendly bunch, in Flint's experience. Willing to take a chance on people.

Mildred's Corner would have been an easy place to hitch a ride going in either direction. Even for a woman with a baby in tow.

Which probably meant it would have been easy for Oakwood to hitch a ride a few miles along the road on either side of Mildred's Corner, too.

But not if the truck drivers knew what had happened inside the store, unless they had a grudge against Mildred or something. Otherwise, they'd want to help find the killers, not help them escape.

Flint saw what he'd been hoping to find on the windows of two big rigs parked near each other at the end of the row.

Yellow-and-blue decals proudly displayed.

The drivers were standing outside, talking. Both wore plain white T-shirts with left breast pockets. Both had their hands shoved down into the front pockets of their jeans. Their boots were sturdy and worn. They looked tired.

One guy was about forty, Flint guessed. The other was maybe a decade older. Beards covered their jaws and squint lines marked the corners of their tired eyes.

When he approached, they looked up and nodded a friendly welcome.

"Hot out here," Flint said, to get the conversation started. They nodded again. "Where you boys headed?"

The younger man said, "Houston."

The older one said, "Phoenix."

"Long ride ahead, then." He offered his hand. "I'm Flint. I saw the decals in your rigs. Road Warriors against Human Trafficking, right?"

He felt big callouses on their palms when they shook. These were honest workingmen. Reliable.

"I'm wondering if you might be able to help me," Flint said. "I'm looking for anybody who might have been traveling this route maybe twenty-five, thirty years ago. Any old-timers around?"

The older one shook his head. "Sorry. I've been running that long but only on this route for about five years."

"Name's Tom Manning," the younger guy said. "Why are you asking?"

"I'm looking for a girl, Tom. Runaway teenager. We think she might have caught a ride from here. We're not sure what happened to her after that." Flint shrugged. "Been a while, though. I know it's a long shot."

Most truckers were willing to help find missing kids, in his experience, even if they weren't formally involved in the volunteer effort against human trafficking.

Flint showed a copy of the best photo he'd found of Laura Oakwood when she was a seventeen-year-old cheerleader. He had age-progressed pictures of her in his pocket, but she had probably looked more like the kid she'd been in high school.

CHAPTER TWELVE

THE OLDER TRUCK DRIVER took the picture and looked at it, then shook his head again and passed it along to Manning.

"I don't know her." Manning studied the photo briefly and returned it to Flint. "But my Uncle Larry used to run this way between Houston and Amarillo. He knew Mildred Tuttle, the woman who owned the place back in the day. He's been helping locate runaways for years."

Flint nodded. "Why would runaways end up here? Seems pretty remote. Where would they come from?"

"We've got a few cults around here now, but we had a lot more back then. Before the David Koresh thing ended, you know?"

Flint knew.

Koresh's compound was the site of one of the most notoriously bad FBI raids in history.

But it didn't happen until years after Laura Oakwood robbed Mildred's Corner. And the Koresh compound was over in Waco. Quite a long way from here.

Flint glanced around at the acres of nothing. "What kind of cults? And where do they hang out?"

He hadn't considered the possibility that Oakwood had been involved in a fringe group, but given the times, she could have been.

"There's a few abandoned properties around this area where they congregate. I've heard about some over at a place called Clovis Ranch. Groups of druggies, faith nuts, and stuff like that." Manning shrugged. "Local sheriff chases them off and then another batch shows up a few months later."

Flint nodded. "The Koresh group was active for a long time. Are there any cults around here now that might have existed back then?"

"Hard to say. Far as I've heard, the cults come and go. People are always coming here, looking for teenagers or lost souls, and we tell them about the cults, you know? I'm not sure what happens after that."

Manning moved the toothpick around with his lips and chewed the end a bit.

"Uncle Larry knows the area well. Answers the trucker's hotline couple times a week now. He might know where to start looking for your girl, at least."

If Oakwood and Prieto had been living with a cult near Mildred's Corner, they'd have known everything about the place.

Robbery, and general lawlessness, was one way some of the cults kept food on the table and drugs in their systems.

The cult could have hidden Oakwood after Prieto was killed. Maybe helped her get away, too.

She had needed help to run and disappear the way she had. A cult was the perfect answer.

Researching local cults and finding a connection to Oakwood was a task better suited to Scarlett's resources. But it was a solid possibility. When he could, he'd hand it off to her.

"Think I could talk to Larry today? We really want to find this girl. People are worried sick about her." Flint fished around in his pocket as if he was looking for a business card and couldn't quite find one.

"Hang on a minute. I'll see if I can get him on the horn for you." Manning pulled his phone out of his jeans, pressed a quick-dial number, and waited while it rang.

He shook his head and shrugged and finally left a message. "Larry, I'm at Mildred's Corner. Got a guy here looking for a missing woman. Thinks she may have hitched a ride from here a long time ago and maybe got into trouble. Could have been involved with a cult, maybe. Guy's name is Michael Flint. He'll give you a call."

When he disconnected, Manning walked over to his truck and retrieved a business card. He handed the card to Flint. "Sorry I couldn't reach Larry. But call him later. He'll be glad to help you if he can."

"Thanks." Flint looked at the card briefly before he shoved it into his pocket and shook hands with the two truckers again. He walked along the row of semis but didn't see anyone else to approach.

When he turned to make his way back to the Navigator, a dancing knot of broad backs and flying fists consumed the area in front of the convenience store.

The only broad back he recognized was Drake's.

"What the hell?"

Two truckers were pounding on Drake, but he was holding his own.

Drake could take care of himself. But he rarely demonstrated those skills these days, particularly against petty insults. He said his bones took too long to heal.

After he'd lost the battle to Baldy and Earless earlier, Drake was probably defending his pride more than anything else.

Flint hustled over to break things up, but before he reached the huddle, a scrawny guy wielding an aluminum baseball bat overhead burst through the door and ran into the parking lot screaming like a hockey referee.

"Go on! Get the hell outta here!"

Drake looked up just in time to catch a swing of the bat on the meat of his left bicep. He turned to grab the bat with his right hand, but a bigger guy grabbed it first and wrenched it away from the scrawny guy, knocking him to the ground.

Flint heard the sickening sound of skull on concrete, and a split second later, the knot of truckers who had been cheering the fight piled on Drake like angry wasps.

The one holding the bat swung it like a club, landing a couple of solid blows on Drake's shoulder. Drake fought back.

Flint heard sirens approaching fast.

The last thing he needed right now was another night in jail.

He looked at the fight again. Drake was holding his own against four burly truckers, but Flint needed to get him out of there before the cops showed up.

He hurried to the Navigator and fired up the engine. He threw the transmission into reverse and stomped the accelerator.

Tires squealed as the shiny black behemoth sped backwards directly toward the knot of fighters.

Flint slammed to a squealing stop and laid on the horn.

The noise penetrated at least one thick skull because the fighters' knot burst apart like an explosion from the center, inches behind the Navigator's back bumper.

The first two truckers, the ones who had initially jumped Drake, were still vertical, but barely.

Drake took two final swings, one uppercut to each chin. The blows pushed them back far enough to give Drake room to move.

Drake dashed to the Navigator's passenger seat and scrambled inside. The door was still open when Flint punched the accelerator.

The limo leapt forward.

Momentum closed the heavy passenger door with a solid thud.

Flint glanced toward Drake to confirm that all his limbs were intact before he pressed the accelerator to the floor. The big vehicle rolled out.

He grinned. "You look like crap."

Drake scowled his reply as he wiped blood from a cut near his hairline. "How kind of you to notice."

Flint put a dozen miles between the Navigator and Mildred's Corner.

"What the hell did you do to get those guys so pissed off?"

"You tell me. I bought a Coke and chips. Put them on the counter and paid for them." Drake had pulled antiseptic wipes out of the glove box and was cleaning the blood from his hands. "I said I was looking for Laura Oakwood. Everybody said they'd never heard of her. I picked up my stuff and walked outside. Next thing I know, they're on me like bees protecting the hive."

Flint thought about that for a second. "Who was the scrawny guy with the baseball bat?"

Drake shrugged, looking in the mirror to remove the blood and dirt from his face. "He was behind the counter. I heard somebody call him Steve."

"Why did he come after you like that?"

"I'm not sure he was after me. Maybe he just wanted to break up the fight."

Drake had used half a dozen antiseptic wipes to clean himself up. Most of the blood and grime was gone, but he'd have some dandy bruises tomorrow.

"Did you see Steve after he fell? Was he okay?" Drake asked.

Flint had been thinking about the fight. "He hit his head and didn't get up again."

"That's just terrific." Drake scowled and ran his hands through his hair. "I didn't even grab the bat. That other guy wrenched it out of his hand and threw him off stride or something."

"Nothing we can do about it now. We'll check on him when things calm down back there."

The whole thing was odd, though. Why would those two truckers just jump on Drake for no reason?

"Swell." Drake slumped deeper into the passenger seat.

The stop had been a success as far as Flint was concerned. Drake was fine. Steve was probably okay, but even if he wasn't, Drake wasn't the one who had taken him down.

The better news was that Flint had identified solid leads. Larry, the trucker who located runaways. The possible cult connection. And whatever made those truckers attack Drake simply for mentioning Laura Oakwood's name.

Any one of which could point to Oakwood if he had unlimited time to do the job.

Which he didn't.

Still, he was farther ahead than he had been two hours ago. Something would turn up. It always did.

He'd absorb as much as he could of Laura Oakwood's experience. He'd add that to what he'd learned from the cold data.

From there, all he had to do was keep unraveling the mess.

Fast.

He had a few more quick stops to make before he went back to Houston.

CHAPTER THIRTEEN

FLINT COVERED THE FIFTEEN miles of dusty road from Mildred's Corner to the old Maxwell place in less than twenty minutes. Drake didn't ask any questions and Flint didn't offer any answers.

He was already late for his promised check-in call with Scarlett, but she could wait. If she had anything helpful to report, she'd have called him.

The Navigator passed under the Lazy M's rusted iron archway at the entrance and rolled easily up to park in the driveway in front of the ranch-style house.

Blinding sunlight bounced off the metal roof of the dilapidated building, flooding Flint's retinas even inside the air-cooled vehicle. He peered through the glare from behind his sunglasses, immediately absorbed by the bubble of desperation that surrounded the place and everything in it, as if he'd never left.

There was nothing wrong with the house that a good fire wouldn't cure. What had been white paint a couple of decades ago was faded and chipped and stripped from the weathered clapboard building's exterior. The wood screen door had been attacked by termites and hung crookedly from its bottom hinge.

Flint assumed the inside was at least as rundown as the outside, but he hoped to avoid the experience. When his vision cleared, he saw the porch was occupied.

"Well, I'll be damned." Flint shook his head. He figured she'd died long ago, but all these years later, she was still here.

A tiny old woman sat on the porch in a rocking chair, shelling peas.

A basket of purple pods rested at her feet and a plastic dishpan in her lap collected the peas as she shelled them.

No doubt some well-meaning farmer had given her the peas. The Lazy M's sunburnt land hadn't been fertile enough to grow anything much for decades, although one of his jobs when he'd lived here had been to make the effort. His fingers curled to touch the remembered callouses on his palms caused by hours of hoeing weeds in the unrelenting sun.

Bette Maxwell had been worn down by life long before eight-year-old Michael Flint arrived at her foster home and boarding school—abandoned and broke and damned near crushed by her husband's betrayal. The bastard had bailed ten years earlier and their two sons had gone with him.

Bette had shriveled to bones and sinew held together with leathery wrinkles as her enthusiasm for life evaporated, but she was a kind soul. The type of woman who'd been kicked around and beaten down and never seemed to find the tiniest seed of anger to fuel her comeback.

But she kept going somehow, and Flint had admired her perseverance. The woman was an amazing survivor. She'd filled her home with foster kids out of necessity. She survived on the state funds she collected by caring for the kids.

And thank God for that, for where would he and Scarlett be otherwise?

She'd been the closest thing to a mother Flint had ever known. He winced. He should have come back to see her long before now. He'd been a coward and he knew it.

Flint opened the door of the SUV. "Let me have a couple of minutes alone with her, okay?"

"No problem. I'll just stretch my legs a bit while we wait for the helo." Drake glanced at the dashboard clock. "Should be here in thirty minutes or less."

"Roger that." Flint stepped out and closed the door before he called out to her. "Mrs. Maxwell?"

Her thumbs paused inside the pea shell she was working on. She looked up. Watery eyes blinked a few times, as if she had difficulty focusing across the distance of the dusty front yard.

"Yes?"

He closed the gap between them in a dozen long strides and climbed the three steps to the porch.

"How can I help you, sir?" Her voice was weak but friendly. She slid her thumb the rest of the way down the pea shell and dropped the peas into the dishpan.

He knelt down to her eye level. "Don't you recognize me? It's Michael Flint, ma'am."

She tilted her head slightly and squeezed her eyes shut. She opened them again and a tear leaked from each outside corner.

When her lips widened into the broad, kind smile he remembered from childhood, her gold front tooth gleamed and pierced his heart.

She put the peas down and jumped up to hug him, knocking him slightly off balance—physically as well as mentally. No one had been that happy to see him since his dog had died two years ago.

"Whoa!" he said, as he plopped onto his ass on the porch, the old woman still in his arms, careful not to drop her.

She felt light and bony.

No weight to her at all.

Bette Maxwell laughed like a child when she squeezed him, burying her head in the side of his neck. "When you left, I was sure you'd be dead in a month. That day, I thought I'd never see you alive again, Michael."

He felt the lump in his throat.

He had never, for a single instant, considered that she might worry about him.

When he'd lived here, she'd always seemed stretched paper-thin by all the responsibilities of running the boarding school and keeping the two-legged wolves away from the door.

She'd paid him no more attention than any of the others, and no less, either. He'd assumed she'd forgotten him long ago, even if he'd never forgotten her.

Bette cleared her throat and pushed herself upright. She wiped her tears and smiled again.

"Well, come on. Get up. I've got sweet tea brewed and shortbread made." She glanced toward the Navigator and waved. "Bring your friend, too. Dust settles in your throat out here. He's got to be thirsty."

"Thanks, but he needs to stay with the vehicle," Flint said.

Bette pulled the screen door aside and walked through into the dark interior of the house.

Flint lifted the door and replaced its top hinge. It wouldn't stay there because the termites had damaged the wood and the hinge pin was missing.

He followed Bette inside, leaving Drake.

Flint crossed the threshold, removed his sunglasses, and waited a moment as his pupils widened to absorb light in the cooler darkness.

He blinked and shook his head to clear the strange images.

The outside of the house hadn't changed, but the inside had been transformed. Gone were the battered pine floors, sagging couches, and broken chairs he remembered. This traditional Texas ranch decor could have graced the pages of *Modern Texas Interiors Magazine*'s most recent issue.

Also missing were the three-dozen noisy, ragged kids running through the house, fighting, screaming, and tearing the place apart faster than Bette could put it right.

And the smell.

His nose wrinkled and he inhaled.

No more grimy shoes, sweaty clothes, and faint whiffs of urine mixed into the locker room odors of his childhood.

Bette Maxwell's place had been gentrified. How the hell had that happened?

CHAPTER FOURTEEN

FLINT JOINED BETTE IN the kitchen, which was as new and improved as the rest of the interior. She had poured iced tea into glass tumblers and placed a china plate laden with shortbread cookies between the glasses on the table.

She gestured toward the chair opposite hers. "Have a seat. Enjoy the cookies I made this morning and tell me why you're here."

Flint settled into the chair. "This place looks great, Bette. Where are all the kids?"

"We closed the boarding school two years ago, when the last group finished high school and our teachers retired." She grinned and sipped tea, which, if memory served, was so sweet her teeth would rot before she swallowed. "And you're wondering where the money came from to do all of this, aren't you?"

"Frankly, yes." He leaned forward, elbows on the table.

"I know, I used to barely have two pennies to scrape together." She wiped a tear from her eye. Her lip trembled and her voice was weak. "We really lived hand-to-mouth when you were here,

Michael, and I'm sorry about that. I did the best I could, but it was never enough, was it?"

"Of course it was." He placed his hand on her arm and squeezed. "I would have died without you, Bette. You know that. Katie Scarlett, too. You kept us fed and clothed and educated for ten years. No one else in my life has ever done that much for me. I want you to know how grateful I am to you."

"Thank you for saying so, even if it's not true." Bette covered his hand with hers. "And Katie Scarlett. How is she?"

"She's fine. Fiery as ever." But he wondered why Scarlett hadn't already been here ahead of him.

Maybe she'd thought Bette was long gone after the school closed. Sloppy work not to have checked. Which was unlike Scarlett. Yet he'd been no better.

"So. The money." Bette swallowed and nodded and coughed to clear her throat. "Turns out part of the ranch sits on some natural gas deposits. I didn't know that I still owned any mineral rights. Lots of folks around here sold off rights years ago. I figured my ex had done the same."

"No doubt he would have stolen them from you in the divorce if he'd known."

Flint had met Bette's husband only once, when Flint was still a kid. He would have unloaded on the bastard if he'd come around when Flint was older.

She shrugged and patted his hand again. "When the oil company found out about the gas and did their title research, they had to go back about four generations. Hired heir hunters and everything. Took 'em a good long time to get to the bottom of it. Eventually, they discovered my granddaddy never sold the mineral rights and I owned everything."

"But that's great news. You can finally get a little rest. Fix up the outside of the place, too." He leaned back and stretched his legs out to cross at the ankles. "I'm really glad to hear all of this. No one deserves a good life more than you."

She cocked her head and chewed her cookie thoughtfully, waiting for him to come to the point, probably. Which he needed to do. Time was running short and he had two more stops to make.

He cleared his throat. Twice.

"I'm a private investigator now, Bette." Not the whole truth but close enough.

"I heard something like that a while back, when I found out you weren't dead." She grinned. "Got a girlfriend? A wife, maybe?"

"No wife."

Flint raised his left hand to show his empty ring finger.

He thought briefly about Ginger. She was fun. She traveled as much as he did, so they weren't together often. He cared about her, certainly, but was she a girlfriend? More like a friend of the moment, which was all either one of them wanted.

"You're not getting any younger, Michael. Don't wait too long." She flashed her gold tooth again. "You get too set in your ways and no decent woman will have you."

He smiled by way of transition. "I'm looking for a missing woman. The last time anyone saw her, she was down at Mildred's Corner." He watched Bette carefully. She'd probably heard more about him that was less flattering, but there was nothing he could do about that now. "You've been here a long time and this isn't a place where news stays secret for long. I thought maybe you'd heard something that might help me find her."

"I'm not much of a gossip." Bette nodded, thinking about the question, maybe. "Don't see many people since we closed the school."

"Well, this would have been a few years ago. When your school was still open. Long before I came here, actually."

"What's her name?"

"Laura Oakwood. Went missing back a couple of decades ago."

A cackle erupted from Bette's throat. "Decades ago? Honey, I can barely remember last week."

Flint nodded as if he believed her. "That's the problem, all right. She's been missing quite a while."

"I'd like to help you. But that's a long, long time ago." She cupped her chin in her palm as if she might think more clearly that way.

She shook her head. "I didn't know anyone by that name as far as I can recall. What did she look like?"

Flint showed her the old cheerleader photo from the Wolf Bend, Texas, high school yearbook he'd found in Scarlett's files. Bette squinted at the grainy image for a while.

"She looks like a lot of other girls would have looked back then, I guess. Long brown hair. Cute. Young. I had more than a dozen just like that here over the years." Bette shook her head and pushed the photo back toward him on the table. "She wasn't one of my students, if that's what you were hoping. I remember each and every one of my kids."

"I'd hoped she might have been one of yours." His lips pressed into a grimace. "Apparently she had no family around here. She wasn't a student at the closest public school either."

"Sometimes the state would park kids here for a few days. They weren't really enrolled in my school and I don't remember all of them. I guess she could have been one of those." Bette shook her head slowly, still staring at the photo. "Anything at all unusual about her?"

For the briefest of moments, he considered how to answer the question. He didn't want to believe Bette would lie or that she might have been involved in the robbery at Mildred's Corner. Or that she'd harbored the fugitive responsible for the killing.

But he'd be a fool to ignore the possibility and let sentiment cloud his judgment. He was a kid when he'd lived here. A kid with a warped perspective. His knowledge of Bette Maxwell and what went on at the Lazy M was necessarily limited to that kid's-eye view.

Still, Oakwood must have had help from someone, and the Lazy M was the closest possible hideout from Mildred's Corner. She'd been wounded. Maybe hauling the baby. On her own. Her boyfriend dead. Surely, she'd been in shock, at the very least.

If Oakwood hadn't come here, where had she gone? If he told Bette any more, if she realized he knew about the baby, would she find a way to warn Oakwood? Or would Paxton and Trevor come here and hurt Bette to get whatever she knew? That was more than possible.

Bette pushed the photo a little farther away. "Why are you trying to find her after all these years?"

"Why now, you mean?" He nodded, a decision made. "She's kind of in the same situation you were. She's entitled to a lot of oil and gas money, and she doesn't know about it. If I find her before the time runs out, she could be a very wealthy woman."

If Bette knew where Oakwood was now, maybe she'd get word to her about the money. Maybe Oakwood would show up to collect it. It was a long shot, but long shots were all he had. He drained the last of the syrupy tea without heaving and glanced at the clock on the stove.

"What happens to the money if you don't find her?" Bette folded her paper napkin like a fan and then pressed out the folds with her index finger.

"She'll lose out forever. Someone else gets the money." He pushed back his chair and stood. "Seems a shame. She could probably use the cash. I mean, who couldn't use fifty million dollars, you know?"

"Wow! That *is* a lot of money." Bette peered up from her chair. "I can ask around, if you'd like. I knew Mildred. And she knew everybody."

"Mildred died about ten years back, didn't she?"

"Her son's still running the store, though. Steve Tuttle. He's about the same age as that Oakwood girl, too, if my memory's right. Mid-forties? He might have known her." She pushed herself up and stood on wobbly knees. "Let me give him a call right now. You can go talk to him, if he knows anything."

Flint heard the blades of Drake's helicopter in the distance. "I'm short on time today. Where does Steve live?"

She rested her body down into the chair again. "He lives behind the store. He hardly ever leaves the place. Says too much trouble can get started if he's not there to stop it."

"What kind of trouble?" Flint couldn't go back to Mildred's Corner without a whole boatload of problems arising. And he figured Mildred's son was probably lying in a hospital somewhere being treated for that concussion he got when his head hit the concrete.

"The usual kind. Fights, mostly. But they've had a few robberies over the years, too. One time, two people were shot and killed. But that was a long time ago."

"Was Steve in the store at the time?" The helicopter came closer.

She shook her head. "He and Mildred were sleeping. They lived in a trailer on the back lot at the time. Her husband was working the store like Steve does now." Bette's nose wrinkled. She grimaced. "Those two might still be alive if Mildred or Steve had been working that night instead of Oscar. He was a good shot but trigger-happy, if you ask me."

Flint nodded and pushed his chair into place at the table. "Why do you think Steve Tuttle might know something about this missing woman?"

"Mildred's is what passes for a town around here, Michael. Folks hang out there. Talk. Make friends. And Mildred was better than a local newspaper. Knew everything about everyone," she flashed him a pointed look, "and didn't mind sharing."

"Sounds like it's too bad I can't talk to Mildred."

"Steve isn't as friendly or as well liked as his mother. But he might be willing to help. Most folks will help take care of people around here. Have to. Place is too hard to live isolated from what little company exists."

The helo was flying directly over the house, hovering, the pilot seeking the best place to land. The house's metal roof seemed to dance with the vibrations. The noise was deafening.

"One other thing. If she wasn't one of your kids, do you think this girl could have been living with a local cult?"

"Maybe. I've chased ragtag cults off my property more than once. They're unsanitary, for one thing. Bad behavior. Thieves and such. Lot of drugs involved. I kept them away from my kids as best I could." Bette cocked her head and tapped her index finger against her cheek to help her think back. "Your girl could have been living with one of them, I suppose. Hard to say. It's not like they kept a list of members or anything, I'll bet. Lord knows, there's been too many young people gone missing because they got involved with the wrong crowd."

"Who would know about cults living in the area back then? Besides Mildred, I mean, since I can't figure out how to communicate with the spirits." Flint smiled and Bette rewarded him with another big laugh.

She seemed to think about the problem at bit more. "Our local sheriff was pretty short-staffed back then. Current one still is. We didn't have a lot of crime around here, other than the petty stuff, which can be pretty annoying. But he'd have been aware of the cults or anybody else just hanging around, causing trouble. You could have asked him about it, but he died a few years ago, too. Throat cancer got him."

Flint nodded. "I see."

And then she put her hand on his arm and looked directly into his eyes. "Michael Flint. You listen to me. Your mother was not a drug user. And she wasn't involved with one of those crazy cults either. Her situation was entirely different."

His head snapped back as if she'd slapped him. What the hell was she talking about?

"You've come back to ask about your mom, haven't you, Michael?" Bette smiled across her dear, sun-wrinkled face, which looked like nothing so much as a dried apple. "I hoped you would."

Flint nodded. He crossed his legs and folded his hands on his knee. "Tell me what you know about her, then."

"Not much. Back then, closed adoptions were the rule. Women gave up their babies and never saw the children again." She shrugged.

"That's the way it was."

"I understand."

"She brought you here when you were about two months old. She wanted me to adopt you and keep you here. But I couldn't adopt you. The state wouldn't have given me a baby back then.

And you were too young for me to take care of at the school. I wasn't set up for infants." She paused and bowed her head for a second. Then she looked up again. "I told her you couldn't stay here, but I'd find a good home for you. She made me promise I'd get you back when you were old enough. Assuming you weren't adopted before then, of course."

"I understand," he said again. All he planned to do was to hear the full story. Or as much as she knew of it. And then he'd put this all behind him. He had work to do.

"She said she didn't mean to get in the family way. Said she wasn't married to the fellow. Said they couldn't get married, but she didn't say why. She was very upset about leaving you. Said she was a schoolteacher, and she'd get fired if they found out she had a child." Bette patted his hand and he covered her small, wrinkled claw with his palm. "By the time she left here, Michael, she was so upset. She cried and cried. She didn't want to give you up. I know she didn't. I just tried to make her feel better. I told her you'd be here for a few weeks while I found you a better home. I told her she could come back and get you any time."

"But she never did come back for me, did she?"

Bette shook her head. "Don't judge her too harshly, Michael. That's the way things were back then. I took good care of you, like I promised. You turned out okay, didn't you?"

He placed his big hand over her small one on the table. "Yes, I did, Bette. I turned out just fine. Thanks to you."

Bette grinned from ear to ear. Her eyes were glassy. She cleared her throat. "Well." She cleared her throat again and blinked her tears away. "Well, that's all I know about her. She didn't leave her name. I never saw her again."

"Did she tell you where she was teaching?"

"I've talked to so many young girls over the years." Bette cocked her head and closed her eyes. Thinking, maybe. When she opened her eyes to look at him again, she said, "West Texas, somewhere? I'm not sure. I might be confused about that, Michael. But that's what I seem to remember."

"You don't have any records or anything, I guess."

She shook her head and pressed her lips into a straight line. "We never had many records and the ones we had were shipped to Austin when we closed the school a couple of years ago. I'm sorry."

"Was her name Flint?"

Bette laughed out loud. "Lord, no. I have no idea what her name was. She said your name was Michael and we kept it for you because you looked like such a little angel. And Flint because you were as stubborn and hard as they come, even back then. You'd fall down and bleed but you never uttered a sound. You were tougher than rocks."

"I still am, Bette." He patted her hand again. "I've gotta go." They rose and she hugged him again. "Good-bye, Michael."

"Until I see you again." He gave her one last squeeze.

The helo had landed. The noise from the front yard overwhelmed the conversation completely.

He stood and walked around to her chair and took her into his arms. She cried on his shoulder a bit. "It's okay, Bette. I promise."

He wasn't sure whether she could hear him or not. But she raised her head and gave him a little kiss on the cheek. She talked into his ear. "Come back and see me soon, Michael. Maybe I'll remember something else about your mother. I'll try. You're a man now. It's normal that you'd want to know."

Normal for some men, maybe. But not for Flint. Nothing about his life had ever been normal. He lived in the moment. Always had. Always would. He liked it that way.

As for his birth mother, experience had taught him that parents who leave their kids have good reasons for doing so. Flint believed he was better off than he would have been if his parents had made a different choice. He was better off not knowing what their reasons were. No need to know, no desire to know. Simple as that.

Maybe he should find out what Bette wanted to tell him while she still could. But not today. He slipped his sunglasses into place and strode through the door into the dust storm out front.

CHAPTER FIFTEEN

A HARRIER JUMP JET would have better served his purposes,
but the four-bladed, twin-engine Sikorsky S-92 was the fastest
helo Flint had easy access to without calling attention to his plans.

With a competent pilot, the Sikorsky could cover the distance
from Bette Maxwell's Lazy M to Wolf Bend, Texas, in under
two hours. The downside was deafening noise and teeth-rattling
vibration levels.

Drake waved Flint over to the Lincoln. The Sikorsky's rotor
wash and big engine volume made conversation difficult. "I can't
pilot the helo today. I'm not even close to 100 percent. Can you
handle the Sikorsky from here? Or do you want my pilot?"

"Do I know him?" Flint peered into the helo, but all he could
see was the guy's back and the bubbles of his headset.

Drake shook his head. "Name's Phillips. Freelance. We've
used him before. Just your kind of guy. Trained in the Navy. He
was a SEAL. Knows his stuff. All business. No chitchat."

Flint flashed a thumbs-up. "You can pick me up when we get
back to Houston."

"Will do." Drake returned the thumbs-up.

Flint touched Drake's forearm to grab his attention. "That envelope the courier gave you while you were waiting for me outside Scarlett Investigations this morning is in the back of the SUV." Drake nodded. "Hand deliver it to Scarlett yourself, okay? Do it first thing. Soon as you get back to Houston."

"Will do." Drake stood aside and Flint joined the pilot in the helicopter.

Phillips grinned, lifted his palms in question. Flint got seated and settled his headset and flashed a thumbs-up. Phillips's electronic voice in his ear parodied a flight attendant. "Sit back, relax, and enjoy the flight."

Flint grinned back. He checked his watch. Less than forty-five hours until Shaw's option expired and Crane would win Juan Garcia Field by default.

He felt his heart beat steadily in his chest, but was that due to Shaw's ticking clock or the vibrating Sikorsky? Flint didn't really care which of the tycoons won this contest. But he'd promised Scarlett he'd find Oakwood before the deadline, and if Shaw lost because Flint failed to deliver what he'd promised—he wouldn't go there. He'd never failed and he'd never let Scarlett down, and he wouldn't start now.

Flint watched Bette Maxwell's ranch shrink as the Sikorsky lifted into the air. He had to admit she'd aroused his curiosity with all that talk about his mother. Maybe he cared about his origin story more than he realized.

He shook his head rapidly. No. Everybody came from somewhere. DNA might be destiny, but it was what you did with your life that mattered. His mother couldn't be bothered with him? Well, he couldn't be bothered with her, either.

He'd been heir hunting, skip tracing, and looking for all manner of missing people and things long enough to know that sometimes the smartest thing was to apply the sleeping dogs doctrine and let it lie.

The best method he knew of for finding someone like Laura Oakwood was to crawl inside her head for a while and feel the world the way she had. The moment he'd seen the maps and the photos of Wolf Bend, he'd understood why a young woman like her wanted to escape the place. One look at the cute teen in the cheerleader uniform explained why Rosalio Prieto wanted to go with her. The pregnancy would have chased them out of town ahead of her father's shotgun, but her father had died a few months before and the timing suggested she wasn't pregnant when they left, anyway.

The rest of Scarlett's file held more motivation for the runaways, if more was needed. Laura's mother had died the year before graduation. Cancer, the long and painful kind.

From the statements Scarlett's investigator had gathered, friends and neighbors said Laura's dad was already depressed and drinking himself to death long before his wife passed. So there was nothing anchoring her to Wolf Bend. No pull factors and lots of push factors.

Laura began dating the cutest of the local bad boys, Rosalio Prieto. Dangerous looking and a year older. He owned an old car. A couple of days after Laura turned eighteen, on an ordinary Thursday afternoon, they left Wolf Bend in Prieto's car. The vehicle was found a couple of days later, but Laura and Rosalio never came back.

There had to be more to that story. She wasn't pregnant yet, so why did they leave on that particular day? And where do two teenagers go without a car? Wolf Bend wasn't the kind of place where anyone could live in the shadows. Back then the entire population was only 1,237 souls.

Laura had no siblings. Rosalio came from a larger family. Two brothers and a sister, still living in Wolf Bend. Maybe someone would talk if Flint pushed the right buttons.

Flint looked down from four thousand feet. The land below the Sikorsky became drier and more barren as they flew the southwest course.

Almost two hours into the flight, Phillips turned on his headset and pointed off to the right side of the helo. "Ladies and gents, welcome to Wolf Bend, Texas."

Flint had already seen the satellite photos of the place. Wolf Bend was nothing but a few unremarkable buildings in the middle of nowhere, Southwest Texas. Total population was barely twelve hundred people today. The town was larger once, but the boom times had ended long before Laura Oakwood was born. She'd only have known the lean years.

The downtown occupied land at the intersection of two blacktopped Texas roads. Three, maybe four, low block buildings occupied land on all four corners. A blinking traffic light anchored the center of town, such as it was.

His research said most of the younger people who lived here went to work in the oil fields over in Mount Warren, in the next county. The ones with good jobs often packed up and moved closer to the fields.

Residents remaining in Wolf Bend tended to fall into three camps: the down-and-outers with no choices, the ones who'd been there too long to leave because Wolf Bend had always been their home, or the ones who had nowhere else to go.

If Laura Oakwood had stayed here, what kind of life would she have had? A pretty desperate one, Flint figured. Desolate didn't begin to describe the place he saw from the helo's viewpoint.

Flint shook his head slowly. Better times were coming, when Baz Shaw or Felix Crane acquired all the rights for the Juan Garcia Field. Flint wondered how many people around here knew about their plans. When either Shaw or Crane had their way, Wolf Bend would become a boomtown again. No one looking at the place right now could argue against such progress, and it was hard to imagine anyone would want to.

"Do you want to set down?" The pilot's garbled voice came through the headset's speakers.

"Not yet." Flint pointed north, toward the site.

Much of the land north of Wolf Bend had once been Juan Garcia's cattle ranch. Ranching was a bust after the water supply dried up. The Garcia ranch didn't look much better than anything else surrounding Wolf Bend. It looked hot and dusty and barren.

In the 1960s, oil was discovered on the property. Garcia wasn't interested in selling, and domestic drilling wasn't permitted then, anyway. The full extent of the field was never explored.

Garcia finally died a few years ago and his family wanted to sell. The business climate had improved, too, making drilling a viable business opportunity. But Garcia didn't own all the mineral rights for the huge field. That was when Shaw and Crane and maybe a few others started trying to acquire the rights, including all the surrounding parcels.

The Sikorsky veered northwest. They flew over the Garcia property toward the abandoned Oakwood ranch, which was immediately across the property line. The Sikorsky covered the distance in about fifteen minutes—which meant maybe a thirty-minute drive for earthbound vehicles traveling a reasonable speed, should anyone try to follow.

"I'd like to get a better look at the place," Flint said into the microphone. "Circle around a couple of times, okay?"

From the air, the abandoned Oakwood ranch looked even less appealing than in the photos Flint had seen. The fences were down and the dirt driveway was overgrown. The house was a one-story wood structure with a covered porch that once ran all the way around. One side of the porch roof had collapsed onto the decking a while back. On the east side, he saw three outbuildings, probably barns, all in worse shape than the house. Otherwise, nothing but dust and weeds in the yards, front and back, and all around.

Flint pointed his thumb down and Phillips nodded. Without fanfare, he landed the Sikorsky near the house.

Flint removed his headset and stepped out onto hard brown earth. The temperature must have been about ninety degrees. No breeze. No clouds. The kind of relentless unfiltered sunlight that burned exposed flesh in minutes.

The noise from the helo drowned any sounds that might have indicated life on this scorched earth.

Phillips didn't move from his seat or shut down the engine. He set the Sikorsky to idling, and the engine switched to its familiar grating whine while the blades slowed rotation. He'd wait inside the helo. They'd be leaving soon.

Every place Flint had been since he left Shaw's office this morning had been for one purpose: he wanted a feel for the places and the people who occupied them.

Who was Laura Oakwood? Where did she come from? Where did she go? What drove her away? Where was she likely to go next? Asking questions like these and finding the answers was what set him apart from other hunters and drove his success where others failed.

Any heir hunter could look at old records and documents and trace family history. Any decent private investigator could knock on doors and interview witnesses. The better detectives could apply logical thinking to lead them from lost to found.

But when they hit a dead end, even the good hunters didn't have a feel for the missing. Didn't know what motivated them. Couldn't suss where they'd gone or entice them to show themselves.

Which was why the others failed and Flint succeeded. He'd find Laura Oakwood. No doubt about it. But first, he needed to entrench himself in who she'd been. Wolf Bend was the best place to start.

The Sikorsky's noise became slightly less deafening while idling. Not ideal but workable. Flint preferred his hearing unobstructed, but he didn't plan to be on the ground long enough to justify the preflight startup procedures if they shut the beast down while he explored the vacant property.

Flint shouted, "Fifteen minutes!" He flashed all five fingers three times.

Phillips gave him a thumbs-up.

Flint moved away from the Sikorsky toward the house. The rotor wash had stirred up the dust and rearranged it over the weeds. As he walked, the dust settled on his boots and wafted up to tickle his nostrils.

From this vantage point, the house looked worse than it had from the air. The reports Flint read in the files said the property had been abandoned when Laura left home.

Flint didn't expect to find anything important here. He just wanted to get the feel of the place.

He still didn't have a sense of the girl or why she'd become a runaway, a criminal, and a fugitive. Was she simply going with the flow of her life? A girl who attracted the wrong stuff and floated from one disaster to the next? Or did she drive her own life off the cliff?

In short, had Laura Oakwood been a bad person or simply an unlucky one? Flint knew the correct answer to that question wasn't always the obvious one based on observable facts. His life proved as much. Scarlett's, too.

The old Oakwood ranch house was a rectangular box. Small. Maybe about eight hundred square feet. The wraparound porch made it seem larger from the air. If it had been painted once upon a time, that paint was a distant memory. The entire place was as weathered and cracked and dry as the ground around it.

The Sikorsky's relentless soundtrack overwhelmed Flint's hearing as he moved toward the house. When Laura Oakwood lived here, the silence must have been all-consuming. The nearest neighbor was miles away. This was no place for a girl. She'd had to have been tough as nails to thrive out here.

The front door and windows were hidden by the porch roof's shadows. Flint didn't see the man standing in the doorway until he shouted out, "Who are you and what do you want?"

At least that's what Flint thought he said.

Even wearing sunglasses to shield his eyes, Flint couldn't see well enough through the bright light into the darkness. The guy might have been sixteen or sixty.

But there was no way to mistake his intentions. His feet were braced apart and his arms were raised to hold a shotgun, aimed straight toward Flint's chest, center mass.

As his eyes began to adjust, Flint noticed the guy's arms trembling. Maybe from the weight of the shotgun. Or nerves. Or something even less predictable.

"Get the hell out of here!" he shouted over the Sikorsky's clamor.

Flint took another four steps, eyes straight ahead, focused, watching, waiting.

He saw exactly the movements he'd trained himself never to miss.

Saw them as if they occurred slowly, one millimeter at a time.

The guy's shoulders leveled.

His torso twisted.

He lateraled the shotgun's barrel to his left.

His index finger squeezed the trigger.

Flint could barely hear the thundering noise and the sound of the pellets hitting the ground on his right, raising more loose dust not ten feet from where he stood.

The pellet storm lasted less than a full second.

Flint's instinct was not to root himself to the spot, which was probably what the guy was expecting.

Instead, he rushed forward as the shooter attempted to adjust the barrel back to center, aim, and fire the shotgun at the now fast approaching target.

Flint covered the distance in three strides. In one fluid motion, he pushed his arms up and knocked the shotgun away from the man's shoulder before he body-slammed the shooter backward.

The shotgun flew up in the air and out of the shooter's hands.

He fell backward, through the open doorway, into the room and down to the floor on his back. Flint landed squarely on top of him and pinned him flat.

The shotgun clanged onto the rough floor.

The interior of the house was dark. Flint still wore his sunglasses. He could barely see. He squeezed his eyes shut and opened them. Rapidly. Again and again.

The Sikorsky continued to fill the air with thundering noise that slithered through the holes in the walls as if the helo had invaded the house.

The man felt puny under Flint's body. Wiry. He wiggled and fought to get away.

Flint pressed down with his torso while he pulled back his fist and punched the shooter squarely in the face. His skull bounced on the wood floor. He stopped moving. He was out cold.

Flint rolled off the shooter and stayed low to the floor. He pulled his sunglasses off and looked quickly around the room for the guy's backup.

Three doors led from the room's central living area. Two on the left and one on the right.

Flint pushed himself up to a squatting position, snagged the shotgun, and checked the other rooms.

When he was sure the house was unoccupied, he returned to the unconscious shooter. Flint patted the assailant's empty pockets. No wallet. No ID. No belt.

He hadn't hit him that hard. He'd be coming around soon.

Flint went into the bathroom and found two threadbare bath towels. He secured the guy's wrists and ankles as well as possible and left him on the floor.

Flint moved from room to room, conducting a quick search of the place.

The house had seemed abandoned, but at close range he saw that it was furnished and lived in. There must have been a generator somewhere. There were no overhead electrical lines outside, but the light switches worked. He flipped them on. He found moldy cheese and sour milk and six longneck bottles of beer in the refrigerator, stains in the toilet, and dirty sheets on the bed. Whoever this guy was, his housekeeping skills needed improvement.

Flint used a nasty toothbrush he'd found in the bathroom to swab around inside his attacker's mouth. He wrapped the toothbrush in a plastic grocery bag he'd found in the kitchen. It wasn't perfect, but it was the best DNA collection he could do quickly. There was probably a first aid kit in the Sikorsky. If he had time, he'd grab a syringe and get a blood sample and fingerprints, too.

Flint grabbed the shotgun again and went through the back door to make a quick tour of the outbuildings. Distance from the Sikorsky helped restore his hearing a bit, but he heard no competing sounds except his own boot steps.

All three outbuildings might have been part of a working ranch once, but they had been abandoned long ago. He found an extension cord and slipped it over his shoulder. The cord would make better handcuffs than the threadbare towels.

He found no vehicles of any kind. No animals either.

How did that shooter get his supplies from town if he didn't have a truck?

Most likely there was another resident here. One who had taken the truck today. One who might be coming back soon.

Flint hustled back inside the house. The guy was still bound on the floor, but his eyes were open. He'd rolled onto his stomach and inched himself across the floor toward the kitchen. Flint pulled a straight back chair from the kitchen table, flipped him onto his back with a booted foot, placed the chair astride the shooter's thin calves to prevent him from kicking, and sat.

The Sikorsky's overwhelming whine continued unabated.

CHAPTER SIXTEEN

"WHO ARE YOU AND what do you want?" the guy shouted. Flint could hear him but not well enough for a lengthy conversation.

Flint yelled back, "Who are *you*?"

"Get the hell out!" The man's eyes were furious. He thrashed from his waist, trying to get free of the chair-leg prison. His face reddened with the effort and the frustration of failure. "Get out! Get out!"

Conversation was impossible and Flint was ready for some answers. But did this guy have any? Or was he merely wasting time until his housemate returned?

Flint went out to the Sikorsky, opened the door, and retrieved the first aid kit. The pilot looked up from his charting. Flint flashed his open palm, five fingers splayed, twice. "Ten minutes!" Phillips gave him another thumbs-up.

Flint hurried back inside. He opened the first aid kit and found wide tape. He tore off a six-inch swath with his teeth, shoved the guy's chin with the palm of his hand to close his gaping mouth, and slapped the tape over his lips. Not as good as duct tape, but it would do the job for now.

He rummaged through the kit's supplies until he located a syringe, alcohol, and a cotton ball. He held the shooter still with one knee on his shoulder and the other on his forearm, swiped his elbow, and drew blood. When he capped the syringe, he pulled out his phone, ripped the tape off the man's mouth, snapped a few pictures of his face, and slapped the tape into place again.

The first aid kit didn't contain anything good enough to lift fingerprints. He found a glass in the kitchen and wiped it off with a sterile wipe from the first aid kit. Then he pressed the man's fingertips onto the glass. He had an app on his phone for collecting fingerprints, but it required precise placement of each finger. This was easier for now.

The shooter had slowed his struggling. Whether from exhaustion or resignation, or something else entirely, was impossible to guess.

When Flint finished gathering the bio data, he looked up toward the clock over the mantle. He'd been here longer than he'd planned already.

Should he leave him here? He'd gathered more than enough evidence to identify him. He couldn't do a lot of harm bound and gagged on the floor. But after that? When his partner came back? What harm could they both do then?

Flint moved the chair, tied the guy's wrists and ankles with the electrical cord, and removed the towels. He reached down and grabbed his arm.

Flint lifted him off the floor, set him on his feet, and tossed him across his shoulder. He stooped to collect the shotgun on the way out the back door.

The third outbuilding was far enough from the Sikorsky to ask questions and hear the answers. Flint plopped the shooter down on its dirt floor and yanked the tape off his mouth again. The shooter glared.

Flint aimed the shotgun at his knee. "What's your name?"

The guy narrowed his eyes. Flint touched his knee with the barrel of the gun. His eyes went wide and the thrashing began again. "Don't shoot me, man! Don't shoot me!"

He touched the gun to the guy's knee again. "What's your name?"

"Jeremy Reed."

"What are you doing here?"

"I live here, man. Been living here a long time. Dude died. Place was empty. Nobody cares. What's your problem?"

"Who lives here with you?"

"Just me, man."

Flint nudged his knee with the gun barrel again.

Reed's eyes went wild. He thrashed his head back and forth. "And my girlfriend. She's at work."

"Why'd you shoot at me?"

Reed's belligerent tone turned whiny. "Because those other two beat the crap outta me. This time, I was ready."

"What other two?"

"I don't know, man. Two ugly dudes. Came here a few weeks back. Asking a bunch of questions about the guy who used to own this place and his kid."

Flint pulled out his phone and found the picture he'd taken of Trevor and Paxton after he'd hit them with the Taser shots back in his alley. He showed the picture.

Reed's eyes widened and bulged out. He nodded his head vigorously. "Yeah. That's them. They wailed on me but good."

"What did you tell them?"

"Nothin'. I don't know nothin'. We own this place now. It's ours. Guy died a long time ago. Nobody came around." He shrugged. "We needed a roof, so we moved in. Stayed on. Not like people are lining up to live in this dump. Nobody cared until those two showed up."

Flint narrowed his gaze. He was no lawyer, but he knew a bit about adverse possession, the law that says squatters can get title to real property if they claim title to it long enough. There are a few requirements, but it can be done in a thousand ways. If the real owner doesn't find out and object before the statute of limitations runs out, then Reed would own the place. Maybe he already owned it, like he said.

And if he owned the land, that didn't necessarily mean he owned the mineral rights, too. If he owned those, Shaw and Crane would already know. They wouldn't be looking for Oakwood.

This guy was smarter than he looked. Or maybe his girlfriend was the smart one. Or maybe Shaw and Crane were behind this. Hedging their bets. If they didn't find the rightful heir in time, one of them would simply steal her land and everything under it. Couple of princes.

Flint bent down and slapped the tape back on Reed's mouth. All the fight had gone out of him, though. He didn't struggle when Flint picked him up in a fireman's carry and hustled over to the helo.

Flint plopped him in the back of the Sikorsky, settled into the passenger seat, and gave the pilot two thumbs-up. Phillips revved up the helo without further conversation.

As the Sikorsky lifted off the ground, Flint retrieved his headset and turned on his microphone.

"Who's our passenger?" Phillips asked. It was the first question he'd asked since Flint came aboard.

"No idea."

"Where are we taking him?"

"Not sure yet."

"I'm going to need to refuel soon. Where are we going?"

"Wolf Bend High School parking lot." He'd chosen the school because its parking lot was the only one he'd seen during the flyover that was large enough to land the Sikorsky.

"Can I drop you off and come back? Maybe an hour?"

"Sure."

"What about him?" Phillips tilted his head toward the guy in the back.

Good question. He was already regretting his decision to bring Reed along. The guy was probably exactly what he claimed to be. Most likely the bio data wouldn't turn up anything either. But the alternative was to leave him to make trouble for Flint with Shaw or Crane or someone worse.

The simple matter of absorbing Laura Oakwood's past through direct exposure to her habitats had become way more complicated than Flint had expected. "Take him with you."

"Will do."

The big Sikorsky rose higher and turned south toward the town.

CHAPTER SEVENTEEN

WOLF BEND, TEXAS, WASN'T the most godforsaken place Flint had ever seen, but it was far from the most desirable. It contained nothing resembling the standard indicators of twenty-first-century life in America.

No big-box stores. No multiplexes. Not even a single fast-food joint.

Did they even have internet access? Back in the day, residents probably ordered what they needed from a catalogue and things were delivered by US mail. Maybe they still did.

Across the street from the high school, he saw four buildings. A gas station and car repair shop. A small grocery store. A diner. And something like a dollar store for everything else, he guessed. The sign out front said, "If we don't have it, you don't need it." He grinned. All problems solved.

Most of the next block was occupied by a church and an open space that might have been a city park. On either end and behind the buildings of the main town were a few two-story homes on half a dozen residential streets.

The Sikorsky set down in the school parking lot long enough for Flint to get out and then left to find fuel. No doubt the Sikorsky's coming and going drew attention, but it was Sunday afternoon and the streets were almost deserted.

The few pedestrians who were milling about glanced at the helo and went on about their business. Which might have meant they were somewhat used to such arrivals and departures. Seemed unlikely that even the smallest thing would go unnoticed in a place like this.

The two school buildings, one slightly larger than the other, sat on the north edge of what only a prankster would call the city. Both U-shaped buildings were cement block with flat roofs and big windows facing Main Street.

Flint was surprised the town had enough kids to justify two schools. The larger one was the high school. Next door was the school for kindergarten through eighth grade. Behind the buildings were the parking lot and the athletic field.

Fortunately, the entire school complex was closed on Sunday. The high school's back door faced the parking lot. The school principal was waiting for him outside. Flint was late. He'd have to check out the town after their meeting instead of before, as he'd planned.

"Thanks for giving me the tour on a Sunday, Mr. Mason," Flint said, hand extended, a polite smile on his face. "I won't take up too much of your time."

Dan Mason looked like the online photo Flint had found before he made this appointment. Sixtyish. Balding. His skin was weathered and his handshake bony. "No trouble at all. Come on inside. My office is up front."

He looked exactly how Flint had imagined a high school science teacher and principal in Wolf Bend would look. He'd had the principal's job for eighteen years. He'd been the science teacher and football coach before that. In a school this size, Flint suspected, everybody wore more than one hat.

As they walked shoulder to shoulder through the empty halls, Flint absorbed more of Laura Oakwood's world. Beige tile walls, beige tile floor, lockers lining the entire trip from the back door to the front. What would high school have been like for her? Nothing but contact with the same people, day in and day out, for all the years she lived here. Except for the lack of bars on the windows and barbed wire around the perimeter, it could have been a prison. Oakwood probably felt like a prisoner. No one tries to escape from a happy place.

Mason's office was just inside the double front doors, along with the other two administrative offices, one for the nurse and one for everything else.

Flint stopped a moment to look at the wall dotted with group graduation photos dating back to 1960 when the school was built.

Each of the photos included faculty and staff, which hadn't changed much for the past dozen years. Two or three pretty teachers showed up in the earlier photos now and then but disappeared from the later ones. A few years' photos were missing, probably because they'd had no graduates those years.

Laura Oakwood's class was a year before Rosalio Prieto's. There were no role models for Laura or Rosalio. No pretty women teachers or men younger than fifty.

Flint pulled out his phone. "Would you mind if I took pictures of these?"

"Not at all," Mason said.

While Flint snapped photos, Mason looked at the framed gallery as if he hadn't seen them in a long time. "One class of graduates looks pretty much the same as the next when they're dressed in those caps and gowns, doesn't it?"

After Flint dropped the phone into his pocket, Mason turned his palm toward the small office and preceded Flint into the room. He settled into the brown leather chair on the opposite side of a battered wood desk while Flint took one of the heavy wood chairs across from him.

This was the kind of meeting in the principal's office that had instilled fear in students and their parents for generations. An experience Flint had never endured as a kid. There had been no principal at Bette Maxwell's boarding school. Not enough kids to justify the state paying for one.

"I don't see how I can help you, Mr. Flint, as much as I'd like to. Laura Oakwood was a nice girl and she's had a tough life. I'm glad she stands to inherit something after all these years." Mason rested his forearms on the arms of his chair and folded his hands across his paunch. "But as I said when you called, I haven't seen Laura Oakwood or Rosalio Prieto since they left Wolf Bend the summer she graduated. Nineteen eighty-eight, was it? Her dad passed not long before that. She didn't have any other family, far as I know. None that lived here in Wolf Bend, anyway."

"You seem pretty sure about that."

"Look around, Mr. Flint. This is a small place. Everybody knows everybody and everything that happens to them, too. If Richard and Selma Oakwood had family left here in Wolf Bend, I'd have known about it."

"Selma? I thought Richard's wife was Sally."

"Sorry. You're right. People called her Sally. I forgot." Mason smiled. "She hated the name Selma. But that was the name on Laura's official school records. I'm not great with names, so I refreshed my memory before you arrived."

"I see." So Laura Oakwood had named her daughter after her own mother, which was usually a loving gesture. But she'd saddled the girl with an awkward name that her mother hated. Laura Oakwood was a complicated female, all right. Even before she'd robbed Mildred's Corner and disappeared.

"So you knew the Oakwood family, then. What can you tell me about them? Anything at all might help me locate Laura." He'd fed Mason a line of bull that was partly true. The same story he'd told Bette Maxwell. That if he found Laura Oakwood, she'd inherit some oil and gas money. It was a common thing in Texas and encouraged cooperation from people who might not want to gossip. Most people were likely to help the little guy get money from Big Oil and keep it out of the hands of the government.

"Richard came here in the 1960s, I think. To work in the oil fields over in Mount Warren. Jobs were thick on the ground over there at the time. Like so many others, he didn't have much education or many skills, but he was a hard worker." Mason leaned back like he was warming up to tell a long campfire story. "Richard wanted a ranch, and land around here was some of the cheapest in Texas at the time."

"Still is."

"Right. That place he got from old Juan Garcia wasn't ever going to be a working ranch, but he didn't know that for a while."

"What happened when he found out?"

"By then, he'd already fallen in love with the girl next door, literally. Old Juan's daughter, Sally. About a year after they married, little Laura was born," Mason continued. "Richard was too prideful to quit ranching for a long time. Poured every penny he made into that old place. He and Sally tried to make the ranch work until Sally got sick."

Flint let the story seep in through his pores.

Mason said, "After Sally died, seemed like the last straw for Richard. He fell into the bottle and never climbed out. Never tried to, near as anybody could tell."

"What about Laura?" Flint asked.

"She finished high school. Shy girl, standoffish, I guess. But friendly enough once you got to know her. In a small school like this, all the kids are involved in everything because, well, what else are they going to do besides get into trouble?" He shrugged. "So she was a cheerleader and a debater and she was on the school paper. Like I said, she was a nice girl. Most people felt sorry for her, but she didn't appreciate the pity."

Flint understood. The well-meaning people were sometimes the hardest for a kid to take.

"What happened after she graduated? Why did she leave Wolf Bend?"

"Well, not much to keep her here, was there? I'd guess Richard was probably pretty hard to deal with before he died. He had a temper. Always had. And drinking didn't make him any easier, you know?"

Flint nodded. "When did she start dating Prieto? They left town together, you said, right?"

Mason closed his eyes and tilted his chin, as if he was thinking back. "I want to say they were dating in her last year of high school, but it could have been before that. He'd already graduated, I know that. He wasn't the kind of kid who wanted college. He was looking for work and not having a lot of luck. That's always a frustrating thing, no matter how old you are."

"Tough country out there." Flint tilted his head toward the window to the hot, dusty world outside. "Anybody go after them when they left? Try to find them? Bring them back?"

"Why would anyone do that?" Mason's eyes met Flint's.

He shrugged.

"Look, Wolf Bend's no place for young people. Never has been. There's nothing to offer them here," Mason said. "Laura's father might have been the only one to try to bring her back, but he was already gone, too. She wasn't close to anyone else. Not close enough, at any rate."

"You said her mother was Juan Garcia's daughter. What about the Garcia family? Wouldn't they have tried to find Laura and bring her home?" Flint was trying to wrap his head around the life Laura had left behind.

Mason shook his head. "Afraid not. The rift in the Garcia family goes way back."

"How about Prieto's parents? Weren't they interested in getting him back?"

Mason looked down at his hands and seemed to mull something around in his head for a bit. He cleared his throat and met Flint's gaze.

"Rosalio wasn't the best apple in the barrel over at the Prietos, I'm afraid. They're a fine family. God knows, they tried. And he might have grown out of his rebellious phase eventually."

"But?"

"I'm not saying he was running from the law when he left here, because I don't know why he left." Mason cleared his throat and straightened his shoulders. "But the police chief was about to put him in jail again. He'd have been convicted again, and this time he'd have served a couple of years, probably."

"What crime did he commit?"

"Stole a car. Went joyriding in it. Wrecked it." Mason raised his gaze. "The usual hijinks that boys his age do when they've got a girl and pals they want to impress and no job and too much time on their hands."

Flint nodded. He recognized the truth in that story. "Had Rosalio ever done anything like that before?"

"A few times, he'd been in trouble. Drinking. Petty larceny. Fights. But nothing quite that serious."

"What caused him to escalate to grand theft auto?"

"Well," Mason cleared his throat again, "he'd fallen in with a drifter. The guy was older. Not a good influence."

"Do you know his name?"

Mason shook his head. "I'm not good with names."

"What happened to the drifter?"

"He wandered out of town right around the time Laura and Rosalio left." Mason looked down and then up again. "Some folks said they might have all left together."

Flint nodded and resisted the sarcasm that sprang to mind. "You said there were more members of the Prieto family living here. Are they still around? I'd like to talk to them, if they're willing."

"Won't help much. They don't have a lot of lost love for Laura Oakwood. They blame her for leading him astray, although I've always thought it was the other way around." He shrugged again. "Anyway, Rosalio's younger sister, Teresa, works over at the diner. She might be there today. The others have all scattered. Like I said, there's not much Wolf Bend has to offer people these days."

"You said Richard Oakwood moved here in the 1960s. Any idea where he lived before?"

"I'm not sure I ever heard." He pursed his lips and frowned a few moments. "Canada, maybe?"

Flint noticed the time on the big clock on the wall behind Mason. He leaned forward. "I'm sorry, Mr. Mason, but I need to get going. Do you still have any files for Laura Oakwood or Rosalio Prieto from back then? There might be something in them that I could use to help me find her."

"Like what?"

"Like a birth certificate for her parents or other forms that showed where they were born. So I can check with the extended family to find Laura."

"We don't keep files after about five years." Mason shook his head. "We send the transcripts in to the state, though. State of Texas might have more information on the Oakwoods. Did you check?"

"We didn't have any luck in Austin, I'm afraid. And immigration was pretty lax back then, too." Flint stood. "Thank you for coming in today, Mr. Mason. Can I call you if I think of anything else?"

"Like I said, I'm glad to help Laura, if I can. When you find her, give her my best, will you?"

But the interview wasn't a total waste of time.

Now he knew Laura Oakwood was related to old Juan Garcia and Richard Oakwood might have emigrated from Canada.

Scarlett must have chased the Garcia lead down already and found nothing. But she hadn't looked in Canada for Richard Oakwood's family.

Perhaps Canadian records would be better than the ones Scarlett had already checked in Texas.

CHAPTER EIGHTEEN

FLINT LEFT WITH MASON through the back door of the school. After Mason drove away, Flint pulled one of the disposable cell phones out of his pocket to call Scarlett.

Drake should have returned to Houston about an hour ago and delivered the original medical records for Laura Oakwood's baby. Scarlett would have seen the low hemoglobin report. She'd also have examined the blood reports from the crime scene. By now she'd have figured out what any follow-up hemoglobin report on the baby revealed.

The phone fired up but registered no cell signal. Maybe the school complex was in a dead zone. Flint looked around for a tower. He didn't see any. Surely there was someplace in this town where he could make a cell phone call.

He walked from the parking lot to the front of the high school, turned south across the side street, and walked through the pulsing heat to the end of the next short block.

The sign on the front of the only building likely to hold a jail cell and the post office sat across from the church and declared itself "Wolf Bend, Texas, City Offices."

He'd briefly considered dropping Jeremy Reed with the sheriff and lodging a formal complaint for the attempted assault. Reed had shot at him, after all. Locking him up for a couple of days would keep him out of the case until the deadline passed.

He'd like to ask the sheriff about Rosalio Prieto, too. The sheriff was probably the one who notified the next of kin when Prieto died. He might be willing to say more than the information in his files that Scarlett had already collected.

If there was a sheriff or a chief of police, he wasn't on site at the moment. There were no cars in the lot. And still no cell signal registering on the burner phone.

Flint crossed Main Street and walked north. The city park was quiet. A few kids playing across on the other side of the park. The general store and the grocery store were closed. Only the diner and the gas station seemed to have business hours late on Sunday.

Flint checked the phone along the way, but no signal registered.

If the follow-up blood test was done on the baby, Scarlett should already be checking hospitals in Texas and Mexico. But would she be checking in Canada?

He shut down the phone and returned it to his pocket.

Flint walked into the Wolf Bend Diner and stood in the doorway a moment. Cool air felt welcome on his overheated body. He pushed his sunglasses onto his head and scanned for a place to sit.

The diner was nice enough. It had been decorated a few decades ago, but it was clean and tidy. More than a dozen steel tables with green laminate tops and green vinyl-padded chairs were strewn about the open room's cement floor. Four of the tables were occupied. Maybe they'd come for dinner before Sunday-night church.

A long counter ran along the right side of the diner. Steel bar stools, with seats covered in the same green vinyl padding as the chairs, lined the floor on one side of the counter. On the other side were the usual walkways, food displays, working countertops, and a window through to the kitchen in the back.

Everything about the diner, and the town, seemed like a movie set for a 1960s-era film. Edward Hopper, the American realist, might easily have painted the place and he'd been dead since 1967.

There was no hostess stand and only one waitress. She was the right age, about forty-five, Flint guessed. Dark hair pulled back in an elastic band. Dark eyes. Slender. Maybe five seven or so. Her uniform was a pair of khaki slacks and a polo shirt the same green color as the diner's vinyl seats.

Flint found an empty table near the front window and sat facing the door. The waitress came over after five minutes with a glass of water, a plastic menu, a brown plastic mug, and a coffeepot.

She put the water and the menu on the table. "Coffee?" Her voice was pack-a-day husky. Stale cigarette smoke lingered on her breath.

"Yes. Thank you."

She poured the coffee and put it in front of him before she pulled a knife and fork wrapped in a paper napkin from her pocket. "Special's meatloaf today. It's pretty good. Joey learned to make it from his grandmother. Mashed potatoes and gravy. Side salad. $6.99."

"Sold." Flint handed her the menu.

She held it against her chin for a moment. She must have known every resident of Wolf Bend, and he didn't number among them. "You came in on that helicopter, didn't you?"

"I did." No reason to deny it.

"We don't want any trouble." Her voice trembled.

"Nor do I. Why would you think otherwise?"

"Order up!" Joey, the cook, yelled through the open serving window behind the counter.

"I'll be right back with your food." She returned to the counter and spoke to Joey. She delivered an order to a guy sitting alone at a table in the back and refilled coffee for several diners on her return trip.

When she had everyone satisfied for the moment, she swooped past the kitchen and then headed his way, carrying a brown plastic bowl for the small green salad doused with ranch dressing in one hand and the rest of his meal under congealing gravy on a separate plate in the other hand.

She placed both on the table and sat across from him.

"After you eat, you should go. Joey has already called the police chief at home and he's on his way." Her tone was quiet, earnest. She didn't want to be overheard, but she wanted him to leave.

"Is this how you greet all visitors to Wolf Bend?" He picked up the fork and tasted the meatloaf, which was surprisingly good. He hadn't realized he was hungry. When had he last eaten? Steak in London? "This is great meatloaf."

"Meatloaf's been on the menu every Sunday since Sam Houston was a pup." Briefly, the frown left her face and something like pride replaced it. "When you're the only game in town, everybody's counting on you."

"Well, Joey's grandmother must have been an amazing cook."

"She was. She and her husband owned this place until they died. She did the cooking and he did the serving."

He nodded and took a few more bites. He glanced at the plate. He'd eaten more than half his food already. He put the fork down and looked across the table. "Speaking of family, you're Rosalio Prieto's sister, aren't you? Teresa, right?"

She gasped and her hand flew to cover her mouth.

He reached over and placed his hand on her forearm to keep her from bolting. "What kind of trouble do you think I'm likely to cause, Teresa?"

"Why are you interested in my brother after all these years? Can't you let him rest in peace?" He could feel her trembling under his palm.

"I'm looking for Laura Oakwood. Dan Mason over at the high school told me you might be able to help me because she left town with your brother." He lowered his voice so she had to lean in to hear him. Given the small town and Teresa's age, she and Laura Oakwood must have known each other. He took a chance on the rest. "She was your best friend, wasn't she? You knew they were planning to leave Wolf Bend. You knew where they went, too, didn't you?"

Teresa's eyes widened and a frown settled across her features. She tried to pull her arm away, but he tightened his grasp.

"Joey called the police chief, Teresa. I don't have a lot of time before he gets here. If we're not going to have any trouble," he didn't raise his voice, but he put more urgency into it and squeezed her arm a little tighter, "I need you to help me find Laura Oakwood."

"I don't know where Laura is. I haven't heard from her since before my brother . . . died. We didn't know where they went." She stopped for a breath and her lip quavered. "I swear. I told those other guys I didn't know where she is. It's the truth. Didn't they tell you?"

So she thought he was with Paxton and Trevor. Maybe even their boss or someone worse than the advance team. Not a bad assumption.

No wonder she was scared.

He willed her to calm down a bit. Odd that Mason hadn't mentioned that Paxton and Trevor had already been around. Even if they didn't interview him, Mason should have known they'd been asking about Laura Oakwood. Why didn't he mention it?

"Mason said there was another friend of your brother's. A man. A drifter. Mason said Rosalio and Laura might have left town with him." Flint cocked his head when he saw her nostrils flare.

"Leo. My brother's name was Rosalio, after my grandfather." Her tone softened again. "But those of us who loved him called him Leo."

"Did Laura call him Leo, too?"

Teresa nodded. "She loved Leo. More than the rest of us realized."

Flint nodded. "The guy who left town with them? Mason didn't know the guy's name or anything about him."

"John David, he said his name was." She caught her breath. Her chin quivered. "He was bad news. He had them both wrapped around his little finger, though."

"How's that?"

"Drugs to start. John David seemed to have an endless supply of marijuana and a bunch of mind-bending chemicals, I guess. And Leo was wild. Always had been. Not bad. A daredevil. He'd try anything. Crazy stuff, you know?" She paused and her tone softened a bit more. "Laura was shy. She was thrilled when Leo started paying attention to her, even though he was just bored at first and she was handy. She'd never had a boyfriend before, and after her mom died, her life with her dad was pretty miserable."

Flint felt the instant irritation that always triggered when he learned someone like Leo was taking unfair advantage of a girl like Laura. If that's what happened. He forced the annoyance from his voice. "What kind of crazy stuff was Leo involved in with John David?"

"People here in Wolf Bend tend to be Christians. I am. Laura certainly was. And so was Leo. John David comes along and says he's a Satan worshipper, which Leo found exciting, he said. Something different. Another way to rebel, I guess. Piss off our parents." She shrugged and took a deep breath. "And by that time, Laura would do anything Leo wanted. So they started doing stuff with John David."

"Stuff like what?"

"Dumb crap. Dancing naked in the moonlight. Getting high. All that crazy stuff you'd see in old horror movies." Her voice was stronger as she recounted each outrage. "When they started killing animals, I told Leo to stay away from John David, but he wouldn't listen to me."

"And Laura?"

"Laura wouldn't listen to me either. I begged her to stop. To get Leo to stop. She followed Leo around like he had her on a leash."

Flint's voice was quieter. "I see."

Teresa heard the anger in his tone. She began trembling again. "But it was John David that did all the leading. He was the one who stole the car and blamed it on Leo. He said they wouldn't put Leo in jail, but he was wrong about that, too, wasn't he?"

"Yes, I'm afraid he was. Grand theft auto is a felony everywhere."

"Damned straight." She stuck her chin out.

"Where did they go, Teresa?" He lightly squeezed her forearm again.

Some of her spirit seemed to collapse. "Some camp. A place John David knew about called Clovis Ranch. They said they were going to live there for a while. Not far from where Leo . . . died."

"Did you tell that to the police?"

She nodded. "'Course I told the police back then. They said they already knew. They figured Leo had been hanging there before he . . . died. They went out to that camp a few times, but John David wasn't there. And the creeps said Leo and Laura hadn't been there, either."

"Maybe they weren't. Maybe they actually went somewhere else."

She didn't respond for a moment, and then she whispered, "They'd be alive now if they'd stayed in Wolf Bend."

"Maybe so." He couldn't argue about what might have been. He released his hold on her arm. "How about the other two guys who were here asking about Laura? The ones who frightened you. Did you tell them about John David and Clovis Ranch?"

"Hell, no. They didn't even ask about Leo. Those jerks thought they could intimidate me. Well, the hell with that. They came to my house and I let my dog after them. He bit one in the ass and took a good chunk out of the other one's ear." She smiled, satisfied. "They haven't been back."

Flint smiled, too. Paxton and Trevor weren't having much luck so far, but they wouldn't give up. They had to be getting desperate. The finder's fee Crane promised them was too high to simply give up. "I need to find Laura. She's due a lot of money. Those two guys are looking for her, too. If they find her first . . ." He let his voice trail off.

Teresa's eyes widened and her mouth formed a little O. She shook her head. "I'd help you if I could. I haven't seen or heard from Laura since she left here. I swear."

"Do you know what happened to John David? Where can I find him?"

"He's dead, I hope." She glared and then shrugged. "Cops said he was at that convenience store where Leo . . . died. They were looking for him. I've never seen him since he left here. And don't want to."

"Do you think he could be with Laura?"

"Not likely. He was a creep." Teresa shook her head and chewed her lower lip. "John David tried to put the moves on both of us a few times. Laura punched him right in the face. Left him with a big black eye for a week."

He watched her face a bit longer. He believed her. "Okay. How about this. Do you know a guy named Jeremy Reed?"

"No."

"He's squatting at the Oakwood ranch. He says he has a deed and everything."

"Well, that's a lie. I have no idea who that guy is. And if he was from Wolf Bend, I'd know." She took a deep breath. "I knew Richard Oakwood. He was a mean son of a bitch. He wouldn't have given anybody anything. Not willingly, anyway."

"Reed says he's living out there with a girlfriend who works in town. Any idea who that girlfriend might be?"

"In this town?" She shook her head. "Are you sure he didn't mean Mount Warren? That's over in the next county. Lots of folks around here work in Mount Warren. Richard Oakwood worked over there. Lots of oil field money available in good times. Plenty of jobs. You might find her over there."

From the kitchen Joey called, "Order up!" Flint suspected he was worried about Teresa, because no one could have ordered anything since she sat down at Flint's table.

"I need to go." She pushed her chair back. "Joey didn't really call the police before. But he will if he thinks you're going to be a problem."

"Just bring me my check. I'll get out of your way." Flint smiled at her. "And thanks for recommending the meatloaf. It really was great."

"If I hear from Laura, I'll let you know. But I don't think I will. She hasn't contacted me in twenty-eight years. No reason to think she'll call now. She's never coming back here." She stood up and puffed up her chest and stuck out her chin a little. "Nobody wants her here either. Far as I'm concerned, she killed my brother. I'll never forgive her for that. You find her, you tell her that for me, okay?"

"I will." He touched her hand again and softened his tone. "But you were Laura's best friend."

"That was a long time ago."

For a moment he considered telling her about her brother's child. Her niece, Selma. But the girl could be dead by now if his suspicions about her health proved out. And he didn't know where she was or have the time to find her at the moment. He didn't have it in him to bring Teresa more heartache. Instead, he suggested, "You might change your mind, Teresa."

"Why? Because she'll be rich now or something? I seem like the kind who would forgive her because of that?" Teresa pulled her hand away. "She didn't shoot Leo. But she didn't help me keep him here in Wolf Bend, either. She could have. He'd have stayed for her. And I'd still have a brother."

"Don't make up your mind yet." He heard the Sikorsky headed in toward the school parking lot across the street. "Wait and see."

Teresa folded her hands over her chest. "I'll be right back with your change."

She took his twenty, turned, and walked toward the cash register. Before she returned, he polished off the meatloaf and headed out to meet Phillips for the trip back to Houston.

CHAPTER NINETEEN

THE SIKORSKY LANDED WITH the same ear-splitting volume. Only a dead man could fail to hear it. Litter and dust took flight, washing away from the downdraft.

Flint crossed the street and waited for the air to clear before hurrying to the high school parking lot.

He climbed up into the passenger seat, donned his headset, and gave a thumbs-up. Phillips pointed to the seat belt. "You might need it." He shrugged. "You never know."

Phillips had been a decent pilot so far, but Flint latched the four-point harness as requested.

Phillips ran through a series of checks. The engine spooled up. A long, slow increase in the jet engine's whining pitch. The giant blades beat the air. The big helo rocked for a moment before easing off the ground.

A gentle lift, ten feet, before Phillips tilted the craft forward, nose down, tail up. The big blades caught the air, pulling the helo forward. As they gained speed and altitude, Phillips brought the helo almost level.

The Sikorsky left Wolf Bend as efficiently as it had arrived.

Couldn't have done it better myself.

Flint watched the flat-panel displays in front of him. The heading looked right. An aeronautical chart was on one of the displays, a thick blue line marking their route back to Houston. One turn, roughly halfway along. The altitude scale showed the helo at five thousand feet and still climbing. Several displays showed engine RPM and a series of temperatures, all higher than normal with the effort of lifting the giant bird. "Sorry I'm late. Harder to find fuel than I'd expected," Phillips said.

"No problem. How's our passenger?" Flint turned in his seat to look for himself. Reed was no longer lying on his left side on the floor where Flint had plopped him. Phillips had moved him into one of the backseats and strapped him in.

Reed's wrists and ankles were still hog-tied with the extension cord. The paper first aid tape covered his mouth, but it had curled at the edges. Reed's head rested on the back of the seat. Angry eyes narrowed and watched Flint like a predator in the wild. "Quiet as a baby," Phillips said, grinning.

The Sikorsky leveled off. Flint checked the map. They were spot-on the blue line, heading east toward the turn and on to Houston. A number in the top corner of the display showed that the flight time should be under three hours, but that was three hours too long.

Flint pulled out a disposable cell phone and fired it up.

"It's illegal to make cell phone calls in flight. Fines are huge. Stiff penalties," Phillips said.

Flint wasn't worried about fines and penalties. He had bigger problems.

A call from the Sikorsky would be worse than broadcasting on live radio. The signal could reach towers fifteen miles away.

Anyone could listen in. The other option was to wait the almost three hours until he reached Houston. Far from ideal.

Paxton and Trevor already had a significant head start. An additional three-hour lead might be too great an advantage to overcome. But they weren't the sharpest knives in the drawer, either.

So far, Flint's ace in the hole was that everyone who came into contact with Paxton and Trevor was pissed off and all too happy to strike back. It wasn't much of an advantage, but now that he knew it existed, he could exploit it.

Flint was starting to feel like a quarterback who'd elected to run with the ball. Everybody on the field was trying to tackle him.

He pulled off his headset and dialed the cell phone as soon as it registered a signal. Scarlett's phone rang three times before she picked up the unrecognized number. "Yes?"

Cryptic conversation was all they could manage over the noise and vibration of the Sikorsky. "Did you get the package?"

"Yes."

"I'm on my way."

"ETA?"

"165." One hundred and sixty-five minutes.

"Everything okay?" She sounded a bit worried.

"Excellent. Any progress to report?"

"Not much. We found—"

The call dropped. He considered calling back, but the altimeter showed the Sikorsky passing through six thousand feet. Too high for a good cell phone connection, perhaps. They were traveling faster than they had on the two inbound flights earlier. The Sikorsky's RPM and engine temps were still higher than normal.

Phillips was pushing it, and the flight time had dropped ten minutes. Flint wasn't about to complain. The sooner he reached Houston, the better.

Texas lay below. Mostly wide and empty. Long, straight roads connected small towns that had the same sunbaked tan color as the wilderness around them. One road looked like the next. One patch of sunbaked earth the same as the rest. Patches of green were sparse.

The Sikorsky's engine droned on. Phillips stared ahead, turning his head every minute or so to scan the horizon for any sign of errant aircraft.

Flint adjusted a rearview mirror to see the passenger without craning his neck. Reed simply glowered, his eyes narrowed to focus his anger on Flint.

The towns grew even more sparse. Roads took right-angle bends at the corners of property lines. Many simply ended at a small cluster of buildings, likely a house and a couple of barns. Nothing but blacktop over what had once been gravel farm-to-market paths.

Flint leaned back in the copilot's seat, folded his hands across his lap, and closed his eyes. A nap wasn't a bad idea. Once the helo set down in Houston, he wouldn't have much time for sleep. The clock was ticking.

The helo nosed down a fraction. Flint raised his head and looked as Phillips pointed to the flat-panel display. "We're running a little hot." The temperature gauge had definitely risen since they left Wolf Bend. The needle was bordering on the red zone. The altitude scale showed they were just over six thousand feet.

They could increase altitude, where the air was cooler, but that would also be slower and consume more fuel. The current altitude was a reasonable compromise.

Flint checked the map. They were approaching the turn in the blue travel line. Halfway. He watched the temperature gauge, willing it to go down.

A buzzer sounded. He looked at Phillips. The pilot was busy finessing the flight path, keeping the nose of the helo angled down slightly. He pressed a button and the buzzer stopped.

Flint glanced back at Reed, who was still staring. Still as angry as ever. Reed couldn't hear any of what was happening because he wasn't wearing a headset. His anger was fueled not by the buzzer but by Flint.

Too bad. Flint wasn't all that thrilled with him either.

Another buzzer sounded. Louder and angrier than the first. The engine's whine stuttered. The helo shook, solid thumps as if it had traveled over a speed bump.

Phillips was pressing buttons. He cinched his four-point harness tighter. Flint followed his lead, tightening himself to his seat.

A bell joined the buzzer.

Large red symbols flashed on the display. The temperature gauge was well into the red.

The altitude scale showed fifty-nine hundred feet. They were dropping.

The engine coughed.

Flint knew what was coming next.

CHAPTER TWENTY

FLINT HAD EXPERIENCED HELICOPTER free fall before. A trained pilot should be able to get things under control. Flint didn't interfere.

Phillips was familiar with the aircraft, and Flint had never flown this particular Sikorsky before. Smart money was on the pilot, who knew the particular machine inside and out.

He would give Phillips as much time as possible to handle the big bird before taking over.

He might die today. But not because he failed to save himself.

Phillips twisted the throttle. The engine made a plaintive attempt to spool up before slowly winding down. There was a feeble *whump* sound, and the engine's whine was gone.

A bell sounded, regular, insistent. A female voice came over the headset. "Flameout. Flameout."

It was the automatic warning system. Redundant. They already knew the engine had stalled; the flame needed to keep it running was somehow gone.

Phillips was leaning forward. Scanning the ground.

The helo was traveling forward.

Momentum. Nothing more.

Then it wasn't.

Flint's stomach shot up into his mouth. His body lurched up against his harness as the helo dropped away below him.

Reed's harness was not as tight as it could have been. He plopped up in the air and slammed down on the seat. His angry glare was replaced with wide-eyed shock. His head was pushed sideways by the impact, and the curled edges of the tape over his mouth caught in the harness and were ripped off his face.

"We're falling! We're going to crash!" Reed screamed.

The bell rang on.

"Restart, restart," said the woman's voice, calmly.

Phillips was straining to see over the helo's nose, looking for a landing spot.

Read's screaming continued, but Flint couldn't reach him to shut him up.

"Restart," Flint said.

Phillips shook his head. "Too hot."

Flint pointed to the temperature gauge, rapidly dropping out of the red. "It's cooling." He pointed to the RPM dial. "And the air is spooling up the engine."

"Landing," Phillips said, angling the helo forward and down.

Reed's frantic yelling from the backseat was loud enough to be heard over the noise. "We're gonna die! We're gonna die!" Flint and Phillips ignored him.

Below, the ground was not flat. The roads and buildings that had dotted the route since they'd left Wolf Bend had vanished.

Flint gripped a handhold beside his seat. The engine's noise had been replaced by a howling gale of rushing air and the grinding of metal. The helo's blades were back-driving the giant gearbox and jet engine.

Reed's screams continued. "We're gonna die! We're gonna die!" Flint blocked the screaming out of his mind.

Phillips pressed the "Push to Talk" button and recited the helo's tail number into the ether. He added the words, "Flameout. Going down. Request assistance."

Phillips's voice was calm, but Flint had no doubt the radio tower could hear Reed's panicked screams in the background.

Flint's nostrils twitched with the assault of hot metal and oil odors. And something else—urine. Reed had pissed himself.

The helo rocked from side to side. Phillips battled with the cyclic to keep the flying brick upright. The blades were a blur, seeming to spin just as fast as if they had been powered by the engine.

The helo was on a slow, curving descent. The meager lift from the spinning blades and the big bird's momentum helped to keep it flying.

Only it wasn't flying.

It was falling.

"Caxton tower," said the voice of an air traffic controller from their headsets. "Do you see a clear place to put down, sir?" The controller's voice sounded more tense than Phillips's.

"Affirmative," Phillips said before rattling off their GPS coordinates.

A few moments of silence passed before the controller came back.

"I've notified the emergency services. They're on their way."

"Two thousand feet," Phillips said.

"If we lose radio contact, stay near your helicopter until EMS arrives."

"Roger."

"Godspeed, sir."

Flint heard a distinct click. The controller had nothing else to say. There was nothing else he could do. Flint tightened his grip on the bracing handle and stayed out of the way.

Reed was thrashing and screaming in the backseat.

Flint looked down and out through the plexiglass canopy that allowed a clear view of the ground below. The feature was vital to fine maneuvering in tight landings, but at that moment he was glad Reed didn't have such a detailed view of the rocks below them.

The helo was still moving forward. Phillips was still finessing the controls. Perhaps a half-mile ahead, Flint saw a smooth patch of ground covered in something green. A tiny lawn in a desert of rock. Which meant there was water nearby as well.

The rocky hills on the ground grew larger. The helo's forward speed blurred them like the swipe of a painter's brush.

They were going to crash. All Phillips could do now was simply decide where they crashed. And how.

Flint glanced into the backseat. Reed's eyes were still wide but he'd stopped screaming. He was blubbering now and repeating, "Ohmygodohmygodohmygod!" over and over without pause.

Reed could feel that the Sikorsky had been falling for a long time. He must have known there was an inevitable end to their fall. It was just a matter of whether he would survive. Flint would have tried to reassure him, but Reed was beyond reason.

They had almost reached the tiny lawn. The ground was close—a hundred feet at most. But even if forward speed was dropping fast, they were going to hit beyond the softer green at this rate.

The woman's voice that had warned them of the engine conditions came back. "Terrain, terrain," she said. She repeated her warning at two-second intervals. It was the kind of warning to which a teenager might have snarled, "No joke, Sherlock."

They were directly above the tiny lawn. It was time.

Come on, Phillips. Do it now.

"Autorotating," Phillips said, as he pulled up on the collective.

Finally.

The sound of rushing air grew to a gale-force storm. Metal groaned and creaked. The Sikorsky shook.

The helo's nose tipped up like a motorboat. Flint was shoved down into his seat. Reed was pressed into his, still blubbering,

"Ohmygodohmygodohmygod!"

The big helo decelerated hard.

The nose lowered.

They were horizontal.

The blades spun slowly, each one visible as it whirled by.

Dust swirled into the air. Flint lost sight of the ground when a sandstorm caused by the rotating blades engulfed everything.

Flint and Phillips watched the horizon bar on the display in front of them. The outside world was gone from view.

Phillips twitched the stick, keeping the helo level with the horizon.

The helo hit the ground.

It bounced. Inched sideways.

Bounced again.

Bounced a third time.

On the fourth bounce, the massive Sikorsky passed six thousand feet's worth of momentum onto mother earth.

Metal creaked.

The helo leaned down on the right, the pilot's side.

Phillips had waited too long. Flint braced himself for the craft to roll over, visions of scenes from movies like *Blackhawk Down* running through his mind.

But Phillips was a good pilot. He struggled but ultimately managed to keep the helo upright.

The churning of the rotors and their gears finally slowed to a stop.

Flint relaxed his grip on the handholds. He breathed out. Surrendering the helo's controls to Phillips had been harder than the landing.

Flint was alive today because he relied on one man—himself. He'd never trusted anyone else. Except, occasionally, Scarlett.

But Phillips had done okay. They were on the ground and all in one piece.

He glanced at Reed. He looked like a child at a stage show right after the magician sawed the pretty girl in half and she waved to the crowd without bloody guts spilling all over the stage.

After a while, the dust cloud settled.

All sounds eventually stopped, even Reed's blubbering, halting breaths.

The Texas twilight poured into the cockpit.

Flint looked down through the plexiglass. The Sikorsky was perched firmly on the tiny lawn. Dead center. If he hadn't lived through it, Flint would have said Phillips's landing was perfect.

Phillips clicked his radio on. "Caxton tower, we're down." No reply.

"Caxton tower," repeated Phillips, "we're down." Radio silence.

Phillips glanced at Flint, and shrugged. "Looks like we lost the radio."

CHAPTER TWENTY-ONE

FLINT LOOKED AROUND INSIDE the Sikorsky. Everything was as expected.

"We're stuck here for a bit. After a landing like that, almost anything could be damaged," Phillips said, not even breathing hard. "We can't leave until mechanics arrive and declare the helo fit for flight."

Flint didn't argue. "How far away is Caxton Field?"

Phillips was flipping switches and completing paperwork. "Ninety minutes, give or take."

Flint unlatched his harness and left Phillips sitting in the cockpit.

In the back, Reed had finally stopped blubbering, but his eyes were still wild. His pants were soaked with urine and his shirt was spattered with vomit. He smelled like an outhouse.

Flint checked him for signs of physical injury and found none. His skin was pale, cool, and clammy. Respiration and pulse rapid. All signs of mild shock.

He untied the extension cord from Reed's wrists and ankles and tossed it out of the way. He pulled the dangling tape from Reed's cheek. He unlatched Reed's harness and laid him on the floor, feet elevated. He raised his head and offered him a few sips of bottled water.

By the time EMS arrived, Reed should be physically fine. Which meant he'd be talking and making trouble. More delay was likely. The last thing Flint had time for was extricating himself from local law enforcement again.

Flint rummaged through the first aid kit for something that might work as a sedative. He found a blister pack of narcotic painkillers. They could make Reed's symptoms worse, but that was a risk Flint was prepared to take. He pushed four pills through the blisters and opened Reed's mouth. He dropped the pills inside, offered more water, and held Reed's lips closed with a firm palm under his chin until he swallowed. Reed didn't struggle. He'd relax and sleep awhile, which would be better for all of them.

When he'd finished with Reed, Flint found antiseptic wipes in the first aid kit. He cleaned Reed's stench from his hands as well as possible and then left the helo.

Outside, Flint noticed the layer of dust that covered everything within a twenty-foot radius. The grassy spot was not quite as green under the dust blanket. It was still hot out. Though it was lower in the sky, the sun's glare continued unabated. The silence, now that the big bird was dead, felt surreal.

He glanced around the area for a quick threat assessment on this side of the Sikorsky. He didn't have a 360-degree view, but the inbound helo's racket and rotor wash should have scared away predators like wild pigs, cougars, and coyotes. No water nearby for alligators, stingrays, or other killers. The most common threats of nature in Texas, besides humans, were venomous spiders and snakes. He hoped they'd all scattered, too.

When Flint was a kid, he'd been bitten by scorpions, spiders, and fire ants more times than he cared to remember. A few scars from the welts still dotted his ankles. He didn't dwell on them. The memories made him itchy.

Once, Scarlett shot a snake not ten feet from Flint's side. They'd been shooting targets out behind one of the abandoned barns at Bette Maxwell's ranch. He'd never forget it. She was eighteen and had packed to leave for good the next day. She said she was never coming back. They didn't know if they'd ever see each other again. They were horsing around, trying not to focus on her departure, not paying attention to the ground.

The small venomous creature slithered up behind Flint and to his left, in his blind spot. Scarlett saw it, raised her gun, and fired without so much as a gasp or a blink or a moment's pause. He'd jumped ten feet and landed flat on his ass, screaming and cussing at her for shooting so close to him.

Until he saw the thick red-and-yellow-banded viper separated from its head on the ground not twelve inches from where he'd been standing. He'd screamed and she'd laughed, and he'd wanted to kill her on the spot and hug her at the same time.

Ever after, Scarlett insisted she'd shot a rattler that was about to impale his ass. He'd countered that the little snake wouldn't have been able to jump that high. He was already over six feet tall at the age of sixteen. And it wasn't a rattler. It was a coral snake. Not that its precise species mattered. The childhood rhyme popped into his head: "Red into black, venom lack. Red into yellow, kill a fellow."

According to Scarlett, that day wasn't the first time she'd saved his sorry ass. His memory of childhood events was a bit different. He recalled several times when he'd returned the favor by saving her, although she disputed every instance.

After she left the next day, Flint spent several hours with the encyclopedia in Bette's school library, memorizing the pictures of every dangerous animal known to inhabit Texas. These learning sessions had served him well over the years he'd spent in service to Uncle Sam, and after.

He saw no such creatures around this side of the helo. They'd probably run far enough to make the area fairly safe for now. He'd keep a watch, though, just in case.

What had caused the engine to flame out? Flint ran through the day's flights in his head.

The Sikorsky had been fine on the inbound trips from Houston to Bette Maxwell's to the Oakwood ranch to Wolf Bend. Nothing at all out of the ordinary in several hours of flight, three takeoffs, and two landings.

He reviewed the Sikorsky's behavior on departure from Wolf Bend. The helo's takeoff and initial ascent had been practically textbook. During the flight, Phillips had pushed the engine a bit, but it was nothing Flint hadn't done before without consequences. He saw the instruments again in his mind's eye. Nothing seemed amiss.

Yet the engine temperature had risen too high, and the engine flamed out.

In Flint's experience, fuel issues were the most likely cause. Probably slow fuel delivery, which was usually an obstruction of some kind in the fuel line. Not the kind of thing that simply manifested out of the blue.

Must have happened when Phillips refueled while Flint was in Wolf Bend. Maybe Phillips allowed someone else to refuel the Sikorsky. Flint always did those tasks himself. Certified pilots were expected to perform certain routine maintenance functions, and refueling fell into that category.

"That guy stinks." Phillips jerked his thumb over his shoulder toward Reed as he jumped to the ground. "EMS should be here in due course. Caxton is a pretty good airfield. We might be able to get another helo over from Houston in a couple of hours. Pick you up there and deliver you to Houston before midnight."

Flint didn't intend to wait any longer than necessary, but there was no reason to argue with Phillips. "Engine on this bird overheat like that before?"

"Not that I'm aware." Phillips pulled out a stick of gum, unwrapped it, and stuck it in his mouth. Flint could smell the sweet pungent strawberry as he chewed.

Flint nodded. Scanning the ground for snakes, he walked around the Sikorsky to the sponson and opened the door covering the fuel cap. The door was held steady in the open position by a single flexible strut, which wasn't standard on the Sikorsky. This one was a modification, probably classified as a fatigue life-limited component. It was frayed and weakened, close to the end of its useful life.

But not the cause of the engine trouble. Certainly not ideal, but it was noncritical and didn't impact the fuel delivery system. As long as the strut was tucked inside the fuel door and not baking out in the hot sun, it should be okay until it could be replaced in Houston. Worst case, if the strut failed and snapped, the metal cover would slam down or flap around or fall off during flight.

Flint reached inside to test the fuel cap. The cap was securely locked into place. It wasn't missing or faulty. No air or debris sufficient to clog up or interrupt the flow of fuel should have been able to enter the fuel line at the cap.

He pulled off his sunglasses and bent his neck to look inside the fuel door toward the fuel line. Barely inside the metal door, on the side adjacent to the weakened strut, he saw it.

A crimp in the fuel tube. Definitely crimped enough to choke the flow of fuel through the line, causing a flameout.

He heard two snaps and smelled the strawberry before he turned around.

Phillips stood ten feet behind him, legs braced apart in the proper stance, holding the pistol carried by Navy SEALs. The pistol that set the standard by which all other combat handguns are measured. A Sig Sauer P226. Pointed directly at Flint.

CHAPTER TWENTY-TWO

"I'D RATHER NOT SHOOT you, Flint." Phillips snapped the sweet pungent strawberry gum.

Maybe he'd been a smoker. Or a ball player. Regardless of its origin, the chomping and snapping habit was annoying.

Phillips said, "We wait here for the EMS. Get back to Caxton. And then you can go on to Houston. You'll be a few hours late, that's all."

Flint was standing directly in front of the sponson. If Phillips shot the Sig, he'd hit the fuel tank. The Sikorsky wouldn't be fit for even limited flight. Flint had to move. "Late for what?"

"Late for whatever you're planning to do when you get there." Phillips held the Sig steady. Textbook for a man with his training.

"Which is way better than arriving dead, don't you think?"

"Can't argue with your logic." Flint hadn't raised his hands or anything silly like that.

"Toss me that Glock in your pocket," Phillips said.

Flint briefly considered arguing about it before he pulled his weapon out and tossed it toward Phillips. He didn't try to catch the gun. It fell to the ground near his feet.

"Now what?"

"We wait. Sit on that rock to your left." Phillips pointed with a nod of his head to an area behind Flint.

Flint couldn't see the rock, but changing a potential bullet's trajectory from the fuel tank is always a good idea. He sidestepped away from the Sikorsky without taking his gaze off Phillips. He didn't expect Phillips to shoot him. But he hadn't expected him to sabotage the fuel line and bounce the helo to the ground either.

So far, this was the sort of gun-waving that experts called threat display. A warning. Showing how far Phillips was willing to go to persuade Flint to change his behavior. Phillips was simply offering him a choice. The classic fight or flight.

Phillips wasn't attacking him. Not yet. But his attention never wavered. He could change his plan and shoot to kill in a fraction of a second.

George Patton once said that a good plan, violently executed, is better than the perfect plan next week. Flint figured Patton's good plan required a weapon in hand and probably wasn't recommended against an armed Navy SEAL, one of the best-trained combat fighters on the planet.

Flint's peripheral vision picked up the brown boulder jutting above the others on his left. Not that he was planning to sit. "So you're working for Crane, then?"

"He pays well." The gum snapping and strawberry scent traveled across the quiet distance.

"So I've heard. Shaw pays well, too. Whatever Crane's offered you to keep me here, Shaw will pay you more to let me get back on the job." Maybe he would. Maybe he wouldn't. But it sounded like something Shaw would do.

"Sit." Phillips moved the gun slightly toward the boulder. "We've got about sixty more minutes to wait."

"You're working with guys like Paxton and Trevor. You could do better." Flint was quick on his feet but not faster than a round shot from a P226. He moved closer to the boulder.

He felt the hot sun and knew the weakened strut on the fuel cover door wouldn't hold up long exposed to the heat. It would fail. And when it did, the cover would drop.

Could he use the clanging as an adequate distraction? "Paxton and Trevor attacked me with Tasers, did they tell you that?"

"They told me they tried." Phillips grinned and snapped and chewed. "They suggested I use more firepower."

"It's too hot to sit out here for an hour." Flint had lain in wait under worse conditions for much longer, but Phillips didn't know that.

Phillips nodded. "We can't fire up the engines for air-conditioning."

"There's got to be some shade around here somewhere. We're standing on grass. Grass needs water." He tossed his head back. "Over that ridge, probably."

A smirk settled across Phillips's face. He gestured with the Sig's barrel. "After you."

Flint shrugged. Moving was better than sitting. Momentum could be used to his advantage. Much harder to launch any kind of attack from a seated dead stop.

Flint sidled around the big rock and took a few slow backward steps toward the most likely shady spot over the ridge. He calculated the distance between them. Considered how quickly he could subdue Phillips and fire. He scanned from behind his sunglasses to find even a mediocre plan. Where was George Patton when you needed him?

Phillips followed leisurely, close enough to shoot without the need to aim, cracking the strawberry gum all the way.

Over the ridge, Flint could hear running water. A creek. From the sound, he judged it fairly narrow and shallow and protected, which was why he hadn't seen it from the air. He kept walking until he reached the first shade. He welcomed the cooler air.

Phillips reached the shade and the creek a moment later. He bent down to scoop up a palm full of fresh water, but he kept his weapon pointed at Flint.

Flint heard the running water splash onto Phillips's face and fall back into the creek. He heard the rustle of the trees as the breeze gusted through. And something else. Another sound almost any Texan who had ever held a hunting rifle would recognize.

Flint stopped moving. He turned his body sideways to present a smaller target to Phillips and glanced quickly around the little oasis of trees surrounding the creek. Two of the three basics right there, water and shelter. But what about food?

The food source had to be there. Probably on the other side of the trees. If Flint were foolish enough to walk over there, he'd find a few roll barrels filled with corn or even field crops sufficient to keep a small population alive.

Phillips straightened up. "What's the problem? Change your mind about sitting in the shade?"

Which was when Flint once again heard the unmistakable sound. He knew what to do: turn and run. Fast. Try to make it to the Sikorsky and get inside and hope for the best.

CHAPTER TWENTY-THREE

PHILLIPS SEEMED UNAWARE OF the noise or the danger.

"Have you ever been wild pig hunting, Phillips?"

"Not much of a hunter, actually. Not since two tours in Fallujah hunting humans, if you get my drift."

Phillips continued to snap the gum, and the overpowering strawberry smell wafted toward Flint on the breeze that would carry the scent around the oasis.

Strawberry was one of the scents most attractive to wild pigs. Hunters used it as bait in their boar traps.

"Wild pigs are a serious problem in Texas. They're even overtaking some of the urban areas now. They're vicious and dangerous." Flint took a deep breath through his nose, checking for scent. "Hogs are intelligent beasts. Fourth smartest creature in the world, they say. Only dolphins, apes, and some humans are smarter."

"Good to know. What's it going to be? Sit and wait here or back in the sun? I'm not standing around for an hour, Flint."

Flint pointed deeper into the little stand of trees and the running creek. "Do you hear that noise? Not the water but the little squeals?

Those are piglets. There must have been a group of wild pigs down there when we flew in."

"None here now." Phillips shrugged. "They'd have fled when the Sikorsky came down."

"Yeah, maybe. Unless the piglets were newborns. They'd duck down in a clump of grass or behind a log, trying to hide. And the sow wouldn't go far from her litter." Flint scanned the area from behind his sunglasses. "She can smell us. Sows have been known to lie in wait."

"I've got a weapon." Phillips's smirk was back as he pantomimed his plan of attack. "Right between the eyes. We can handle it."

"Let's go." Flint shook his head and turned to face the creek, walking backward as he scanned for wild pigs. "Hogs are hard-headed. Literally. If we have to shoot, aim for the vital organs, between the shoulders."

No sooner had Flint issued his warning than an ominous rustle from across the creek reached his ears. He backed up faster. Phillips didn't notice his increased speed. He didn't move out of the way. Flint ran into him and knocked him off his stride.

Phillips fell to the ground at the same time the charging sow broke through the trees.

She ran straight at Phillips at top speed. She was huge. Flint had seen bigger males, but the sow was easily two hundred pounds of momentum traveling like a battering ram at ten miles an hour.

Flint reached down to pull Phillips to his feet. "Come on!" Phillips stood his ground, braced, and aimed at the sow's head.

She kept charging until he'd fired two rounds. Each hit weakened her, but she kept coming. Until she got close enough to Phillips and lunged. She knocked him to the ground and his Sig flew out of his hand.

The feral hog ripped into Phillips's legs with her tusks. The shorter upper whetters lashed as she lowered her head, and the bottom canines gashed deeper when she tossed her head upward. She slashed, stabbed, and bit Phillips as he screamed and kicked and tried to escape.

Flint scrambled to retrieve the weapon. The Sig had landed too close to the fighting sow. Flint darted toward it several times before he was able to grab it. He steadied his grip, aimed, and emptied the magazine with accuracy and precision, placing all remaining shots between her shoulders until she finally gave up.

Phillips writhed on the ground. Blood flowed from the gashes to his legs and torso. His clothes were pasted to his body by sweat and gooey coagulating blood. His face was contorted with pain.

Flint helped Phillips to his feet and supported him. "No broken bones, right? Can you walk?"

"Hell, yes." Phillips leaned heavily on Flint's shoulder and limped back to the Sikorsky.

"Worst case, you'll have infections from those wounds. Any hospital will clean you up and treat you with antibiotics. You'll be okay."

"I've been worse, Flint. Don't trouble yourself." Phillips's face was whiter than it should have been. He pressed his lips together. Sweat dotted his forehead.

Flint said, "I'm going to Houston. Do you want to come along or wait here for EMS?"

"How likely is it that the sow was a loner?"

"Not at all likely."

Phillips looked a little green. "I'm coming with you."

Flint helped Phillips into one of the backseats. He found a bottle of water and handed it to Phillips along with the first aid kit. Phillips could clean his wounds and apply disinfectant, at least. Anything more would have to wait until they reached Houston.

Reed was still out cold on the floor. The flight was bound to be rough and the landing might be more so. He could be seriously injured during the rest of the flight. Or he could regain consciousness and become a bigger problem.

No. He couldn't stay unrestrained on the floor.

Flint hoisted Reed up and strapped him into the seat he'd occupied before. The man's stench was overwhelming. Flint bit back the urge to gag.

With luck, Reed wouldn't wake up before they reached Houston.

Flint went back outside and did a quick visual check of the Sikorsky.

He squinted to see the shadowed fuel line more clearly and identified small, shiny scratches on the crimp. Shiny enough to prove the crimp had happened recently. Phillips had probably used pliers to apply just the right amount of pressure. Too much pressure applied to the line, and fuel flow would have been stopped completely. Too little, and they'd have made it all the way to Houston.

The good news was that decreased fuel flow wasn't a fatal problem for the Sikorsky. Fuel flow was slowed but not stopped. The engine was probably not irreparably damaged. Once it cooled down, the engine could function well enough to fly the rest of the distance to Houston.

He saw nothing that would ground the bird. No obvious structural damage to impede flight. The strut on the fuel cover door had snapped, as he'd feared. He pushed the door into place and latched it. Maybe it would stay in place. Or at least not cause serious damage when it ripped off.

Flint stepped back, replaced his sunglasses, and swiped his hands together to knock off the dust that had settled on every inch of the Sikorsky.

He found his Glock where he'd tossed it on the ground at Phillips's feet what seemed like a lifetime ago. He slipped the weapon into his pocket along with the one that belonged to Phillips.

He ran back around to the Sikorsky's entrance, jumped up and into the pilot's seat, and spooled up the engine. Caxton EMS should be here soon. He needed to be airborne before they arrived.

Flint strapped himself into the harness, pulled it tight, and focused on getting the Sikorsky off the ground for the tough ninety-minute flight to Houston.

CHAPTER TWENTY-FOUR

TWENTY MINUTES BEFORE LANDING, Flint flexed his shoulders and squeezed his eyes open and shut a few times.

The strain of flying the wounded Sikorsky, on top of everything else that he'd done today, was catching up with him.

His entire body felt fatigued. He needed sleep. What he didn't need was any more interference.

He found his phone. Not the disposable cell phone but the one Shaw, Crane, Paxton, Trevor, and hell, maybe even Bozo the Clown were monitoring.

He wanted to make one call, not five.

So he chose the one number they'd all notice.

He removed his headset, turned the phone's volume all the way up, and pushed the speed dial number.

"Scarlett Investigations," Scarlett said automatically when she answered the phone. She must have looked at the caller ID. "I can barely hear you over the helo noise. Where the hell are you?"

"Landing at Shaw Tower in fifteen. Can you get over there?"

She hesitated. "Sure. I guess."

"Bring Crane with you. And Paxton and Trevor, too, if you can find them. Tell them I have something that belongs to them. I want to give it back." The signal cut out. He waited a second for her to call back.

When she didn't, he put the headset back on. It filtered out some of the noise inside the big bird but not enough.

He contacted the control tower closest to Shaw's skyscraper and received clearance to enter the airspace and land on the rooftop helipad. After that, every ounce of his attention was focused on getting the helo down safely.

When the Sikorsky was perched firmly on the pad, he shut the engines down and sat for a moment in the blissful quiet.

Shaw's private two-man ground crew ran out to the Sikorsky and attached the tie-downs. Flint unlatched his harness and made his way from the cramped cockpit.

Reed was still groggy, but his eyes were open. His head lolled to one side. Now that the urine, vomit, and fear sweat had dried on him, he smelled worse than a full port-a-john after a frat party. Flint was loath to touch him again. As it was, Reed's stench had permeated Flint's clothes. Everything he was wearing, including his favorite leather jacket, would have to be burned.

One of the ground crew had a pair of gloves sticking out of his back pocket. "Hey, buddy! Loan me those gloves?" The guy handed them over.

"Got a wheelchair? This guy's unable to walk."

"Just inside the door. I'll get it." He trotted to collect the conveyance and returned to steady it on the helipad.

The gloves were snug on Flint's hands, but he yanked and tugged and finally got them on before he released Reed from his harness and pulled him to his feet. He lifted him out of the

Sikorsky and plopped him into the wheelchair. In the still, warm air, Reed's body gave off a noxious odor like a mushroom cloud, rising and expanding as it hit the atmosphere.

Flint pulled the gloves off and handed them back to their owner, who shook his head as if they were toxic. Flint completely understood. "Thanks for the help. The other passenger needs a ride to the hospital."

"Will do."

Flint pushed the wheelchair toward the entrance and dropped the gloves in the trash can on the way, sorry that the bin wasn't large enough to dump Reed in, wheelchair and all.

Flint pushed him to the elevator and rode from the roof to the penthouse. Was it only this morning that he'd met Scarlett and Shaw here for the first time? It seemed like a lifetime ago.

The elevator went down one flight. The doors opened onto the big, empty space. Scarlett wasn't standing there tapping her impatient foot this time.

Flint pushed Reed toward Shaw's office along the polished granite floors. In a place with no light pollution, like Wolf Bend, the glass curtain walls might have been blank windows on the night sky. Here in Houston, they provided views of the city.

Before he reached Shaw's end of the open floor plan, he noticed the small crowd gathered in one of the seating areas. Three of them. As requested.

Only Paxton and Trevor were missing. Which couldn't be a good sign.

Crane and Scarlett stood facing the panoramic display of downtown Houston, which was spectacular. Shaw was standing with his back to the window. He was the first to see Flint's approach.

Flint made steady progress toward the group. "Crane. Brought you a present." He gave the wheelchair a shove and it rolled between a black leather sofa and a black leather sling chair into the center of the open room. The stink, of course, preceded Reed.

Scarlett wrinkled her nose. "Who is this odious creature and why is he smelling up the place?"

"So glad you asked. His name is Jeremy Reed. He's been squatting at the old Oakwood ranch. He says he owns it. Says Richard Oakwood gave it to him." Flint turned to Crane. "Know anything about that, Felix?"

"No." Crane glanced at Reed. He put a stogie to his mouth and inhaled to cover Reed's smell. He blew out a batch of perfect O rings. "Which leaves my pal Baz here. What about it, Baz? This your guy?"

"Never saw him before in my life," Shaw said. Which wasn't exactly a "no."

Flint ran his hands through his hair. He bowed his head for a moment and then took a deep breath. "Okay. Here's how this is going to go. Crane, you tried to hire me to find Laura Oakwood for you, or, barring that, to prevent Shaw from finding Oakwood. I declined."

Crane pushed his lips around and stuffed the stogie between his teeth and said nothing.

"Your boys Paxton and Trevor claim they already have Oakwood. They say they're holding her hostage until the deadline passes, at which point their plan is to let her go and collect your finder's fee." He stared into Crane's eyes. "So you don't need me."

"And Shaw." Flint turned his attention to the taller man. "I agreed to help you find Laura Oakwood because you pressured Scarlett. In the hours since I took on this case, I've been attacked by Crane's men and everyone they've pissed off on their bungled hunt for Oakwood. Reed here shot at me with a shotgun. One of you hired Phillips to crash our helo and strand me in the middle of Texas to keep me out of the way for a while. He says it was Crane. And a good friend of mine was attacked twice, once with a baseball bat. At least two other men are in the hospital."

He paused for reaction. Neither Shaw nor Crane offered any excuses or defenses. Which pissed him off all over again. "I'm sorry, Scarlett, but I'm done here. You guys can arm wrestle or something to decide which of you is the bigger dick. I have better things to do."

Flint turned and walked out. His heels tapped on the polished granite floors all the way to the elevator. No one followed.

But they would.

CHAPTER TWENTY-FIVE

FLINT FOUND A TAXI on the street in front of Shaw Tower.

The cabbie covered his nose and coughed when Flint settled into the backseat. "Yeah, I know I smell like I fell into a septic tank. I'm sorry, pal. I'll pay to have your cab fumigated. Market Square Park, please."

The cab dropped him off at the corner. Flint tossed the guy a hundred bucks for the ten-minute ride and the fumigating and walked toward home. Pedestrians on the sidewalks gave him a wide berth. When he reached his house, he went around through the alley into the backyard and stripped. He emptied his pockets and dropped his entire wardrobe into the dumpster behind the garage.

He walked naked in the dark to the back porch, disarmed the security system, allowed himself inside, and rearmed it. He carried the contents of his pockets and his gun upstairs to his bathroom and dumped it all into the empty sink. Later, he'd figure out how to decontaminate everything.

He turned on the hot water full blast and stepped into the shower.

After he'd drained the hot water tank and applied strong soap with stiff-bristled brushes over his entire body, he looked more than a little like a lobster, but he'd finally shed the *Eau de Reed parfum*. He took several deep breaths through his nose for the sheer pleasure of breathing clean air.

He padded into his bedroom, donned a pair of boxers from the top drawer, jeans and a shirt from the closet. He slipped his feet into supple leather slippers and returned to the kitchen.

It was full dark outside. He closed the plantation shutters over the kitchen windows. He stood in the blinding light from the refrigerator for a moment before he grabbed a bottle of water, closed the door, and carried the bottle into the den. The glow from the cable box cast a soft blue sheen over the room.

He found the remote next to his favorite chair and punched up background music. He adjusted the volume. He added a layer of frequency interference to confound the listening devices it was safe to assume targeted the house.

"You definitely smell better," Scarlett said from the shadows.

"I see you hacked my security code again." His eyes had adjusted to the dim blue light. She stood in the far corner of the room and she hadn't changed clothes from the meeting at Shaw Tower, which meant she'd come directly here. He'd thought she might detour to check on her daughter. "Would you like a drink?"

She raised the whiskey glass in her hand. "Thanks."

"No problem." He lowered himself into his favorite leather chair and propped both feet onto the ottoman. "How can I help you, Miss Scarlett?"

"That was a fine tantrum you threw back there in Shaw's office."

"Glad you liked it." He unscrewed the cap on the plastic bottle and took a good long swig of icy-cold spring water.

"We're running out of time, Flint. We've got less than thirty-five hours to find Oakwood. The deadline triggers automatically, like Cinderella's pumpkin. One moment past our deadline and we're done."

She sipped his oldest single-malt scotch, the one she'd bought him for his last birthday. "We've got work to do."

"I resigned back there during my tantrum. Didn't you hear?"

She closed her eyes and rested against the wall for a moment, not bothering to argue. He never quit anything. And Scarlett knew that better than anyone.

With luck, Crane and Shaw would believe he'd quit, though.

"You might have told me about the baby this afternoon," she said, weary.

"You might have told me about the mistake of the clerk thinking the second gunman was a man before I got to Shaw's office this morning, too," he replied, wearier.

"We're even then. Pax." She sipped the scotch and waited a couple of beats for him to argue. When he didn't, she moved on. "So I found the medical records and the follow-up blood work on the Oakwood baby. Looks like Oakwood and Prieto kept the child. At least initially."

"That could be helpful. Gives us something more to go on."

"Maybe. The low hemoglobin was confirmed a couple of days before the robbery at the only other hospital within twenty miles of where the baby was born. Definitely sickle cell disease, the report said. Both parents were carriers, too. Confirmed from the blood evidence left at the crime scene. Poor kid." Scarlett's tone sounded a little sad and a lot tired. "But I don't see how that helps us find Laura Oakwood."

"Don't you?" He drained the rest of the water from the bottle. "No luck in Mexico? Or with your US connections?"

"Would I be standing here now?"

He grinned, but she probably couldn't see that in the dark with her eyes closed. "I guess not."

"I'm waiting, Flint." She sounded just like the ferocious ten-year-old he remembered. Funny how voice tones and timbres don't change that much as humans age. Not females', anyway.

"Or what? You'll hold me down and twist my arm and rub my face in the dirt?" He grinned again and rubbed the scar on his chest and his voice was a little less defiant. "Maybe you're going to aim your bow and arrow with your eyes closed, like William Tell, and shoot me in the chest?"

"Don't tempt me." She plopped down on the sofa, pouting. But he knew she regretted the day she'd almost killed him with a straight arrow to the heart. She hadn't meant to hurt him and he hadn't even tried to duck. She'd been devastated as she rode in the ambulance with him to the hospital. It was one of the many times when their childhood games went too far off the rails.

He laughed. He walked to the bar in the corner and poured himself a glass of scotch before she drank it all. Ginger was a scotch drinker, too. The last time she was here, before he went to London, she'd reminded him to replace the bottle, but he hadn't done it yet.

He returned to his chair with the heavy crystal glass. "I saw Bette Maxwell today."

Scarlett's breath caught, but she didn't reply. Scarlett's affection for Bette had never been as great as his. Their relationship had been filled with bickering and challenge. But he knew Scarlett loved Bette all the same. Bette knew that, too.

"She's still living at the Lazy M. She's closed the school and all the kids are gone. But she's still there." He paused. Sipped. Savored. "Did you know?"

"I, uh, didn't know." She cleared her throat. "And I don't see how she's relevant."

"I thought maybe Laura Oakwood had been a Maxwell kid after she ran away from home. Bette's place is the only thing anywhere close to Mildred's Corner where a reasonable young woman might have been living." He sipped again and swished the scotch around in his mouth before he swallowed. "Or maybe she just went there for help with the baby, either before or after the robbery. Bette would have helped her if she'd turned up." He sipped again and leaned his head back on the chair and closed his eyes. "I thought maybe Bette would know something about where she went."

"And did she know anything?"

He thought about Scarlett's question for a while. He replayed Bette's responses to his questions in his head. "You know, I think maybe she did."

"Maybe?"

"Well, Bette never said she didn't know the girl. And that's unlikely, isn't it?"

"Why?" Scarlett studied the glass of scotch as if it were a crystal ball that might hold the answers.

"This convenience store, Mildred's Corner. It's fifteen miles straight south from the Lazy M. You know what that area's like. Nothing but dirt and tumbleweeds as far as the eye can see." He paused and sipped and savored and swallowed and felt the liquid warmth all the way into his toes. "How many times did we try to hitch a ride along that road when we were kids? Instead of adventure, all we ended up with were sore thumbs and tired feet."

"Don't remind me." Scarlett was definitely not overcome with warm fuzzies by reminders about Bette Maxwell or their days at the Lazy M. Which didn't matter much. He was really thinking out loud at this point, anyway.

His voice had taken on a lazy, meandering quality. "After the robbery, Oakwood had to go somewhere. And now we're thinking she either had the baby with her or she was traveling to collect the baby before she moved on. And she'd been wounded during the robbery, so she'd have needed first aid, at least."

Flint sipped again, thoughtfully. If Oakwood and Prieto had been at the Clovis Ranch before the robbery, she might have gone back there, too. But that seemed too risky. The police would have considered members of a cult like that to be suspects. She was more likely to have been found out there.

He rolled the crystal glass between his palms. "The Lazy M was her only real choice. I don't see how she could have kept running that night. Someone had to have helped her."

"Bette was always helping kids one way or another. It's possible she might have sheltered Laura. Especially if she had a baby with her. But not if she knew about the robbery and the murders." Scarlett took a breath and shook her head. "Bette wouldn't have helped a killer. Not knowingly anyway. But that was years ago. Look, I didn't keep in touch with her and you didn't either. And we lived there for a long time and Bette petted you like a favorite bunny, so you loved her. Why would Laura Oakwood have kept in touch when she'd only known Bette for less than a year, at the absolute most?"

He shrugged and then realized she couldn't see the gesture. "You know how I work. I was looking for a thread to unravel."

"Was Bette able to help with anything at all?"

He might have told her what Bette said about his mother, but something made him hold that back. "She said Mildred's husband was the one at the store that night. Oscar Tuttle. He was the clerk. Both he and Mildred are dead now, but their son, Steve, handles the store these days. Bette said Steve Tuttle was home with his mother that night, not in the store. He might know something helpful."

"That's pretty thin." She swigged her scotch. "Not worth wasting more time on."

"It's worse than thin. Steve Tuttle's in the hospital now. Couldn't talk to him even if we wanted to. Not before Shaw's Tuesday-morning deadline, anyway."

CHAPTER TWENTY-SIX

SCARLETT SHOOK HER HEAD like her ten-year-old know-it-all self would have. "You got into a fight? With the one guy who might have been a lead?"

"Not me. Drake did. And it wasn't his fault. He asked about Oakwood, and Steve's pals came after him. One of them accidently hit Steve. His head hit the concrete." Flint tipped the glass to his lips again. "We thought at the time that the problem might have been Paxton and Trevor. Maybe they were there before us. Probably acted like their usual charming selves."

"Meaning they either busted up the place or pissed people off and you got the brunt of it? Figures." Scarlett sighed. "Okay, so what did you find out by applying your considerable charms all day? Anything? Or did you just burn too many hours of our time?"

"I wanted a feel for Laura Oakwood. See where she came from. Maybe get a lead on where she might have gone. Talk to people who knew her so I could see and hear for myself. At the Oakwood ranch and Wolf Bend, Crane's men had definitely been there first. I'm not sure about Mildred's Corner, but it seems likely."

"And? What did you find?"

"Let's just say that nobody rolled out the red carpet for me and leave it at that."

"Figured." She nodded. "Did you find anything remotely useful?"

"Maybe. I put stuff in a file and sent it to your private server. Look at all of it. Tell me what you think." He pointed to a black nylon bag by the door. "There's some hard forensic stuff in there on Jeremy Reed. Bio data. Prints, blood, photos. And a business card with fingerprints from Paxton and Trevor. Check it all out. See if you find anything worthwhile."

"None of that is going to tell me where Laura Oakwood is, Flint.

Did you find anything else?"

Instead of answering, he shrugged. "Tell me what you found out today. Everybody except me already knows."

Scarlett grinned. "I thought you'd quit this case. No reason to tell you anything."

He lifted his glass.

She smiled and lifted hers in return. "The biggest thing was the baby, which you already knew. And she's definitely sick. It's possible she's dead. Sickle cell disease kills if it isn't managed properly. And it's been twenty-seven years."

She was silent for a while, maybe processing the reality of an infant diagnosed with a serious lifelong blood disorder. Scarlett had a daughter she adored like crazy. She was devastated when Maddy suffered so much as a paper cut. For all of Katie Scarlett's toughness, she could be frighteningly vulnerable.

She took another sip of the scotch and cleared her throat. She took a deep breath to deliver one of her long-winded explanations. But her voice was stronger when she continued.

"Once we knew about the sickle cell disease, we began searching for the child, but it's like panning for gold in a stream. We've come up with a bunch of rocks. The disease is not rare, and it's more common in the Hispanic population. There are a lot of patients. We started searching registries and hospitals, but we haven't found any records on a female that might be Oakwood's daughter yet. We've broadened the searches, starting in Texas and moving out. We did the same in Mexico. If we had unlimited time, we might find a trail of her medical treatment and it could lead us to her mother. But finding either Laura Oakwood or her daughter through the sickle cell treatment before Shaw loses to Crane will require divine intervention."

"Yeah, well, neither one of us has ever been that blessed." Flint tapped his fingernails absently on the scotch glass to the music's beat. "Keep looking. It might be our turn to win the lotto, you know?"

Scarlett scowled. "No way you could narrow our search down a bit?"

"Not yet. Look, here's what I know about the disease, which is not much. The red blood cells are deformed. They block blood flow through the body. That causes pain, fatigue, infections, and pretty often requires medical intervention." He couldn't afford to let Crane, Paxton, and Trevor get ahead of him again. Right now, she was saving him from chasing down false leads. But he couldn't spend the whole night talking to her. He had other plans. "What do we know about standard treatments? Anything that we could use to find and identify the girl now?"

"Like most medical conditions, symptoms and treatments vary, according to the experts I talked to." Scarlett grabbed her wild hair and held it at the nape of her neck. "She should see her doctor every three months or so. Like you said, SCD patients are more susceptible to infections, so she could be on daily penicillin for the rest of her life as a preventative measure. We're checking pharmacies. She could have more serious medical conditions, but we haven't found any connection that we think is her. Stuff like that."

"And what about continuing treatments besides penicillin? What does she need? Where does she get it?"

"Regular lab tests. Monitoring for organ damage. Ultrasound screening for stroke prevention. Eye exams. Cognitive screening." Scarlett sighed. "There's a long list. And it never ends. Cradle to grave, as they say."

"Sounds pricey. Even back then, that kind of regular medical care wouldn't have been cheap. How could Laura Oakwood have paid for it? She took the money from the robbery, but it was only about thirty thousand. Even with stellar management, that much cash wouldn't have lasted twenty-seven years."

Scarlett cocked her head, but she didn't go any further. She'd suss it out, though. He was counting on that.

Flint figured Oakwood would protect the child. She'd have been living somewhere close to good medical care while the girl was a minor, for sure. And probably long after that.

The reasonable options were limited. Living inside the United States under a false identity with great medical insurance was one option. She could be working in the medical field. Or living in Canada as a citizen entitled to national health care. There were other possibilities, but he didn't have unlimited time either, and these three were the most likely choices. They'd found nothing so far to rule any of them out.

Scarlett said, "So what do you want me to do besides play decoy and chase an endless stream of medical issues?"

"I'd like to know who Jeremy Reed really is. Get all of that bio data in the bag over there checked out. And find out who installed him at the Oakwood ranch and when that happened. And how." He paused.

"And why."

"So you said. I'm on it. What else?"

"You followed up with the Mexico branch of Rosalio Prieto's family.

Find anything helpful at all?" She shook her head.

"Her mother was related to Juan Garcia. Maybe there's a Mexico family connection to the Garcias."

"No kidding. Like we didn't already chase that to the dead end of the trail." She straightened her shoulders and her nostrils flared. "I know you're holding back. I've got a big team. Let me help, Flint. It's important to me that we nail this and get Shaw what he wants."

She was right. She was running out of time. She'd asked for his help. Maybe it was time to give it up. "I was in Wolf Bend today."

"So you said."

"I have to sort of soak up what I can." Her scowl didn't faze him. He'd made a decision and he didn't want to talk himself out of it. "One of the things I found out is that Oakwood and Prieto left Wolf Bend with another guy. A drifter. Prieto's sister said he was a bad apple. He had a criminal record. Allegedly, the three were headed for a place called Clovis Ranch to live with some crazy satanic cult or something. It was all the rage, I guess."

"Sex, drugs, and rock and roll? That's the best you can do? Seriously?"

"Sounds ridiculous, yes. But here's the thing. Clovis Ranch is not too far from Mildred's Corner." He paused again. "So I figure it could have been Oakwood and Prieto's home base for a while before the robbery. And that guy could have been the known associate that the cops figured for the second gunman."

"The police reports we've got don't include the name of the known associate. We're digging for that now." She frowned. "But wouldn't the cops have chased all that down at the time?"

"Prieto's sister said they tried. But just because they didn't find anything doesn't mean there was nothing to be found." He paused. "And after all these years, someone might be willing to talk about things they weren't willing to say back then."

They'd run into that before. People change. Circumstances change, too. Someone knew what had happened to Laura Oakwood. They knew now and they knew back then, too. Flint had only to find the people with the right answers.

That was always the secret to locating people. Somebody knew where they were. Find the right somebody, and he could find the missing. Every time.

Or they could simply get lucky. Old crimes were sometimes solved when quirky, unpredictable things happened. Which wasn't a strategy to either count on or ignore.

She nodded. "Does the cult still exist? Most of those things flame and burn out after a few years."

"That's what I'd like you to find out. The drifter called himself John David. Which sounds like a fake name and probably was. But if there was a cult, we might be able to get a lead on why Oakwood robbed Mildred's Corner." He closed his eyes, visualizing the area again and the people he imagined were living there. "Maybe they told someone where they were going. Hell, maybe this John David, or whatever his real name was, helped them. Just because you believe he wasn't the second gunman doesn't mean he wasn't involved somehow. Maybe he drove the getaway car and that's how Oakwood disappeared after the robbery."

Scarlett considered the problem for a bit. "You didn't interview the Wolf Bend sheriff about the guy? Get an ID, a real name, at least?"

"I would have, but the sheriff's office was closed and I was running short on time. I thought maybe you'd have the name of the known associate the local sheriff at Mildred's Corner figured to be the second gunman and we could go from there." He paused.

"We've been running down the second gunman stuff. The old records are atrocious. Everybody's dead and gone. But okay. We'll give it a higher priority. At this point, we're grasping anyway. Can't hurt to take a harder look. But keep in mind that if this guy, John David, was the known associate, then he's dead. So finding him won't help." Scarlett nodded again. She was silent for a while. "I'll see what I can do."

"Do you think you can do it without using any of your office resources? Or leading Shaw and Crane right along with you?"

Her frown jumped back as fiercely as ever. She was touchy tonight. The pressure was getting to her. "I'm as good at covert ops as you are, Flint. I've got as many contacts in the right places, too. Don't flatter yourself."

He grinned. Her melancholy over the sick Oakwood baby was hard for him to take. He preferred ferocious Scarlett any day. She'd always been a woman who could take care of herself. It was one of the things he most admired about her. Not that he'd let her know that.

He sipped his scotch. "Have you found anything more about Richard Oakwood's family of origin?"

"Not yet. Have you?"

He nodded. "Laura's high school principal says that before he fell in love with a local girl, Richard Oakwood might have emigrated from Canada to work in the oil fields. Maybe he had family in Canada. His daughter might have known that. Maybe that's where she went."

"We checked US immigration records a while ago and came up empty."

"He might not even have had a passport. He wouldn't have needed one back then to enter the States." He sipped again. "Of course, he shouldn't have overstayed his vacation time. But that happened a lot back then. Happens a lot now, in fact."

Scarlett said, "Who knows whether he was born in a hospital or not? He might not even have a birth certificate. We might never find his birth family." She sighed and shook her head. "I'll see what I can do, but Canada's a big place. Lots of open country up there." Her voice trailed off.

"Be careful. Crane is desperate to beat Shaw. He's not above killing to get there." He took a breath. "And Shaw's not above killing to keep Crane at bay, either."

"I can take care of myself, Flint." The stiffness returned to her spine.

Good.

"Meanwhile, I need some sleep." He shrugged again. "I'll check in with you in the morning. I put a new burner phone in that bag. Keep it with you. Only use it once and then destroy it."

"I know how to avoid phone taps, Flint." She practically growled at him.

"Prove it. After what happened with Phillips today, I'm taking no chances. And you're not either." He knew she had her back up and he was a little surprised she didn't launch off the sofa and pound him right there. He rubbed the scar on his chest absently. "Can you let yourself out through the front door? Crane needs to see you leave."

She cocked her head briefly and then slapped her empty glass down hard on the table and did as he asked.

They'd never turned the lights on. But Crane would know she'd been here and he needed to see her go. He was watching her or tracking her or even had surveillance equipment aimed inside Flint's home. Didn't matter. Now that Flint knew Crane was always present, he'd use that to his advantage, too.

Scarlett had been inside his house for more than an hour, and Crane wouldn't have been able to hear their conversation because of Flint's defenses. Which meant Crane would be worried. He might keep watching Flint, just to be sure he was standing down as he'd claimed when he quit the job. Certainly, Crane would keep watching Scarlett.

CHAPTER TWENTY-SEVEN

THE BURNER PHONE ON the side table rang. Flint had left the number with only one person. He answered without opening his eyes. "This is Michael Flint."

"This is Larry Manning, returning your call." The long-haul trucker's voice sounded rough and tired. "I'm sorry it's so late, but I've been on the road all day. I just pulled in for the night and picked up my messages. You said the matter was urgent."

"Yeah. Thanks for calling me back." Flint put his glass on the table and raised himself up in the chair and put a bit of urgency into his tone. "I'm looking for a young woman who went missing after a robbery at Mildred's Corner a while back. Your nephew thought you might be able to help me."

"You're talking about the Oakwood girl. That's a bundle of trouble you're opening up right there." He paused and took a big swig of something. Flint heard him swallow. "Steve Tuttle is in the hospital with a bad concussion. Docs aren't sure he's going to be okay."

Flint could feel Manning's hostility through the wireless connection. "Three guys jumped my associate. He defended himself. Can't fault him for that. He didn't hit Tuttle, either."

Manning took another big swig and his tone softened slightly.

"That's what I heard when I asked around."

"Do you know why they did it?"

"Let's come back to that." He paused a long time. "Why are you looking for Oakwood now? You're not a cop. She's got no family looking for her, does she? If she was trafficked, you'll never find her after all these years."

Flint understood what he meant. If Oakwood had been a human trafficking victim, she'd probably have been dead long before now. Maybe without a trace. Normal people left a paper trail when they died, but human trafficking victims too often did not. She could be buried in a shallow grave in Mexico somewhere or out in the desert or a thousand other places.

Which could explain why no one had been able to find her.

But that answer didn't feel right to Flint. For one thing, there was no hint in the investigation files that she'd been trafficked. Human trafficking technology wasn't as sophisticated as it was today. Traffickers were easier to find back then because they left a physical trail. Law enforcement would have found something to suggest she'd been taken instead of running away and trying to hide. If she'd been trafficked. Big if.

"I have a client who wants me to find her. I told him I would." Flint put a shrug into his voice. "Any chance you can help me out with that?"

"Any chance your client would make a donation to Road Warriors against Human Trafficking? We could use more funding."

"I'm sure he would if you have information that leads me to Oakwood." Flint held the connection open through a long period of silence on Manning's end. "Can we meet up? You tell me what you know. I'll follow through. If your info pans out, my client will be glad to write you a check."

"I hauled a load of drilling supplies down here to Mount Warren and I'm laying over until tomorrow. I'm at the Texas Inn on the north side of town. In the morning, after I load up, I'm headed to San Diego." Manning swallowed and paused, thinking things through, maybe. He belched. "Come out here and we'll discuss it. Or we can talk when I get back from San Diego next week."

"Next week will be too late." Mount Warren? A town on the far west side of Texas that Flint had never heard of before his trip to Wolf Bend had now been mentioned three times in less than twelve hours. "I don't have time for a trip all the way out there unless you have something valuable to offer. I'm working on a tight deadline."

"I'll put the coffee on." Manning disconnected the call.

Flint considered what little he knew about Manning. Long-haul driver. In the business more than thirty years. According to his nephew, he'd been working to thwart human trafficking for a couple of decades.

He ran the route that passed Mildred's Corner back in the day.

Manning could know something useful. Or not. Could go either way.

Not much reason to go chasing across the state again, maybe for nothing, eating up the few hours left before Shaw's option expired.

Then again, Flint didn't have any better leads to chase.

By 3:00 a.m., he'd organized the trip. First, as a precaution, he'd run a few quick database checks on Larry Manning. No danger that the trucker would be given the Presidential Medal of Freedom in the next couple of days but nothing to suggest he was working for Crane either. On paper, Manning looked like a normal guy working hard and trying to do the right thing.

Maybe he was exactly what the paper trail suggested, but very few people were. Records were nothing but a place to start looking—and sometimes not even that much, in Flint's experience.

Precautions were a way of life for him. No reason to change his habits now. To keep ahead of Crane, he'd need to improvise more than usual. Which was why he'd given the Clovis Ranch and the Canada-connection assignments to Scarlett. Like the sickle cell babies search, both were probably dead ends, just as she said. But they needed to be checked out and eliminated. The searching would keep her here in Houston, where she could protect herself and Maddy, and keep Crane on guard and out of Flint's way.

He dressed in black jeans, black shirt, and sturdy boots. He collected cash, weapons, and other items he needed from the large safe in his bedroom closet and stuffed them into his pack. He left his personal smart phone in the safe. Too easy to ping off the cell towers. The burner phone he'd used to reach out to Manning was in his front pocket.

He grabbed cap, jacket, and gloves, slipped out through the back door, and engaged security.

Flint melted into the shadows and made his way across the neighborhood alleys. He stayed close to homes likely to have operational electronic interference. When he reached the brightly lit used car lot over on Alamo Street, he sidled toward the shadows there, too.

Drake was waiting in a black sedan with the engine running. Flint tossed his pack into the backseat and slipped into the front. Within moments, Drake had pulled away from the lot, headed north. They had a long way to go. First stop was the twenty-four-hour big-box store two miles from the private airfield. Flint needed supplies.

Among other things, he bought disposable phones. He penned a quick note and dropped two of the phones into an overnight delivery service for expedited delivery to Scarlett Investigations. She'd have them before noon.

Drake's driving skills were honed. He could lose any tail, any time. He applied those skills on the way to the airport.

The drive was a little longer than ideal, but Flint was confident Crane didn't know he'd left the city.

CHAPTER TWENTY-EIGHT

AN HOUR LATER, DRAKE and Flint were airborne, headed west in a Pilatus PC-24.

Drake had turned the transponder off and flew VFR—visual flight rules—to keep the jet's identity off the radar.

Someone might see raw radar return, but they'd have no way to confirm that the return was this particular aircraft or to know who the plane's passengers were.

As long as they stayed clear of major airports and below eighteen thousand feet, the PC-24 could remain practically invisible.

The Pilatus claimed to be the world's first super-versatile jet. It was designed to operate from short paved or unpaved surfaces and remote fields. Flexibility was key. The Pilatus could land in well under two thousand feet. This PC-24 was registered to a CEO client of a friend of Drake's.

All of which meant it would be harder for Crane and Shaw to find him. Such precautions wouldn't thwart them forever. But they'd help for long enough, he hoped.

The Pilatus climbed to cruising altitude and leveled out at about 425 miles an hour. It could travel faster, but after his experience with the Sikorsky, Flint was wary of pushing the engines too hard.

He calculated travel time to Mount Warren at eighty-five minutes. Touchdown should be well before 5:00 a.m. Sunrise was forecast at 7:56 a.m. under clear skies, temperature at seventy-one degrees, light wind. Excellent.

"How long will we be on the ground in Mount Warren?" The flying was easy right now and Drake was ready to talk.

"Hard to say. Not more than a couple of hours, I hope. Three, tops. By the time we land and get out to meet Manning and get back."

"We've got two operatives on the ground. One will stay with me. The other will drive you. Both can provide backup, if we need it."

"Perfect. Both already armed, right?" Flint watched the airspace through the windshield, but there was nothing much to see.

"Correct." Drake rubbed the back of his neck and rolled his sore shoulders. "I'm not going unarmed anywhere with you ever again."

"Good plan." Flint grinned, but he was dead serious. "You've worked with these two guys before. You know them. Not another Phillips situation, right?"

Drake grimaced. "Look, Phillips came highly recommended. We'd worked with him before without problems. We didn't know he was in debt up to his eyeballs."

"Could have happened to anyone." Flint shrugged, but he didn't mean that literally. Phillips had been a mistake. Not that it mattered. Phillips was handled. But Flint wasn't interested in a repeat. He knew Drake was not happy with the Phillips situation either. No reason to dwell on the problem.

Drake nodded. "What do we know about this Manning guy?"

"Not much. He's an Army vet. Vietnam. Sixty-five-ish. Hardworking guy. Seems to have his heart in the right place, from what I could find in a short period of time." Flint paused. "Claims he can help me find Laura Oakwood. For the right price."

"Well, that would be refreshing." Drake's tone implied a shock greater than first news of the sinking of the *Titanic*.

Flint leaned back and closed his eyes. A nap seemed like a good idea. He hadn't slept much since he left London. Flint could sleep anywhere, anytime. It was a skill he'd perfected while working for Uncle Sam. Fatigue caused mistakes, usually at critical crisis points. Fatigue was an unacceptable risk. He avoided it whenever he could.

Flint awoke as the Pilatus began its descent into the Mount Warren area. They'd been flying uneventfully for an hour. It was still dark, but the cloudless sky surrounded a full moon acting like a spotlight illuminating the flat scrubland below.

Drake pointed to the long, straight road that led to an abandoned oil well north of town. Flint had located the road on satellite images earlier. It looked hard-packed enough and long enough for the Pilatus to land and take off again later.

As the jet descended, Flint saw a black Land Rover, lights and engine off, parked well away from their makeshift runway. Likely occupied by the two operatives Drake had hired. The radio silence they maintained meant the identity of the Land Rover's occupants remained unconfirmed. Flint pulled his weapon as a precaution.

Drake's approach was textbook perfect, and he landed the Pilatus like Flint was a flight instructor he wanted to impress. He powered down the engines and Flint opened the exit door. The Land Rover was parked near the bottom of the flight stairs.

Drake and Flint disembarked as the two operatives left their vehicle. They met halfway, boots crunching on the scrub and gravel in the silent night.

Both operatives looked suitably professional, a bearing undeniably instilled by military training. They were dressed in dark clothing similar to Flint's. The taller one was darker, bigger, and heavier. Straight, fit, clean-cut. No wasted movements. They exuded confidence.

Drake greeted the two men and introduced them by last name only to Flint, nodding toward the taller one first. "Brady, Davis, this is Flint." They shook hands all around. "Davis, you're with me. Brady, Flint will tell you more on the way. Meet back here. Give me twenty minutes' notice, if you can, and we'll be ready for takeoff." Four heads, four nods.

Brady turned and led the way back to the Land Rover. Flint glanced at Drake and Davis, who were already climbing into the Pilatus.

"Drake." He turned his head to look at Flint. "Stay alert. We don't know what's coming at us."

"Got it," Drake said, without breaking stride.

Brady had the Land Rover running when Flint tossed his pack into the back and settled into the passenger seat. He'd lost count of how many vehicles and passenger seats he'd traveled through in the forty-eight hours since he landed on that London rooftop.

"Where are we going?" Brady's voice was a deep baritone, almost a bass. The kind of voice Scarlett wouldn't kick out of bed for eating crackers.

"We're meeting a guy at the Texas Inn." Flint gave him the address. "Do you know it?"

"It's not exactly the Ritz." Brady's frown used his entire face, not just his brow. He put the Land Rover in gear and drove around the back of the Pilatus onto the abandoned road. "Who are you meeting?"

"Truck driver. His name is Larry Manning. Know him?"

Brady shook his head slowly. "Why?"

"He's a witness. Says he has information about a missing person."

"You believe him?"

Good question. "Not yet."

Two miles west, the abandoned road connected with another, better graded road. Brady turned left and drove south for three miles until they reached a paved two-lane. He turned west. The land was flat and dark and empty. They hadn't met another vehicle of any kind.

Ten miles from where the jet had landed, Flint could finally see evidence of civilization. Road signs. A few buildings and a couple of intersections. Homes, most of them dark inside, but a few people were stirring, early risers preparing for the work day ahead.

Brady pointed to the right side of the road. "The Texas Inn is up there in the next block. You're armed, right?"

"Always," Flint replied. "You?"

"Yes." Brady wasn't a sparkling conversationalist, which was fine with Flint.

The Texas Inn was an old-fashioned motel, the kind travelers might have seen along Route 66 in the 1960s. A one-story L-shaped block building, with an office at the short end of the L and a string of rooms running the long leg. The office was closed. The sign in the window announced "Vacancy" in steady-glowing red neon.

In front of each room was a single parking space. Only two of the parking spaces were occupied. Both vehicles were pickup trucks of the rusty-but-trusty kind.

The room doors were numbered from one through twenty. On the wall, left of each door, each room's window faced the sidewalk.

"My witness is in room fifteen." Flint nodded his head toward the far end of the row.

Brady parked the Land Rover in the empty space in front of the room. "What do you want me to do?"

"Stay with the vehicle. Keep the engine running." Flint opened the door and put one foot onto the pavement. He turned to look directly at Brady. "But at any time, if you think you should come inside, do that. You've got good training and good instincts, Drake said. I'm counting on both."

"Roger that." Brady nodded.

Flint left the vehicle and closed the door. He stood in the parking lot for a moment, scanning the area. There was a restaurant across the street. He saw lights on in the back, probably the kitchen. It was 5:30 a.m. They'd be preparing for the breakfast rush, such as it was.

The other buildings within his line of sight were dark and quiet, even the two all-night topless bars south of the Texas Inn. Parking lots were empty. He didn't see a tractor anywhere that could belong to Manning. Which didn't necessarily mean much, but in Flint's experience, long-haul drivers tended to stay the night pretty close to their rigs, even if the tractor didn't have a sleeper bunk inside.

Flint walked the few steps to the sidewalk and rapped the knuckles of his left hand on the door of Room 15. A heavy curtain covered the window. The room's air-handling unit below the window was rattling loudly. The door stayed closed.

He knocked again and reached with his right hand to grasp the handle of his Glock. He pulled the weapon out and held it ready by his side. No one opened the door.

He glanced left and right along the sidewalk in front of the rooms. He saw no one. The heavy curtains on the windows blocked all interior light, assuming anyone was stirring inside.

Had Manning lured him out here and then thought better of it? Or had someone—Crane or his men, or Shaw, or someone else—reached Manning first?

He raised his left fist and rapped harder on the door. He called out, loud enough to be heard over the rattling air handler, "Manning! Open up!"

The door to Room 16 opened. Flint turned swiftly toward the noise. A heavyset man wearing a tank-style undershirt and a pair of jeans stepped out. He was barefoot.

"Are you Flint? I'm Manning. Sorry I didn't hear you over the noise of this contraption." He kicked the rattling air handler with his bare foot. "They moved my room after we talked. Something wrong with the toilet in that one. I've got coffee. Come on in."

Manning hadn't shaved in several days. His eyes were bloodshot. Curly gray hair erupted from his skin and protruded everywhere that wasn't covered by the dingy white undershirt.

The top of Manning's head was bald. The rest of his gray hair was gathered into a pink rubber band. The ponytail hung halfway down his back.

Flint glanced around the inside. The room was a standard two-bed layout. It was large enough for two chairs, a small chest of drawers, a television, and a combination open closet and vanity with a single sink. The toilet and tub were in a separate room left of the vanity. A cheap plastic drip coffee maker waited on the laminate countertop beside the sink.

He followed Manning inside, but he didn't release his grip on the Glock.

CHAPTER TWENTY-NINE

MANNING POURED THE COFFEE into two eight-ounce Styrofoam cups and handed one to Flint. He didn't offer powdered cream or cheap sweetener, which made Flint like him a little bit.

"Thanks." The coffee tasted bad. No surprise there.

"I'm too old to be doing this job. When I get back from San Diego next week, I might just hang up my keys." Manning gestured to one of the chairs and sat down heavily in the other. He swallowed a gulp of the coffee. "I've got to be at the yard in an hour and on the road before seven. What do you want to know?"

"Everything you know about Laura Oakwood." Flint had no clue what Manning might be able to offer. He was here because he'd run out of ideas.

"For starters, I don't know where she is now." *Great.*

Manning tipped up his Styrofoam cup and drained the coffee from it. "But I can tell you where she told me she was going. Maybe that will help."

"It's a place to start."

Manning nodded. "Canada. She said her dad's family was there. Said her aunt might help with the baby."

Flint felt no satisfaction in knowing his talk with the Wolf Bend principal might be paying off. The last thing he really wanted to do today was fly to the still-frozen north country. Flint was a Texan. He hated the cold. "Where in Canada?"

Manning shook his head. "See, at the time, I didn't know about the robbery. I picked her up because she had a baby with her. The weather was miserable. Cold and rainy. And she was limping. People limp for all kinds of reasons. I didn't know at the time that she'd been wounded somehow. I was running north as far as Denver so I offered her a ride. Like I'd done a hundred times before and hundreds of times after. Gets lonely out there on the road. Sometimes a hitchhiker is good company for a few miles."

Flint nodded. He'd been a hitchhiker and he'd picked them up more than a few times, too. He understood the allure on both sides. "Did she say anything about where she was running from?"

"Yeah. She said she'd been living with that bunch of whack jobs out on Clovis Ranch. With her boyfriend. Said she was desperate to get away. Said they were vicious to her. Said her boyfriend had stopped a few of the others from raping her a couple of times, even when she was pregnant. How sick is that?"

"Did she tell you anything about the baby?"

"She said the baby was sick. That was why she needed to find her aunt. She needed help with the baby."

Flint nodded slowly. "How is it that you remember all this so well? It was more than twenty-five years ago."

"I dropped her off in Denver. I never heard from her again after that." Manning looked down into the coffee sludge. He lifted the cup and tried to drain it a second time. "But a few weeks later, I was on another run and I stopped at Mildred's Corner again. I usually stopped there whenever I drove that route. That's when I found out about the robbery. And about her boyfriend and the woman, that customer, getting killed."

Flint nodded again, mainly to keep him talking.

"At that point, I probably should have told the cops about picking her up. But they didn't come around asking me. And I didn't have any idea where she'd gone to." Manning walked to the vanity and poured the rest of the coffee into his cup and started a new pot of the vile brew. "Runaways tell some big stories, and most of them aren't true. So I didn't know if she'd gone on to Canada or not. And that damned Clovis Ranch bunch. They were human trafficking back then. We just didn't know to call it that. Few weeks after the robbery, local sheriff had already been out there and questioned everybody a few times. They'd identified the second gunman. Some guy the boyfriend knew. Guy turned up dead, I guess."

Flint nodded again. He had questions, but he let Manning play out his story the way he'd rehearsed it first.

"She'd already been through a lot. Maybe I felt sorry for her." He hung his head. "She was in big trouble already with that sick baby and her boyfriend dead, and nothing anybody did to her could bring those people back. And it was really Oscar's fault that they died, anyway. And I was on the road."

Manning shrugged his big, hairy shoulders. "I dunno. The whole thing was already over by the time I knew it had happened. I guess I just figured there wasn't anything I could do."

Flint quickly sorted through all that. Manning didn't think Oakwood had been the second gunman. That much was clear. Scarlett could be wrong about that, but the blood evidence supported her theory and not Manning's. Not that he intended to enlighten him.

He focused on one particular piece that might have mattered to Oakwood now. "What do you mean it was Oscar Tuttle's fault that two people in the store died?"

"He was a hothead. Always had been. And he was having an affair with that woman, the customer. No question about that. That had to be why she was behind the counter with him instead of in front of it where a customer should be. And if I know Oscar—and believe me, I knew him—he was trying to impress his date when those two came in looking to rob the place. Those kids might have interrupted something, if you catch my drift." Manning stopped to breathe. His belly expanded. "Oscar could have just given them the money. That's what Mildred would have done. No amount of money is worth killing over, you ask me."

"You never told anyone you picked her up?"

Manning shook his head. "Oscar never did a minute's jail time for killing that baby's dad. That dead woman was a mother, too. Oscar never owned up to ruining her family's life, either. Maybe Laura knew about the robbery and that's why she was running, but it didn't seem right to me that a sick baby should have to go through anything else, when it was Oscar killed her daddy."

Flint understood Manning's desire to stay out of it. He'd harbored a fugitive, but as far as he knew at the time, Oakwood was not one of the gunmen. "Where did you pick Laura up?"

Manning looked down at the spotted carpet. He leaned his forearms on his thighs and clasped his hands together. The coffee pot stopped dripping. The aroma of fresh-brewed java filled the room, but Flint already knew the coffee didn't match its promise.

"I picked her up at Bette Maxwell's place. Just at the road, at the end of the driveway." He raised his head and looked at Flint. "I'd picked up kids there before. There was a little bench there because the bus system had once run along that road. Laura and the baby were sitting there. She waved me down."

Flint had interviewed hundreds of witnesses and he was a good judge of them. Manning was telling the truth. Mostly. But he'd left something out. Something important. "Was she sitting there at Bette Maxwell's place by herself? Just her and the baby? Hoping for a ride?"

Manning stalled. He shuffled over and refilled both coffee cups and shuffled back. Maybe he was trying to decide how much to tell. Or maybe something else was bothering him. He didn't answer the question.

"What time did you pick her up at Bette's?" The robbery had happened at 11:32 p.m. on a Sunday. Had he found her there in the middle of the night, miles from the crime scene?

Manning didn't say anything else for a good long while, leaving Flint to work things out on his own. But he didn't know enough to figure it out. Not yet.

Manning had confirmed a few of Flint's deductions, though. Laura Oakwood had headed toward Canada. But that wasn't specific enough to find her. Canada was a big country. He needed more.

She'd been at the Clovis Ranch and her story about escaping the abuse might have provided a motive for the robbery, and it explained how Oakwood and Prieto knew all about Mildred's Corner store. But it didn't suggest she'd made any friends while she was there or tell Flint anything about where Laura Oakwood was now.

Manning confirmed that the baby was with her, so Flint was on the right track there.

Unfair as it might seem, whether or not it was Oscar Tuttle's fault that Prieto and the customer were killed was irrelevant to the law. Oscar was deceased now. He'd probably never have been prosecuted, anyway. Whoever John David had been, he wasn't the second gunman inside the store. The blood trails proved that a woman was there. DNA would establish that the woman was Laura Oakwood. She was guilty of felony murder because both deaths occurred during the course of the felony robbery and she was the one who shot the customer.

"Why did you call me back?" Manning's motive niggled Flint. He probably wouldn't be charged with witness tampering or even aiding a fugitive after all this time. But he was taking a risk he didn't need to take.

Manning didn't reply.

"You've avoided all this for almost thirty years. Why get involved now?"

"I've always wondered what happened to that girl and her baby." Manning shrugged and returned his gaze to the floor. "And if she has money coming, well, the baby deserves that much, doesn't she?"

"Who said she had money coming?"

"That's why you're trying to find her, isn't it?"

"What makes you say that?"

Manning looked up. He pushed his chin forward. "Well, that's what you do, right? You find people who have the right to inherit things?"

"You don't seem like the type of guy who'd have looked me up on the internet." Flint cocked his head. "Someone must have told you Laura would be coming into money if I find her." Manning didn't reply.

"A couple of land men share that info with you? Paxton and Trevor?"

He shook his head. "I don't know those guys. Sorry."

"So who told you? I'm not leaving here without an answer, Manning."

"It was Bette. She called me after you left." He shrugged. "She said we needed to help you find Laura and help the baby. She wants to be sure they get the money they're owed."

The answer didn't surprise Flint as much as maybe it should have.

"And how do you know Bette Maxwell?"

"Bette and I have been together for a long time. She's told me a lot about you and Katie Scarlett." Manning chuckled and the chuckle led to wheezed coughing. "I met you both once, years ago, at the Lazy M. When we were all a lot younger. Bette says you two were a couple of little hellions."

Flint grinned in an effort to keep the conversation flowing. "Can't argue with the facts."

"And there's the money. The donation you promised." Manning's laughter had died and he'd turned serious again. "Laura Oakwood was the reason I started reporting human trafficking to the Road Warriors hotline."

"I don't get the connection."

"Before I picked up Oakwood, I'd give folks a ride and when they left my rig I never gave them much thought after that. But when I found out she was running from the law and I thought more about her limping, I figured she might've been involved in that robbery somehow. Even knowing Oscar Tuttle was probably the one at fault." He lowered his head again for a moment before he looked directly into Flint's eyes. "Well, I didn't want to help the criminals. I wanted to help the victims, you know? Even if I couldn't figure out which was which. So now I call it in. Let the experts sort things out. It takes money to do what they do. And lots of it."

Flint ran all of Manning's ramblings through his head, testing his theories, comparing to the facts he'd already confirmed. Most of what Manning said rang true, and the bits that didn't were probably too old to matter.

"I've gotta get in the shower." Manning stood and moved toward the small bathroom. "Any chance you can give me a lift over to my rig? They'll have it loaded and I can get on the road. Won't be much out of your way."

"Yeah, sure. Get dressed. We'll drop you off." Flint left the cup with the cold coffee on the table. "Come on outside when you're ready."

CHAPTER THIRTY

DAWN KISSED THE SKY with daylight and the promise of more heat as the day developed. Flint stood on the sidewalk in front of the Texas Inn and dialed from a fresh burner phone to the one he'd given Scarlett last night.

It was early, but she'd be awake. Maddy was an early riser.

On the fourth ring, Scarlett picked up. "Yes?"

He recognized weariness in her tone. She'd probably worked through the night, too. "Are you alone? Away from ears and eyes?"

"I wouldn't have answered this phone otherwise." Like she'd said, she was good at covert ops. He hoped she was good enough.

"I'm short on time," Flint said. "Have you seen the option?"

"What?"

"The written document that Shaw claims gives him the right to the Juan Garcia Field when we find Laura Oakwood and get her to sign over her rights. Have you seen it?"

The silence on the other end of the line was all the answer he needed.

"Can you get it?"

"Why? We don't care about the contract. All we care about is our assignment, which is to find Oakwood before two o'clock tomorrow."

"So the question is, how did Shaw get that option? Where did it come from? What did he pay for it?"

"Again, why do we care?"

"It's odd, isn't it?"

"In what way?"

"Shaw and Crane both go after the same field. They both have a colorable claim of right."

"So?"

"That field is out in the middle of nowhere. The owners are people they don't know. How did they even know to look for the owners? How in the hell did they become aware that the field existed?"

"They're oil men. This is their business. They're always looking for growth, like any business. They figure out where the oil is, and they go after the rights to it. You know how this works, Flint." Her tone became increasingly exasperated as she spun her answer. "Somebody brought this field to their attention, and then they both wanted it. They chased down all the owners and got it all worked out down to the very last holdout, and that is Laura Oakwood and now they can't find her. Business as usual."

Flint said nothing. Her theory made sense. But that didn't mean it was true.

Maybe Shaw and Crane were just a couple of billionaire jerks trying to find something to fight about, too. But that didn't ring totally true to him either.

She said, "Don't we have enough rabbit holes we're chasing down without you adding another long list of nonsense?"

"Just do me a favor, Scarlett. Get a copy of that option. I want to see it."

"I thought you'd quit this job."

"I did."

"Yeah, right." She blew a long stream of exasperation out through her mouth. "You might as well tell me. What's the problem?"

"I don't know exactly. Just a feeling, I guess." Which was true and not true at the same time. "But this is a lot of trouble to go to for a single missing girl, isn't it?"

"She's not a girl, Flint. She doesn't know it yet, but she's a very rich, very powerful missing *woman*—she hasn't been a *girl* since she killed that woman at Mildred's Corner. Or maybe even a long time before that." She paused. "She's not a lost lamb you need to save. Remember that."

Traffic had picked up along the road in front of the Texas Inn, making it difficult to hear on the cheap phone. He blocked his left ear with his palm. "Get a copy of the option, Scarlett. Send it to me. I need to see it."

"I'll try. I'm not sure how long it'll take. Shaw's on his way to Montana. That's where he and Crane are meeting to bury the hatchet, I guess. At The Peak Club. Lot of money at stake, so they wanted a posh place. They've planned a big party with all their cronies. Everybody skis and drinks and they have some sort of annual hunt and there's some gambling involved, most likely. They've got some sort of backslapping handover blowout planned. Or something. Whatever billionaires do to celebrate."

The Texas Inn parking lot was still empty, but several of the businesses along the street had begun to show signs of life. Manning would be out shortly. "Tell me what progress you've made on the other matters."

"Let me just give you the highlights. Otherwise, we'll be here all day and I've got a kid to get off to school before I get back to work." She took a breath and launched into another one of her long spiels. "We're skating around the privacy laws, but we haven't found any providers who are currently treating, or have ever treated, Oakwood's daughter. We've broadened our search to all fifty states and we've checked all the major treatment centers in Mexico. We've contacted about half the facilities in Canada, starting with the major ones in the more populated areas. No luck."

"Keep looking everywhere but focus on Canada." Telling her about Canada was a risk because Crane was watching her like a hawk with a field mouse. But she was right. They didn't have the luxury of time to hide in the shadows anymore.

"Why Canada?"

"I'll fill you in later."

She sounded even more annoyed now. "We haven't found any records reflecting Richard Oakwood's birth or where he came from or when."

"Have you found a social security number for him?"

"We chased down the missing records based on the tip you got from the high school. After a lot of digging, we still haven't found a social security number for her, but we finally uncovered one for her father."

Flint nodded. The wind had kicked up a bit now. "You ran the SSN through the SSDI?"

"No luck."

"Why not?"

"You know how the Social Security Death Index works as well as I do."

"And Richard Oakwood is not listed at all?"

"Which isn't as unusual as it should be. The index goes back to social security numbers issued since 1936. But it only lists those people who actually collected benefits after 1962 and were later reported as deceased. In Oakwood's case, he never collected benefits because he died before he was eligible. And as for his death, well, apparently no one reported that, either. Not that anybody had an obligation to."

Usually, death was reported by the family. Often, there were beneficiaries who were entitled to death benefits. Which would have been another way to track Richard Oakwood's relatives, if he had any.

Scarlett was still talking. "If he were alive today, he'd be eligible for benefits. Nobody is impersonating him or collecting on his account, unfortunately, because that could be a solid lead. As it is, bottom line, his SSN doesn't hit in any of the systems because it's too old and hasn't been used in more than two decades."

"Same answer for Medicare, I guess?"

"He was fifty-two when he died. Too young for Medicare." She stopped for a breath. "We used the SSN to run more background checks that we couldn't do before, though. More bank records, real estate, and so on."

A big rig powered down on the road, filling the air with the stench of diesel and more noise. Flint pressed his palm closer against his ear and turned away from the road. "Find anything?"

"Nothing is easily accessible. Physical tax returns are usually destroyed by the IRS after about three years. Electronic filing was too new back when Richard died so it's not likely he filed electronically. But if he did, we could get the tax returns if they still exist. Maybe. Eventually. With a court order. I've got calls in to contacts I can lean on for a favor. Maybe just get the information without the documents. Still waiting." She blew out a long stream of exasperation. "Nothing moves slower than the IRS."

"Unless it's the DMV," Flint teased. She didn't laugh. "How about his application for the social security number?"

"The SS-5? It would have his date of birth, place of birth, and parents' names at least, as you know. We asked. They're looking. He applied for the number after 1962, so the application should be in the system's computers. He has no right to privacy after death, which means we should be able to get access. And we will, eventually. But they wanted a certified copy of the death certificate before they'd look for it. We're getting the certificate now. We had to wake up a judge."

He walked away from Manning's room to the quietest corner of the building. "Read the number out to me." She did and he memorized it. He saw Manning leave his room and motioned him toward the waiting Land Rover. "And you've found nothing else on Richard Oakwood's family of origin?"

"We find anything and you'll hear me whooping it up across the entire state of Texas."

He grinned. "I'll be sure to listen for it. I haven't heard you whoop in years."

"You do that." She hung up.

Flint grinned again and pulled a second burner phone from his pocket and dialed a source inside the FBI. When he answered, Flint said, "I need you to find the family of origin for the man attached to this SSN. Pronto." He repeated the memorized number.

"Got a callback?"

"I'll call you." Flint disconnected and dropped both phones into his pocket until he could dismantle and discard them. He joined Manning and Brady in the Land Rover. Brady rolled out onto the road headed away from the center of town.

Scarlett had come up empty on all leads, but checking off the dead ends made Flint feel like he was getting closer to the right answer. Or maybe that was nothing more than wishful thinking.

CHAPTER THIRTY-ONE

MANNING PROVIDED DIRECTIONS FROM the backseat.
Brady drove along Maple Road and turned north onto Pine. The
street names were fanciful, given that the oil industry had long
ago removed all the trees that had once grown here.

Mount Warren was like other oil towns in Texas. It had seen
booms and busts over the years, its fortunes rising and falling with
the price of crude.

At the moment, oil prices were in a long slump. Which,
according to the financial press, was a perfect time for the likes of
Shaw and Crane to gobble up oil-rich land.

Buy low, sell high was the mantra of every developer
everywhere.

Flint noticed abandoned vehicles alongside decrepit buildings
on both sides of the road. Most of this area had seen better days.

A few miles west of town, Manning pointed to a large
distribution center. Flint had assumed he was hauling oil-drilling
supplies, but this was a consumer goods operation. Flint recognized
the name painted in large orange letters on the building. It was a

discount store favored by low-income workers. There were plenty of those to go around all over America these days.

Brady turned into the distribution center driveway and stopped at the rusty guard shack. Manning lowered his window and passed his ID.

The guard barely glanced at it before he waved them through.

"Pull around the back," Manning said.

When the Land Rover rounded the long, flat building, a row of trailers lined up to loading bays filled Flint's field of vision.

"Fifth rig on the right." Manning pointed ahead to an older tractor unit already attached to a semi-trailer. The tractor cabin didn't have a sleeper, which probably explained Manning's overnight stay at the Texas Inn. "Thanks for the ride."

Manning stepped out of the Land Rover. Before he closed the door, he leaned in. "You owe me a finder's fee, Flint. And I'll take it out of your cut. Not hers."

"That so?" Flint said.

"Don't think you can mess with me. I'll collect from your mother if I have to. Bette's got the money and she'll give it to me. You know she will." Manning closed the door.

Flint wasn't worried about Manning, but the thinly veiled threat to extort the only woman who had ever loved Flint like a mother wasn't lost on him. He'd lost contact with Bette but that didn't mean he no longer cared for her.

Flint watched Manning labor toward his rig, thinking how easy it would be to deal with him should he try to hurt Bette. He put her on his list to follow up with after Tuesday, whether he found Oakwood or not.

Brady executed a perfect three-point turn and headed the Land Rover out along the same route they'd used to enter. When they passed the guard shack, he said, "Where to?"

"Back to the plane, but drive through town this time."

Mount Warren was waking up. It was significantly larger than nearby Wolf Bend. People were walking dogs and riding bikes in the residential sections. Monday-morning traffic wasn't heavy, but it was present, which it hadn't been on the way to Manning's rig.

He counted three churches, all serenely perched on wide lawns. One was a Catholic church and school, Saint Michael's. They passed the usual array of public schools and school buses, office buildings, and worker bees on their way to the daily grind.

The only remotely noteworthy things were the two large buildings in the center of town, one on each side of the street, facing each other. Both seemed prosperous enough. Well tended. Brick buildings faced by large windows and brass fixtures. From the look of them, they were built closer to the turn of the twentieth century than the twenty-first.

Shaw Petroleum on the east side and Crane Oil on the west.

Crane had said he and Shaw grew up together. Perhaps Mount Warren was the town where their granddaddies began the legendary feud that Scarlett had plopped him into. He wondered again what event had sparked their dispute and what had fueled it for so many years. Holding a grudge for decades required serious determination. Not many men could manage it.

Brady sent a text to Davis when they were twenty minutes from the Pilatus. By the time he pulled the Land Rover next to the jet, Drake was ready to go. The wait had been uneventful.

Flint didn't know exactly where they were headed, but the general direction was north. Drake and Flint agreed on a flight plan as far north as Grand Forks, North Dakota. They'd need more information after that. From Mount Warren, Drake handled the jet and Flint turned his attention to ground operations.

CHAPTER THIRTY-TWO

FLINT HOISTED HIMSELF OUT of the co-pilot's seat and moved to a table in the back of the Pilatus where he could work.

He wrote a quick report of his chat with Manning, encrypted it, and uploaded it to his secure server, where Scarlett could collect it later.

His FBI source had uploaded encrypted notes. He found the file and opened it.

His source had been able to trace Richard Oakwood's original SS-5 application form for a social security number, which identified Richard's parents. He'd also been able to confirm that both of Richard's parents were long deceased. With more digging and leaning on a few more sources, he'd uncovered Richard's birth certificate.

Flint grinned. Finally. An actual break in the solid wall of granite he'd slammed into at every turn on this heir hunt.

"You're looking pleased with yourself. Good news of the kind that might tell me where to set down?" Drake asked.

"Possibly. Hang on for about thirty minutes and I should know."

Flint read through the data again. Richard Oakwood had been born in Regina General Hospital, Regina, Saskatchewan, Canada. He had one sister, Melanie Oakwood, born in the same hospital as her brother, three years later.

Pretty quickly after reading the message, Flint discovered everything he needed to know about Melanie Oakwood. Unlike her niece, she wasn't trying to hide from anyone or anything.

Melanie had been born, educated, married, delivered her children, and buried her husband all in the same town, ten miles from Regina.

Flint said, "Find an airport close to Charlestown, Saskatchewan. Population is thirty-five thousand, so you should be able to find a private landing strip. Looks like a winner."

"Will do." Drake turned his attention to the task and Flint went back to his work.

Melanie Oakwood's married name was Barnett. She was still living in the same house she and her husband bought together. The house where they raised their own son until he moved to Switzerland. The house where her husband had died five years ago.

Many women in Melanie Barnett's situation might have retired to a warmer climate after their husbands died. Or become snowbirds. But Melanie hadn't. Which Flint took as a good sign. Maybe the woman was agoraphobic or something. Whatever her situation, maybe he would find her at home.

After he'd unraveled Richard Oakwood's connection to Regina, Saskatchewan, finding Richard's sister had been simple. Flint assumed Laura Oakwood had accomplished the task much faster.

Laura would have known where her father was born. She would have known he had a sister, which was what she'd told Manning immediately after the robbery. Armed with that knowledge, the young Laura Oakwood could easily have located her aunt. The trip from Denver, where Manning dropped her and the baby off, to Charlestown, Saskatchewan, was long but doable, even back then.

When her niece showed up on her doorstep with a sick baby, was Melanie Barnett the kind of woman who would have turned the young mother and child away? Unlikely.

"I might have found a good spot to land. We'll see when we get closer," Drake said. "You already know that Canadian immigration laws are not as relaxed now as they were during the Vietnam War for draft dodgers, right?"

Flint nodded. "Laura Oakwood would have been a Canadian citizen even though she was born in Texas, because her father was a Canadian citizen. She probably slipped over the border, but she'd have been able to get proper documentation on the other side."

"Didn't she have a kid with her? What about the baby?"

"Not sure. The baby might be a Canadian citizen, too, because her mother is."

"Sounds iffy."

Flint nodded and said nothing. The legalities didn't concern him overmuch. He hoped Canada's national health service would have covered the child's medical care, because they kept meticulous records.

Flint was close. He could feel it. The important logic was almost flawless and the gaps didn't matter. Everything was falling into place, as it so often did near the end of a hunt.

"What about those two goons that have been following you around? We still watching out for them?" Drake rubbed the side of his neck reflexively on the spot where they'd injected him in front of Scarlett Investigations.

Perhaps Paxton and Trevor had discovered Melanie Oakwood Barnett, too. His best guess was that either Crane or his two land men had hired Phillips to delay him when he left Wolf Bend. Which suggested they'd learned something new, something they wanted to follow with Flint out of the way.

That lead could have been a desire to reach Melanie Barnett first. Which might explain why they weren't at Shaw Tower with Crane when he'd dumped Reed and why he hadn't seen them lately.

"Let's hope they have been here ahead of us. Those two are the opposite of socially adept. They piss off everybody they come into contact with." Flint grinned. "If they already found the woman we're looking for, she's going to be more than happy to help us."

Drake frowned. "Or we'll be attacked. Or arrested. Odds are about even for all three."

"Keep your sidearm handy."

Drake's frown turned to a scowl. "Concealed weapons are illegal in Canada. Can't carry without a permit. Which we don't have."

"Better to argue about that from a standing position than from a coffin, eh?" Flint hadn't found Oakwood yet, but he had a better chance with his boots on the ground in Charlestown than anywhere he'd been before.

Melanie Oakwood Barnett felt like a long shot, yes. But a long shot that could work. He'd told Scarlett he would find Laura Oakwood, and find her he would. Eventually.

Shaw's deadline was of very little concern to him. He was through worrying about Shaw and Crane. Scarlett mattered to him, although he'd never say that to her.

If he found Oakwood before the deadline, Scarlett would be pleased. Not to mention all the extra money they'd both have if he succeeded.

Besides, at this point he simply wanted to prove he could do it. He loved a challenge. Find Laura Oakwood when no one else could. On time. When Scarlett could not? Sure. No problem.

"What's our ETA?" Flint asked, grinning. He quickly encrypted everything he'd learned and posted it for Scarlett to bring her up to speed.

"Still flying VFR, so we have to avoid the major airports and at lower altitudes. Takes a bit longer." Drake punched some numbers into a keyboard. "We're cruising at 425. Calculations say the flight should take a few more hours."

Flint nodded. He had time to develop a plan.

He pulled up maps. He checked tax rolls, voter registrations, census records, driver's license databases, prison records, death records.

"Do you think the Oakwood woman is living in Charlestown?" Drake asked.

"It's a place to start. Her aunt lives there. Name's Melanie Barnett." Laura Oakwood was smart, clever, resourceful, and probably, like most fugitives, more than a little paranoid. He assumed she wouldn't live near her aunt because she might be easily located by anyone watching Barnett. She'd have moved to a town with a good hospital and good schools. Probably not too far away.

"Where do you expect to find her, then?"

"Working on it. You'll be among the first to know."

Drake frowned and stopped asking questions for the moment.

After a bit of digging, Flint found three good possibilities within driving distance of Charlestown. But he was running out of time and he needed to prioritize. He couldn't thoroughly check every town in Canada before the deadline, even if he'd wanted to.

He stood up and walked to the back of the plane, stretching his taut muscles. The galley was set up for executive travel. He found a coffee maker and brewed a couple of cups. He carried one to Drake in the cockpit.

The caffeine seemed to kick his thinking into higher gear. He paced the narrow aisle.

He wasn't the least bit sentimental. The intense desire for belonging to biological connections wasn't a driving force for him. But most people felt differently. After food, shelter, and safety, love and belonging were right at the top of the list for most people. Normal humans, the theory goes, have a basic need to love and be loved in return.

Flint was no therapist. But he'd grown up an orphan and the orphans he'd known wanted nothing more than to find a real family. Ideally, their own birth family. Failing that, they wanted a family they could love and that would love them back.

For Laura Oakwood, Flint had already ruled out Teresa Prieto and everyone else in Wolf Bend as an ideal family unit. Which left only one option among Oakwood's blood relatives.

Odds were strong that Laura Oakwood had placed her trust in Aunt Melanie. She should know where to find Oakwood, and she should want her niece to receive the money that was rightfully hers.

Or maybe not. Barnett could refuse to help. Flint had a plan for that, too.

He resettled into his seat and spent the rest of the flight time absorbing everything he could find about Melanie Barnett.

Charlestown, Saskatchewan, was nestled along the Trans-Canada Highway, sixty miles east of Regina following a well-traveled bus route. Charlestown's main attraction was Charlestown College, where both Melanie and her husband, Harold, were professors. Harold's specialty had been rural development and Melanie's was health studies. Their son's major was finance, which was probably why he was now working in Switzerland.

CHAPTER THIRTY-THREE

DRAKE SET THE PILATUS down at a private airstrip. Hobby pilots were plentiful here in the Canadian prairie, which made the process easier than it might otherwise have been.

Landing at the local airport would have meant seeking permission from the control tower. They'd have been asked for paperwork.

The red tape would have tied them up for way too long, so they'd come in under the radar. No one seemed to care.

After the Texas heat he'd escaped from, the weather was surreal. A storm was closing in to add more snow to the already-blanketed city.

Dark clouds hovered, making midday seem like the middle of the night.

Snow had begun falling in fat, wet flakes, the kind that piled up into sodden blankets.

At least a dozen people would injure themselves tonight attempting to shovel the heavy stuff out of the way.

Flint easily found Melanie Barnett's quiet, residential neighborhood.

Sidewalks lined the brick-paved streets. Single-family homes perched on small lots.

Well-manicured gardens surrounded them in the spring and summer months, but this March, the gardens were buried under at least four feet of snow.

Garages were detached and set back, afterthoughts, added years later, once cars had become standard transportation. Driveways were long and narrow.

Most of the homes were lit from within and a few chimneys belched smoke in wisps from cozy wood fires.

Flint could easily see inside the rooms where people hustled from one task to the next, preparing meals or watching television. Yellow or blue light spilled onto the snow through the windows.

The Barnett house was perched in the middle of the block. A red brick Georgian-style two-story home with white trim and a black-shingled roof. White mounds of snow, several feet high, were piled on either side of the sidewalk and the front porch and the driveway.

But there his luck ended. The Barnett house was dark. Melanie Barnett was not home.

Flint checked the time. Perhaps she was at work or had gone shopping or to accomplish errands before the storm intensified. How long could he wait for her return?

He'd like to have some evidence that he was on the right trail, at least. Shaw's deadline would expire in less than twenty-one hours. If this was another dead end, he didn't have much time to regroup and follow a new lead.

Inside, Barnett might have pictures or other mementos of Laura Oakwood and her daughter. If she did, then he'd wait to speak to her. But if she didn't, perhaps he should save his time and move on.

The fresh snow made it impossible to approach the house without leaving obvious footprints. He scanned both sides of the sidewalk for approaching residents or visitors.

Every few minutes a car would pass by, silently rolling along the snowy street. He couldn't hang around in front of the Barnett house without arousing suspicion.

He considered his options. Should he break in now and confirm his theories and then wait for Barnett to return? How long would he need to wait?

He shifted from one foot to the other. He'd worn boots, jeans, and a jacket suitable for spring in Texas, not winter in Canada. His hands were red. His ears and fingers tingled with cold. He needed to move.

Maybe he could catch her at work.

Flint turned and tromped through the snow to the end of the block. He kept moving toward Charlestown College. If he hustled, he could get there before the administrative offices closed.

The entrance to Charlestown College was six blocks from Barnett's home. Between the two, East Charlestown looked better covered in a snow blanket than it would have in summer.

Low buildings, broken pavements, rusty vehicles, and panhandlers dotted every corner.

Drug dealers, waifs, and hungry dogs and cats loitered around the buildings for warmth. He'd spent time in worse areas but not recently.

Half a block off the main drag, he walked through the archway onto Charleston College's campus. He might as well have walked through a black hole from one dimension to the next.

The campus looked like an advertisement by the chamber of commerce for life in idyllic Canada.

The buildings were clean and well kept. Students and faculty trudged along the snowy sidewalks in all directions, bundled in down outerwear, heads lowered, lugging heavy backpacks or satchels.

The college experience here was foreign to Flint.

He hustled along, dodging preoccupied pedestrians, until he reached the administration building, which was directly across from the main campus entrance.

He gripped the twisted wrought-iron handle and pulled open the heavy oak door.

A heavily bundled female mumbled something that sounded like "Thank you" as she pushed out and walked into the storm.

Flint stomped his boots to loosen some of the wet-packed snow before he set off down the corridor to the offices at the end of the hall. Inside he found a standard set of office furniture and a middle-aged woman behind a desk typing on a keyboard.

She looked up, distracted. "May I help you?"

"I hope so." He put a smile on his face and in his voice. "I'm looking for Melanie Barnett."

"Professor Barnett has taken a leave of absence." She returned her gaze to the screen, preoccupied with some knotty problem that seemed to have carried away any reticence she might otherwise have had about discussing Professor Barnett with a total stranger.

"It's important that I reach her. Do you know when she'll return?" The woman didn't look up again. "Next semester, I think."

He felt his enthusiasm extinguish with the flame of expectation. He'd come so close. "Where did she go?"

"To Switzerland, she said. To visit her son."

The woman had been surprisingly forthcoming so far, so he asked another intrusive question. "Does she have a teaching assistant I might talk to?"

Before she could respond, a middle-aged man emerged through an open door from an interior office. He cast a disapproving glance at the woman and approached Flint, hand extended. "I'm Ralph Lawson, dean of Charlestown College. Would you like to come into my office, Mister . . ."

"Michael Flint," he said, shaking hands before following Lawson, who gestured toward one of the chairs and closed the door behind him.

He seated himself in the other chair next to Flint.

The encounter reminded him of his talk with Laura Oakwood's high school principal. Flint had never been a fan of educators because he'd been a lousy student, which his teachers rarely appreciated.

This one wasn't any warmer than any of the others he'd met.

"Why are you looking for Professor Barnett?"

"I'm not, exactly. I'm looking for her niece."

"Leslie? Why?"

"Yes, Leslie." He latched onto the name like a lifeline. An alias probably, but it could be a searchable one. "I've been hired to bring her some good news and I don't have an address for her."

"What good news?"

"It's confidential." He saw Lawson's spine stiffen. Before Lawson could change his mind and throw him out, he said, "Can I trust you to keep this just between us?"

Lawson folded his hands. "I can't make that promise until I hear what this is about. But as long as you're not threatening her, I don't see why not."

"Right. Well, Leslie is entitled to some money. Quite a lot of money, actually. But only if she claims it before tomorrow afternoon."

Lawson's eyebrows shot up and his mouth formed an astonished O. "And she doesn't know about the money? How is that possible?"

"It's complicated." Lawson stiffened again, and Flint relented as much as he thought the administrator might expect. "Her claim to some real estate was not known until recently. When the property came up for sale, her rights in the oil and gas underneath the property were discovered."

Lawson nodded. "We have a lot of that kind of thing here in Saskatchewan. Oil and gas production have been booming across Canada."

"Then you know this isn't as crazy as it sounds. I need to find her, pronto. Otherwise, she's going to lose out on what belongs to her. Does she live around here?"

Lawson shook his head. "She used to. When she was a student here and lived with her aunt and uncle. But she graduated and moved away. I'm not sure where she lives now."

A current address might be in the college records for fund-raising purposes. Universities were forever pestering graduates for donations. Flint was sure Lawson wouldn't search for it. He'd put Scarlett on the project. Without a last name, it might take a while. But how many Leslies could there be in a relatively small school alumni list from Charlestown College?

He was closer to finding Oakwood than he'd been since the job started. He could feel it. "I understand that Professor Barnett is on vacation. Do you have a phone number where I might be able to reach her and ask for Leslie's address?"

Lawson shook his head. "I don't. She's out of the country. I'm sorry."

"Is there anyone else on campus who might be able to help me?"

"I can ask around. If you can come back tomorrow, I might have a couple of people lined up for you."

Flint had the feeling that pushing Lawson any further was the wrong way to go. He seemed like the type who took his responsibilities seriously. This was probably the best Flint would get from the old guy, and it was more than the school should have shared with him.

"That would be great. I'll call back tomorrow." He put a big grin on his face and reached out to pump Lawson's hand. "And thank you for your help, Mr. Lawson. I'm sure Leslie and her aunt will be thrilled when they hear my news."

Flint smiled and nodded and Lawson walked him to the exit. He wouldn't return tomorrow. But he'd learned three useful bits of information. He was on the right track. He could look around inside the Barnett home without fear of being discovered. And Leslie, as Laura Oakwood was calling herself now, had been a student at Charlestown College before she moved away.

He could use all that to narrow his search. But could he do it before tomorrow's deadline?

CHAPTER THIRTY-FOUR

FLINT RETRACED HIS ROUTE to Melanie Barnett's home in half the time he'd spent on the way over. He walked past her house to confirm that it remained unoccupied.

Three doors down, he found a home whose sidewalk and driveway were covered in numerous snow prints. He trudged through the snow to the backyard, mixing his boot prints with the others.

There were no fences between the homes in this neighborhood. At least he wouldn't have to climb over them. There were no outdoor lights shining from any of the houses into the back.

He ducked along the shadows behind the third house and then the second house, until he reached the back of the garage at the Barnett residence.

He flattened himself against the garage wall and crouched low to avoid being seen, had any of the neighbors bothered to look into the backyards.

From the garage, he saw that the back of the Barnett residence was as tidy and deserted as the front. A patio extended the length of the house.

There were floodlights, probably connected to motion detectors, near the back door. The setup was low tech, installed more for the homeowner's convenience than for crime prevention.

He stayed close to the garage until he reached a walkway to the house. Flint pulled out his LED microbeam and used it to see the connections for the floodlights.

He didn't want to shut down the electricity.

If he could get close enough without tripping the sensors on the motion detectors, he could simply unscrew the bulbs in the floodlights and screw them back in when he left.

He'd seen no evidence of a home alarm system here or anywhere else on the block. The neighborhood didn't seem like the kind of place where a homeowner would need one. Apparently mountains of snow and bone-chilling cold were sufficient deterrents to crime here, even given the dodgy characters he'd passed a few blocks away.

He scanned the area again, to be sure he wasn't visible to the neighbors. Then he avoided the motion sensors, unscrewed the bulbs, and moved to unlock the back door.

Inside, the first thing he noticed was the darkness. Little ambient light spilled in from the streetlights out front.

The windows were covered by heavy drapes or wooden blinds or both.

Barnett had left the heat on with the thermostat set at about fifty degrees, which meant the power was still on. But if he turned on the lights, the neighbors might notice.

Some ambient light had infiltrated the window coverings, which meant light could no doubt escape through the same crevices.

He pulled the LED microbeam from his pocket again. He didn't have to worry about a watchdog.

He made a quick tour of the house.

It was about two thousand square feet and included a finished basement, where laundry and workout equipment were set up.

The first floor was divided into kitchen, dining room, living room, half bath, a small office, and a room with two chairs, two ottomans, and two reading lamps across from a big-screen TV.

The second floor contained four bedrooms and two full baths.

None of the rooms were occupied by woman or beast or sufficient lighting.

If he hadn't assumed that Melanie Barnett lived here alone, he might have concluded this was still a family home. Instead, it was an unoccupied residence because its single owner was on vacation.

On the second pass, he looked for family photos on the walls and in frames resting on the tabletops. Melanie and Harold Barnett had been a happy couple, judging from all the photographic evidence.

Photos chronicled their courtship, marriage, and major life events, like the birth of their son, Harold, Jr., who grew up to be a handsome young man and became a middle-aged banker. If Junior had married, his parents didn't choose to display photos of the occasion. Which probably meant he was still single. Married to his work, perhaps.

On the second floor, along the corridor walls, Flint found the first photos of Laura Oakwood and the girl who could only be her child.

The age-progression photos he'd prepared back in Houston were fairly accurate. He'd have recognized the twenty-five- year-old Oakwood anywhere.

At thirty-five-ish, she resembled his computer-generated images well enough to hit on facial recognition software at border crossings around the world.

She was in her mid-forties now and she probably hadn't changed much.

The baby, Selma Oakwood Prieto, had been photographed slightly more often than the Prince of Wales.

Walls throughout the house were adorned with her image. Framed candid and studio shots of her at various life events rested atop most flat surfaces. In all of them, she looked healthy.

Her fourth birthday had been celebrated with a chocolate cake that said "Happy Birthday, Sally!" in bright pink script.

So they'd used her grandmother's preferred nickname for her, too.

The most recent photo of Laura Oakwood was framed and perched on the table in the TV room between the two easy chairs.

She looked about forty or so. Her daughter was photographed with her.

There were "Happy Birthday" signs behind her and Selma held a martini glass in her hand.

The legal drinking age in Canada was eighteen in some provinces and nineteen in others, which meant the photo was probably eight or nine years old.

He pulled out his phone and snapped a few pictures of the photos.

He made another quick circuit of the house, looking for more recent photos he might have missed while roaming around in the dark, but he didn't find any.

Which made sense if Laura and Selma had moved on, as Lawson said.

Maybe the Barnetts were like a lot of modern families and they took mostly digital photos now. Sometimes people displayed digital images in an electronic frame, but he didn't see one anywhere in the house.

He'd confirmed that he was on the right track with Melanie Barnett, though.

Her niece had come here.

Lived here.

Raised her daughter here.

Apparently changed her name to Leslie something and began calling her daughter Sally. What last name had she adopted? Was she using Barnett now?

Flint shook his head. Logically, when Laura showed up here with a baby, she'd have told her aunt something about the father. She might have invented a name for him, too.

Because if she'd used Oakwood when she first arrived, unless she told her family why she was running from the law, they'd have expected her to have the family name.

So she'd probably given them the false name from the very outset.

Where was Leslie living now? That was the thing he'd come here to find out. But he'd come up empty so far.

He hadn't found an address book or a list of phone numbers near the landline phone.

The phone itself was old and hard-wired into a jack in the kitchen wall. It didn't have a phone book feature or a list of speed dial numbers.

He found five more phones in three of the bedrooms, TV room, and basement. All were of the same vintage and configuration.

None had a list of numbers or addresses nearby.

Where would Melanie Barnett have kept her niece's address and phone number? Unless there'd been a rift in the family, she'd have been sending cards and gifts to wherever Laura and Selma were living now.

All appearances here in the house suggested she'd have that information written down somewhere. She had a home office. A wired landline phone.

He hadn't seen a desktop computer anywhere. So she didn't seem like the kind of person who would store important information solely in an electronic device of some kind.

He heard a noise at the back door.

The small hairs on the back of his neck stood at attention.

He looked at the clock. He'd been inside the house for twenty minutes.

If he'd triggered some sort of silent alarm, surely the police would have arrived before now.

CHAPTER THIRTY-FIVE

FLINT FLIPPED OFF THE microbeam and slipped it into his pocket. His eyes had adjusted to the darkness and his trips through the house had shown him how to avoid bumping into the furniture.

He hurried to reach the kitchen before the intruder managed to unlock the back door. He drew his weapon.

The inky weather concealed the intruder as well outside as the heavy window coverings concealed Flint inside.

Which could mean the intruder hadn't seen Flint's footprints in the fresh snow since the floodlights were disabled. He thought the house was unoccupied.

Flint heard the gas furnace kick on and rumble and the forced air puff through the ventilation system. Warm air blew across the top of his head. He didn't move.

After a few seconds of inept fumbling, the intruder managed to open the lock on the back door. He pushed the door open and entered the mudroom. A second intruder followed and pushed the door closed behind them.

Flint pressed himself against the wall in the darkest corner of the kitchen.

The two shuffled heavily into the kitchen from the mudroom. One turned on a microbeam and pointed it at the floor. He swept the beam around the kitchen, keeping the light below the windows in an effort to avoid being discovered.

The beam ran across Flint's boots and continued its sweep instead of flashing up to confirm that the boots were occupied.

Flint breathed quietly, readied his Glock, and searched for a better answer.

A gunshot inside the house would surely alert the entire neighborhood and destroy Melanie Barnett's home. Flint wanted to avoid both.

The intruder shuffled past Flint's corner and into the living room, his microbeam aimed like a laser moving toward something specific. The second man followed behind.

The forced-air furnace continued its low rumbling and the hot air blew into the room. The scent of both men wafted with the heat, a scent he recognized. He identified the bulky silhouettes.

He spent no time seeking answers, although plenty of questions presented themselves. Now was the time to deal with these two—before they dealt with him permanently.

Flint moved quickly to disable the second man, Trevor, the one he'd originally dubbed Earless.

Trevor was big. His weight and size placed an undue amount of stress on his knees.

Flint had noticed his gait at the airport and again in the alley fight. He'd likely been injured many times before. His ligaments and tendons were damaged already, which made them perfect targets.

Flint planted his left foot securely on the floor. He aimed the heel of his right boot and kicked the outside of Trevor's right leg, slightly above the joint, bending the knee at an unnatural angle.

The right patella's lateral dislocation was instantaneous.

Trevor screamed and folded onto the floor, writhing in pain. Broken bones and torn ligaments hurt like hell. Surgical repair would be required. He wouldn't be walking easily or sneaking up on anybody else anytime soon.

His screaming was an inhuman howl that might send hunters to silence a beast. Flint pulled back his Glock and punished Trevor's temple with the butt. The screaming stopped the instant he lost consciousness.

Flint stepped back into the deep shadow.

Paxton had been leading the way into the house. When Trevor screamed and hit the floor, Paxton was several strides away, focused intently on his mission.

Paxton turned his big torso as quickly as he could and swung the microbeam toward Trevor. But he was slow. Slower than Trevor had been. The beam took a moment too long.

It illuminated his companion's limp body first. Trevor lay on his side, his right leg at an odd angle, painful to look at.

The microbeam's path aimed forward. Paxton shook his head rapidly, as if to process the bewildering stimuli coming at him too fast. He held the microbeam in one hand; the other hand was empty, hanging by his side.

Paxton's movements were slow and deliberate. He squatted beside Trevor to check his carotid pulse and made another mistake. He balanced on the balls of his feet, giving Flint the opening he needed.

Flint stepped forward swiftly, Glock pointed at Paxton. But he held his fire. Instead, he pushed Paxton's ass with all of his weight focused on the sole of his boot and sent him flat on his belly on top of Trevor.

Paxton landed heavily. His breath pushed out in an audible *oomph*. The sight might have been comical under different circumstances.

Flint raised the Glock and applied the same force to Paxton's thick head that he'd applied to Trevor's, with the same result.

Paxton's body relaxed on top of Trevor, his nose nuzzled in the other man's neck. Flint whacked them both again for good measure and because he could. They were out cold and he wanted them to stay that way.

He stepped back and looked at the pile of brawn. He wasn't sure what they had been looking for inside the house, but he knew they wouldn't have found anything more than he already had.

He spent about a minute working out what to do with them. His choices were limited.

He could kill them both easily enough. But that solution presented other problems. For one thing, he wouldn't leave two dead bodies here for Melanie Barnett to find when she returned.

If she didn't come back soon, they'd decompose into a mess she'd never be able to remove from the only home she'd ever owned. She didn't deserve that.

But the only way he could move them while they were unconscious would require a team of horses.

He couldn't bring them around and then push them out under their own steam either. Trevor couldn't walk, and marching these two around in this neighborhood would attract all kinds of the wrong attention.

Body removal was only half the equation. He needed another uninterrupted hour or so here in Charlestown and then time to find Oakwood before Crane found out his mercenaries were done. More time would be even better.

He'd stopped Crane's relentless interference. He still had time to find Oakwood and get her to sign Shaw's contract before the deadline expired. He intended to use the time to finish this job and be done with Crane and Shaw for good.

Finding Laura Oakwood's new contact information in the Barnett house would have made things easier. This was another dead end, but it wasn't the only answer.

He made his choice. Paxton and Trevor were no threat to anyone now. He checked them for weapons. He found two guns and two knives each and left them in place.

He didn't remove the ammunition and empty the chambers. Loaded guns were more likely to get them arrested and neutralized longer than empty ones.

Added to the long list of offenses they'd already committed, they'd be neutralized for a few weeks at least.

He slipped out the back of the Barnett house and locked the door. He left the floodlights unscrewed. He hustled around the garage and through the neighborhood, retracing his steps in the shadows.

When he'd traveled a mile away from the house, he pulled out one of the burner cell phones and dialed 911.

Breathlessly, with urgency, like a frightened eyewitness would, he reported the crime. "There's a home invasion. Two men. They're inside the house. They've got guns. Hurry!"

The operator repeated his words and then asked his name. Twice.

In reply, he ended the call, dismantled the phone, and dropped the pieces into the wet snow as he walked quickly to the west side of Charlestown while the emergency response system did its job.

There was only one hospital in town where Selma Oakwood Prieto could have been treated for sickle cell disease.

All he needed was her current address.

If she'd supplied one, he should be able to find it in the hospital's electronic medical records. He'd try the personal touch first.

Flint lifted his face into the biting wind when an EMS unit and two police cruisers sped past, sirens blaring, headed toward the Barnett house. He grinned. One mission accomplished. Paxton and Trevor would be pissed as hell.

Their boss, Felix Crane, wouldn't be too happy either. Flint would deal with him soon enough.

Local authorities would be looking for the third man in the Barnett home invasion. When Paxton and Trevor regained consciousness, they'd be pressured to name their attacker.

While neither of them saw Flint inside the house, they could make a pretty accurate guess, and they weren't the type to let him go.

Scarlett would be both pissed and pleased. Happy he'd found Oakwood in time, sure. But mad as hell that she hadn't been able to do it herself.

His grin widened.

Any day he could best Scarlett on a level playing field was a good day. It didn't happen very often.

Flint turned up his collar, stuffed his hands into his pockets, and tucked his head deeper into his jacket. Wet snow packed onto his boots as he walked.

The world was blanketed by silence and cold, but he could smell success headed his way.

CHAPTER THIRTY-SIX

CHARLESTOWN GENERAL HOSPITAL WAS located west of the college campus. It was a teaching hospital.

Charlestown College's health services school provided students for nurses and related medical professionals to be trained there.

The hospital wasn't likely to have a large staff of experts for treating sickle cell disease, but whatever its size, the staff would be competent enough for most issues.

Flint located the hospital's main entrance. He hurried uphill along the driveway to the covered valet parking area. As he approached, oversize double glass doors opened wide enough for medical teams pushing gurneys.

Inside, the hospital's gift shop and information center were on the right, admissions on the left. Ten feet beyond admissions, the wide corridor divided into three paths, each leading to one of the facility's separate wings.

He glanced at the posted directional signs on the walls as he moved through the admissions area and veered right, to the east wing, toward the surgery and general admission floors.

Selma Oakwood Prieto had lived with Melanie Barnett for an unknown period of time.

Inside the Barnett house he'd seen candid photos of her taken before age eighteen, but he'd found none for the years between eighteen and now.

Which could mean that she had been treated at Charlestown General as a child.

While she might have been treated here after she reached majority, he'd have limited time to search the records.

Smarter to investigate pediatric records first. Once he located her Canadian SIN, or social insurance number, her medical records would be easier to trace.

He wasn't stopped at the front desk.

He found the elevators and rode with a group to the third floor. When the elevator opened, he walked toward the surgery wing. Surgery was one of the busier sections in any hospital. Visitors were commonplace.

The waiting room was full. Flint claimed one of the vinyl chairs among the families of surgery patients and watched the process.

A young female volunteer manned the desk, answering questions about timing and location of patients for visitors by checking her computer and contacting staff in the operating rooms.

The phone rang occasionally. From time to time, she left the desk to escort families to the recovery room as patients were moved from the operating rooms and shuffled through the various staging areas preparing for discharge or inpatient beds.

When she was away from the desk, it remained unoccupied.

He waited until the volunteer escorted an elderly man who moved slowly, using a walker. She'd be gone at least a few minutes.

He claimed her chair and attacked the keyboard. After applying a few sophisticated hacks to bypass the security walls, he was able to access patient records.

He searched quickly until he found records listed by diagnosis. Sickle cell patients were a small subset of the hospital's total patient database.

When he sorted based on birth year, he found seven patients in the same age bracket as Selma Oakwood Prieto.

Four were males. Three were females. Only one record listed a child with a single parent.

The child's name was Sally Owen. Born in the right year. The mother's name was listed as Leslie Owen. The emergency contact was Melanie Barnett.

Residence address was listed as the Barnett house.

He moved his search to the next level.

From the first record, he located SINs for both Leslie and Sally Owen. He saw treatments listed for Sally through last month. He forced his lips not to smile.

Before he could review anything more, he heard the volunteer walking back toward the waiting room, chatting with an orderly. He shut down his search and moved away from her desk with moments to spare.

He resumed his seat in the waiting room for a bit before he told his seatmate he was headed to the cafeteria and left.

Within three minutes, he was outside again, trudging through the snow.

An EMS unit pulled into the emergency room entrance, and Flint wondered if Paxton and Trevor were inside. But he didn't wait around to find out.

He walked the back streets to the private landing strip where Drake waited with the Pilatus. Drake spooled up the engines and began to prepare his flight plan. "Where are we going? Home?"

"Hang on." Flint opened his laptop and connected to the satellite.

He pulled up a database and plugged in the SIN for Leslie Owen. He did the same for Sally Owen.

Both listed the Barnett home as current residence.

He had a name. He had identification. But he still didn't know where Selma Oakwood was living. Or her mother, Laura.

He knew they were still in the area somewhere because Sally Owen had been treated at Charlestown General Hospital as recently as last month.

Which meant Sally, at least, had to live within driving distance.

He pulled up a map of Charlestown and surrounding areas. Charlestown's northern border opened onto wide prairies, but it was adjacent to smaller towns on three sides.

All three would have seemed like big cities to Laura Oakwood.

The village to the north and the one to the west had populations in the fifteen thousand range. It was both harder and easier to lose oneself in such small towns. Harder because people tended to know each other, to keep tabs on activities, gossip more. Easier because small towns were more likely to be off the grid for electronic surveillance.

All three towns were within driving distance of Charlestown, but one was larger and boasted a small private airport, more businesses to provide jobs, and a few urgent care clinics in case of medical emergencies or ongoing treatment needs.

Which made the town less intimate. Less likely to have nosy neighbors, perhaps.

There was no time to check all three towns and hit Shaw's deadline. One, maybe two, was all he'd be able to fully investigate before his clock ran out.

Drake was ready for takeoff. "Where to?" he asked again.

Flint wasn't the least bit sentimental, but he had to bet Laura Oakwood was, once upon a time.

Her high school sweetheart and the father of her child was Rosalio Prieto. Everyone who loved him, his sister Teresa had said, called him Leo.

Laura Oakwood's best friend and her high school principal said she'd been in love with Leo.

She ran away from home with him.

Made a baby with him.

Kept that baby when she could more easily have taken a different path.

Robbed a convenience store with him.

Killed a woman because of him.

She'd lived in exile for almost thirty years.

All because of Leo.

When faced with a choice like where to live with their child, would Laura Oakwood have broken that pattern?

Unlikely.

In response to Drake's question, Flint said, "Head to Saint Leo, Manitoba."

Saint Leo was the second-largest city in the nearby province of Manitoba, fifty miles east of Charlestown.

The population was seventeen thousand. More than seven percent of those residents were Latin American, which suggested doctors would have at least some familiarity with sickle cell disease at the local clinics, given the disease's prevalence among Hispanics.

And fifty-two percent of the population were females who could be Laura Oakwood or her daughter, Selma.

He'd hunt down every single one of those women if he had to. But he would find Laura Oakwood.

One way or another.

"You're my captain," Drake replied, as he began preparations for takeoff. "It'll be a short flight."

Flint paid no attention to the warning. He was busy searching the census records and tax rolls for the home address of Laura Oakwood, a.k.a. Leslie Owen.

Seconds after Drake touched down at the Saint Leo Executive Airport, Flint found what he'd been searching for. He also found employment records for both Leslie Owen and Sally Owen.

As a kid, he'd have fist pumped the air and shouted, "Yes!" He grinned instead. He encrypted and uploaded the information for Scarlett.

Not long afterward, Drake had the Pilatus on the ground. Flint unbuckled his harness and grabbed his jacket. "I'll be back as soon as I can."

"Reports say weather is deteriorating. We can't stay here too long. It would be better to fly south as soon as we can." Drake frowned. "We'll head back to Houston after this?"

"Maybe." Flint unlatched the exit door and lowered the flight stairs. "I hope."

Drake nodded. "I'll fuel up and prepare. Call me when you're on your way back."

Flint descended the stairs and left Drake with the Pilatus.

What he needed now was a four-wheel-drive vehicle to navigate the snow covered roads.

He spotted a vintage Toyota 4Runner parked in the back of the executive airport lot with less snow covering it than the other vehicles.

Maybe it belonged to a pilot who was now in the air on his way to somewhere else and wouldn't need the SUV for a while.

Less than two minutes later, he was on his way.

CHAPTER THIRTY-SEVEN

SAINT LEO WAS BUTTONED up for the night. Most of the stores had closed an hour ago. Snow fell in tiny, hard flakes that stung his skin and kept him alert.

The woman Flint believed was Laura Oakwood left work at the Saint Leo Urgent Care Clinic and walked along the snow-covered sidewalk, head down against the cold north wind blowing from the mountains through the corridor between the buildings.

She stopped for the automatic doors to open then entered the drugstore. Inside, she threw off her hood and stamped snow off her boots onto the mat.

Until that moment, he hadn't been sure. But this was definitely the woman he'd seen in Melanie Barnett's framed photographs.

Laura Oakwood. It had to be. All the pieces fit.

Across the street, Flint stood inside the limited shelter surrounding the entrance to an office building, closed for the night.

He turned up the collar on his cheap jacket and shrugged deeper into its meager warmth. He stuffed his hands into the pockets and leaned away from the sidewalk.

Through the window across the street, Flint saw the woman select a few items from the store shelves and then approach the pharmacy counter.

She talked to the clerk for a bit. When she turned, she was carrying her purchases in a reusable fabric bag.

She left the store and turned to walk back the way she'd come.

Flint let her gain a block's head start before he followed. The snow covered sidewalks muffled his footsteps. The icy snow seemed attracted to his warm eyeballs. He blinked away the pellet-like stings.

He could have overtaken her at any time, but he hung back.

When she reached the corner, she turned left. He turned the same corner half a minute later. She was a block farther along, hunched over, watching the ground as she forged ahead.

She didn't act like a fugitive.

No effort to obfuscate her route.

No furtive glances, no attempt to disguise herself.

True, the olive-drab down parka enveloped her from head to calf, and heavy boots covered her from calf to toe. But the frigid weather demanded protection.

Hers was an effective disguise, not a purposeful deception.

She trudged through the unshoveled snow to a house whose front door was painted cheerful Chinese red.

At the landing, she scraped the storm door across the snow-covered concrete landing, pushed the front door open, and walked inside. Saint Leo was the kind of town where people didn't lock their doors.

The interior of the house had been dark, but she turned on the lights in the downstairs rooms as she passed through, and yellow ribbons spilled out to sparkle the snow.

The windows in the upstairs rooms remained dark.

The house was a bungalow with a detached garage. The style and the neighborhood suggested circa 1960.

White vinyl siding with black vinyl shutters attached to the sides of the windows that served no useful function.

Flint scanned the house and yard once more, just in case someone else was watching. He saw no one.

The Queen Street house was listed as owner occupied.

The resident's name, listed on the census, tax rolls, and utility bills was Leslie Owen.

The last census report claimed two women lived here. One would be forty-eight years old now and the other, twenty-seven.

Not exactly the right ages for Laura Oakwood and her daughter, Selma. But close enough.

Was this woman Laura Oakwood?

If she was, he could get her signature on Shaw's agreement before the deadline.

Complete the job. Make Scarlett look good.

Get Shaw and Crane off his back.

Go back to his own cases, because the French woman had been patient enough.

But only if the woman was Oakwood.

And only if she signed before the deadline.

Would she do it?

Normally, giving someone a lot of money they hadn't been expecting was an easy gig.

But this was not a normal case.

He glanced around the empty streets. No pedestrians. No running vehicles.

He marched to the front door, walked up the stairs, and turned the doorknob, like a resident would do. He stepped across the threshold and pushed the door closed behind him.

The front entrance opened into a small foyer.

In the right corner was a wooden coat tree. Oakwood's parka was draped from its top hook.

Straight back was the kitchen. The staircase on the right led to the second floor, where the bedrooms probably were. On the left was a living room and, beyond that, a dining room that entered into the kitchen.

The first scent he noticed was the aroma of pine. Probably from a scented candle or a continuous air freshener.

The house seemed quiet except for rustling from the kitchen.

A moment later, he also heard sounds upstairs.

Which meant both women must be home. Maybe Sally Owen had been sleeping in the dark house before her mother came home.

He ducked into the darkened living room, moving quietly on the carpet, hugging the wall. Carefully, he stepped through into the dining room and beyond, until he reached the open doorway to the kitchen.

Laura Oakwood was alone, making dinner. She moved with practiced economy from refrigerator to sink to range, one task to the next. She reached up above the stovetop to press buttons to start the microwave.

She poured two glasses of white wine from an open bottle in the refrigerator. She grabbed both glasses by their stems in one hand and a serving spoon in the other hand and turned toward the kitchen table.

She spotted him. Standing five feet away, inside the open doorway to the dining room. Her eyes widened.

She dropped the serving spoon. It clanged on the vinyl floor, splattering tomato sauce across her shoes. She covered her mouth with her forearm as if to stop herself from screaming.

"It's okay." He stepped into the open kitchen where she could see him better and held up both hands, palms out. "I'm not here to hurt you."

She pressed her forearm tighter to her lips, still holding the wineglasses.

In her world, visitors rang the doorbell and called out when they entered, even when they came to deliver good news.

Surely, this was her first home invasion.

People who had suffered break-ins bought intrusion detection systems after the insult. And kept their doors locked.

He began with a white lie, simply to calm her. "I knocked on the front door, but you didn't hear me. So I let myself in. I didn't mean to alarm you. I'm sorry." He listened to footsteps in the rooms overhead.

"Who's upstairs?"

A small, strangled sound like a whimper escaped from her throat.

"Look, I just want to talk. That's all. I have some good news for you. Seriously good news. Okay?" He waved an open palm toward one of the kitchen chairs. "Can you take a break from cooking for a minute? Let me tell you why I'm here? I don't have a lot of time."

She nodded her head, but her eyes stayed wide as she whimpered again and remained still.

He waved toward the kitchen table, set for dinner for two. She inched forward and pulled the chair away, placed the wineglasses on the table, and sidled onto the hard seat.

She'd left herself plenty of room to bolt. As soon as she sat down, her legs began bouncing, staying warm, ready to run.

"My name is Michael Flint. I'm a special private investigator. I have good news for you." She listened but didn't speak.

He reached into his pocket and pulled out a Scarlett Investigations business card. "This is the woman I'm working with. She represents a company that owes you a lot of money. She's authorized me to pay you."

She didn't pick up the card. But she read it.

When she saw the Houston address, her eyes widened to the size of plums.

She stood up quickly and knocked the chair backward. It clattered to the floor like a sloppy drumbeat, loud enough to overwhelm the small kitchen.

The microwave had finished irradiating the tomato sauce and it beeped, three staccato blasts, as if to punctuate the clamor from the tumbling chair.

He was getting nowhere. Another approach might be more effective. He reached into his pocket and pulled out the Glock. "Pick up the chair and sit down." She didn't move. "Now!"

She seemed frozen to the floor. He kept the gun pointed at her while he uprighted the chair. He grabbed her arm and pulled her in front of the seat. He put his hand on her shoulder and pressed down.

She sat. "Don't move. Understand?" She nodded.

He stood across the table in front of her. "Look at me." She raised her head, eyes open.

"Can you speak?" She nodded. He waved the gun. "What's your name?"

She had to clear her throat three times, but eventually she croaked, "Leslie Owen."

"How long have you lived here in Saint Leo?"

"Seventeen years."

"Where did you move from?"

"Regina."

"And before that?"

She balked. "Why?"

Oh, the hell with it.

"Because if you are the former Laura Oakwood of Wolf Bend, Texas, you're about to be a very wealthy woman. I've got a check with a lot of zeros before the decimal point that belongs to you."

Which was a slight exaggeration, but it seemed like the right thing to say if she needed motivation.

"And if you're not the former Laura Oakwood, I'll leave now and you'll never hear from me again."

The emotions warred on her face.

Extreme terror was the most obvious.

But he saw a twitch of curiosity around the corners of her mouth and something a little like amazement in her eyes.

Still, she didn't claim her inheritance.

"Okay. Obviously, I've got the wrong person. I'm leaving now. Sorry to have bothered you." He grinned to lighten the mood, maybe peel her a little bit off the ceiling. "I'll let myself out."

He backed out of the kitchen into the dining room and when he reached the living room, he turned to leave.

A dozen steps later, he'd reached the foyer.

He stopped.

Oakwood stood in the middle of the small foyer, blocking the front door.

This time, she was the one holding the gun.

CHAPTER THIRTY-EIGHT

LAURA OAKWOOD HAD ASSUMED a perfect shooter's stance. His mind registered that she'd had some training somewhere.

"Make up your mind." He raised his hands in the air and grinned again. "You want me to leave or you don't?"

She didn't smile. Her tone was a cross between a principal's and a prison warden's. "I want to know who you are and why you're here."

"I already told you that, Laura. If you want to hear about it, just say so." He shrugged. "Either way, aren't you tired of living with your bag packed and your fake passport ready? You've been hiding a long time. Nothing lasts forever. It's time to go home."

She frowned, but she didn't lower the gun. "Why would Laura Oakwood come into money now?"

"A lot has happened since you left Texas. Your father died, but you probably know that." He paused. She didn't nod or reply. "His ranch sits on the last big untapped Texas oil field." She waited, her gun steady.

"There's some question about who owns the ranch now, but I guess your mother owned the mineral rights and she left them to you when she died."

He was getting a little tired of holding his hands in the air.

So he lowered them a fraction and she grunted and shoved the gun barrel his way.

He raised his arms again.

"The mineral rights were worthless back then, but they're not worthless now. Our client wants to buy the field outright. He's already bought all the other rights. Yours is the last." He paused and took a breath. "All I need is your signature and you'll be wealthy beyond your wildest dreams."

"How much?" She croaked the question past her tight throat.

He smiled. Now he had her. When they started asking about the amounts, they were already sold.

"Enough to buy whatever you want for the rest of your life. And enough to take care of your daughter forever, too."

She blinked, as if to clear her head. She didn't lower the gun. "What does Laura have to do to get the money?"

"She has to prove to me that she's Laura Oakwood. And she has to sign over her interest in the Juan Garcia Field." He paused, looking for a sign of recognition when he mentioned the name, but he saw none. "After that, my client doesn't care what she does or where she does it. All he wants is to buy her interest and pay her an exceptionally generous fifty million dollars for it."

Her eyes widened and she cocked her head. The number was astonishing. She'd never have expected to see that much money in her lifetime, surely. "And if she doesn't sign or if you can't find her?"

"Then she loses all her rights to the Juan Garcia Field, and she will never be able to get them back." He paused again to be sure she understood. "This is her last chance."

She blinked again and considered that for a moment. "How will she prove her identity to you?"

"Fingerprints and a DNA sample. Just a cheek swab. Nothing more."

She lowered the gun, but she kept a firm grip on it. "Come on into the kitchen." She waved him ahead through the foyer and followed him toward the back.

But before they'd taken many steps, a young woman walked down the stairs. She was the spitting image of the age-progressed photo he had in his pocket of Laura Oakwood at age twenty-seven.

No doubt about it. She had to be Selma Oakwood Prieto.

He'd expected her to look like a younger version of her father's sister, the waitress at the Wolf Bend Diner. Her Aunt Teresa. But she didn't. The only evidence of her father's gene pool was her dark brown eyes, which were fairly common.

"You're Sally Owen, right?" Flint said, watching her descend the stairs.

"That's right. Who are you?" Her voice was midrange and pleasant to the ear.

"Michael Flint." He extended his hand. "Maybe you can join us in the kitchen. What I'm here to discuss with your mom concerns you, too."

She nodded and walked ahead of him to the back of the house.

Laura turned off the meal she'd been cooking and poured coffee. They sat around the kitchen table.

She laid the loaded .38 she'd been pointing at him on the table within her easy reach.

In Flint's experience, women didn't generally threaten visitors at gunpoint.

Canadians are permitted to own handguns, but storage and use are severely restricted.

A loaded handgun lying around, easily accessible, in a private home was not even close to normal.

If her daughter thought the gun situation was the least bit odd, she didn't say so. Which probably meant she knew something about why Laura engaged in such behavior.

"Sally," Laura said, tilting her head in his direction. Her tone was snide. "Mr. Flint says he's here to change our lives."

"Only if you want me to." He shrugged. "Although I have to say, your behavior is pretty strange. Most people would be thrilled."

"What do you mean?" Sally asked.

"I'm an heir hunter. I find people who are entitled to inherit things and make sure they receive them. In your mother's case, it's oil and gas money. And a lot of it."

Sally's brown eyes widened. "From where?"

"Your grandparents owned a ranch in southwest Texas. It's sitting on what they call Juan Garcia Field. Estimates are that your mom's share, over time, may be worth as much as fifty million US dollars."

"Wow!" Sally's eyes grew as big as balloons. Her mouth had formed a large O. "That's a lot of money!"

"Yes, it is."

As if her full two dozen years of disappointment crushed down on her enthusiasm all at once, she narrowed her gaze and cocked her head. "What's the catch?"

"No catch. All she has to do is sign the documents in my pocket selling her rights to my client."

"What happens if she doesn't?"

He shrugged again. "She loses everything."

"How can that be true? It's either hers or it's not, right?" Sally's voice was belligerent now. "You're saying you can just steal it from her if she doesn't agree to sell right this minute?"

"Not steal, exactly. And not me. I'm just the messenger here."

Sally folded her hands around a coffee mug on the table and leaned in. "Tell me how this works."

"Your mother's land has been abandoned for a long time. Too long, in the eyes of the law. People have been trying to find her for quite a while. And the time for searching is over. Her rights are about to be extinguished." He shook his head. "It's now or never."

Sally nodded, head still tilted, still leaning in. "So, the short version is, if she signs, then she's rich. If she doesn't sign, she loses forever?"

"Exactly."

She looked across the table and met Laura's eyes. "Seems like a no-brainer to me, Mom."

"Me, too." Laura must have felt like she was looking through the mirror of time and staring at her younger self. "Except for one thing."

"Which is?"

Laura went quiet. She lowered her eyes. A tear leaked from one of the corners and rolled down her cheek.

"She's worried that if she admits who she really is, the US Marshals will come looking for her." Flint took a quick breath.

This was the tricky part, and he hadn't found the best way to deal with it. "She's worried she'll be extradited to Texas to stand trial for the murder of two people, including your father, during that robbery back in the day. And if she's convicted, she's worried that she'll be executed."

Sally's wide-eyed expression returned, but she didn't appear shocked to hear that her mother was a fugitive. "Surely, after all this time, none of that would happen?"

Flint shrugged. He wasn't a cop. But he had a conscience and healthy respect for justice.

Laura Oakwood had gotten away with murder for way too long. Even if no one reported her to the authorities, if she signed over her rights to the field, a new deed would be recorded.

These days, that information would kick out electronically to a dozen different places in cyberspace.

This was a big oil field. A lot of money at stake.

Enterprising journalists, interested parties, and those who lost out would all have a motive for digging deeper into Laura Oakwood's background.

She'd be back on the radar.

Questions would be asked.

Answers would be found.

It might take a while, but eventually someone would uncover the truth.

A writ of extradition was likely to come knocking.

Sally took a deep breath and held it. After she exhaled, she said quietly, "What are you going to do, Mom?"

Flint could almost see the wheels turning in Laura's head as she tried to find a way out of her dilemma.

Maybe she could work some sort of deal. Maybe she'd find a sympathetic prosecutor. Maybe she'd get the money and run again, hide better, stay gone forever this time.

Regardless, it was long past time for Laura Oakwood to make a choice.

Her face twisted, even as she fought her demons. She must have known for her entire lifetime that the pain would one day arrive.

That day was now.

And the pain was eating her alive.

"We didn't mean to kill anyone that day," Laura said, looking at Sally with a beseeching expression. "We were kids. We were living in that hellhole out on Clovis Ranch with a sick baby we couldn't take care of. Those people were disgusting. They lived like pigs. Always high on something. So filthy. No running water or indoor plumbing. John David had already run out on us. We didn't know what else to do. We just wanted to get away."

Sally bowed her head. She reached across and squeezed her mother's hand.

"We knew Mildred had money in that store. She made her bank deposits on Monday. We went in late Sunday night, when only Oscar would be inside. We didn't know about Oscar and that woman. She was on her knees behind the counter and he was startled when we went in. He pulled a gun and started firing. Leo shot back. Oscar kept shooting. The woman stood up. I fired, too." Laura's face was open.

She stared into the distance. Her tone seemed to come from a faraway time. "When it was over, I was the only one still conscious. I'd been hit, but I wasn't bleeding too much. We'd left the baby behind the store."

She stopped talking for a few moments, as if she was reliving everything in her head. "I grabbed the money bag. I ran to get the baby. We didn't have a car, but there was an old junker in the back. I hotwired it. The thing barely ran. I made it a few miles before it quit. I got out and hoofed it as well as I could with my wound and the baby and the money and the gun."

She paused again. Softly, she said, "Until I collapsed."

"Were you at Bette Maxwell's place by then?" Flint asked gently.

She shook her head. "No. A couple of her kids were out on the road. I don't know why. But they found me and helped me back to Bette's place. I told her I was trying to get away from Clovis Ranch. I didn't tell her what had happened at Mildred's. My wound had stopped bleeding by then, and I'd covered up with one of Leo's big shirts and she didn't seem to notice. She hooked me up with that truck driver. He took me all the way to Denver. Fed me a couple of times. Helped me get food for my baby."

"What happened when you got to Denver?" Sally wanted to know.

Sally was still crying softly and her nose was running, but something like horror and fascination and admiration mixed together shone in her face.

"It took a few days, but I hitched all the way to Canada. I had some cash, so we hid out for a while. I'd patched myself up, but you needed a doctor. I was just a kid myself. I didn't know what else to do. So I went to Aunt Melanie and begged her."

"You made up a story for her, never told her what really happened?" It was a guess, but Flint figured Aunt Melanie wouldn't have helped Laura run forever if she'd known the truth.

She might have tried to sort things out somehow.

Laura shook her head. "I meant to tell her at first. And later, it all seemed to fade. It was almost like all of that happened to another girl. Not to me."

"You can't go back there, Mom. We don't need the money. We're doing fine the way we are."

Sally's plea was refreshing, in a way. She wanted her mother instead of the money.

Flint was surprised. Usually, the people he found wanted the money more than anything else.

Would Laura give up her own life for the money that would provide everything her daughter could ever need or want?

Tough spot to be in.

But Sally needed a lot of expensive medical care, and fifty million dollars was a lot of money to forfeit.

He wanted more details from Oakwood, but he could get them later.

"What are you going to do, Laura?" Flint's tone was easy, but the question was urgent.

She thought about things a bit more and finally opened her mouth to respond, but before she had a chance, the front door burst open and slammed loud and hard against the foyer wall.

A rush of cold air whipped through the hallway and chilled the room.

CHAPTER THIRTY-NINE

TWO MEN RUSHED INSIDE. Pounding footsteps headed toward the kitchen. "Laura Oakwood! Put your hands up!"

Laura picked up her gun and pointed toward the noise rolling in like a tsunami of danger.

The next few movements happened quickly, but Flint seemed to experience them as if he were watching a video one frame at a time.

Flint turned. He peered behind him toward the front door.

He saw two men rushing forward. Guns held steady, as everyone learns in tactical training.

They each carried a 9mm Glock 19 fitted with a suppressor.

Both were dressed in black from head to toe.

Both wore ski masks and gloves.

Both were well muscled, fit, compact.

These were not amateur killers.

Flint dove for Sally, scooped her up, and shoved her into the dining room.

He heard the deafening blast of the first gunshots.

Which had to mean that Laura Oakwood fired first.

The suppressors on the Glocks would have produced quieter explosions.

"Get down! Get down!" Flint pushed Sally behind the sofa, pulled his weapon, and searched for a clear sight line to the shooters.

Several rounds of rapid gunfire, suppressed and not, exploded.

He could see Laura in the kitchen but not the two men in the foyer.

Laura was hit. She'd fallen backward. Landed legs out, braced against the kitchen range. Facing the direction of the incoming firepower.

Bullets continued to fly with deafening constancy, but Flint couldn't see the two shooters clearly enough to hit them.

He ran through the living room to get behind the men in the foyer.

The house was small and the distance short.

Even so, he reached the front foyer as the last gunshots stopped, before he'd fired a single round.

After the repetitive explosions of gunfire, the immediate silence was eerily foreboding. Time returned to its normal pace.

Flint moved cautiously from the foyer straight ahead toward the kitchen and stopped at the open doorway.

He tasted the metallic flavor of blood on the back of his tongue.

The intruders were on the floor lying in gooey red pools. Blood had flowed freely from gunshot wounds on both men while it was forced out by solid heartbeats.

But the flow had already stopped and the blood had begun to thicken.

Flint checked pulses.

Four glassy eyes stared from two masked faces.

Two hearts had stopped pumping.

Blood no longer spurted from the holes in their corded necks. Nothing could be done for either of them.

He stepped over the bodies, avoiding the pools of blood, and moved into the kitchen.

Laura was breathing, ragged inhales and gurgled exhales. Blood was flowing from several wounds in her belly and one in her neck.

"Call 911!" Flint yelled out. "Call 911!"

Sally rushed into the kitchen. She saw her mother on the floor.

She ran over to Laura and held her, crying, rocking them both. "Mommy, Mommy, Mommy."

Flint picked up the house phone and called in the emergency, knowing three things all too well from long experience.

First responders would arrive too late to save Laura Oakwood.

When they arrived, he couldn't be standing there to take the blame.

And whether he stayed or not would make no difference to the dead men or to Laura Oakwood.

When the 911 operator answered, he reported gunfire and injuries and gave the address, then hung up.

"Sally." He touched her shoulder gently.

She looked up into his face, her eyes and nose streaming, sobs overwhelming her, shaking her entire body.

"Emergency paramedics are on the way. We have to go."

Her brain might have registered his words, but her heart did not.

She continued to hold and rock her mother, crying, sobbing, and heartbroken.

In an instant she never saw coming, her world had changed forever.

She'd lived her entire life in the peaceful cocoon of her mother's love.

But unlike her mother, she'd had no prior experience with violent death.

Flint heard the sirens in the distance, coming closer.

When Sally bowed her head and gathered her mother closer, he saw that Laura Oakwood had stopped breathing.

He pulled out his phone and quickly snapped several time and date-stamped photos of the scene.

Two intruders. Dead where Laura had dropped them with two bullets each. Shots placed to kill even as both men wore body armor.

Marksmanship any sniper would be proud to claim.

Sally might not have seen this moment coming, but her mother had.

Laura Oakwood had been an inexperienced teenager when she participated in the Mildred's Corner robbery all those years ago. But somewhere along the line, she'd learned and mastered her deadly aim, preparing for this day.

He pulled up the face masks. He didn't know these men. He snapped quick photos of them and replaced the masks.

He patted them down, one at a time. They carried no identification.

He found a burner phone on the first guy and flipped to the call log.

Several calls had been made over the past two days to a single phone number.

On the second guy, he found another burner with more calls to the same number.

He snapped a quick photo of the call logs and replaced the phones.

He photographed Laura, back against the range, gun still in her hand. And Sally, holding her mother, still sobbing.

Flint noted the time. Laura had died before signing Shaw's contract. The option that would have expired tomorrow at 11:00 a.m. Central Standard Time was effectively over now.

Which meant Crane would be the only winner here. He'd bested Shaw, finally and forever more.

Flint left Sally on the floor with Laura and moved around the bodies to the living room, past the front door, and took the stairs two at a time.

He grabbed Sally's oversize purse off her bed and found her medications and medical supplies and swept them into her purse.

He hustled downstairs and back to the kitchen.

Sally hadn't moved.

Flint reached down and grabbed her arm and lifted her slowly from the floor until she seemed steady on her feet. "Come on. We have to go."

Sally processed his words through her shock, or maybe she simply didn't care, because she didn't resist. She allowed Flint to lead her from the kitchen.

She looked back at her mother as Flint, stepping over the two bodies, guided her through the dining room and living room until they reached the foyer.

He grabbed Laura Oakwood's big parka from the coat tree and held it for Sally to slide into.

Flint hurried through the front door and pulled Sally along with him, headed out into the miserably cold night.

The blast of cold air when they stumbled down the front steps and into the heavy snow seemed to wake her up. She hung back at first but picked up speed as she realized he wasn't slowing down.

He heard a car door slam closed on the other side of the street. Another black-clad man ran full out toward them.

Flint released Sally's arm.

He turned and ran toward the man to create momentum and get the confrontation clear of Sally.

He balled his fist and slammed all his weight behind the punch to the guy's gut.

The man's momentum carried him forward. He bent at the waist and his head battered into Flint's shoulder, knocking Flint back.

But Flint's gut punch had been harder.

The guy fell forward into the snow.

Flint gave him a hard kick and knocked him onto his back.

The guy tugged off his ski mask, which had shifted to cover his eyes, and raised his gun, another Glock 19 fitted with a suppressor.

Flint kicked his elbow hard and heard a sickening crack near the man's shoulder. The man wailed like a wounded animal as he raised the gun to shoot.

Flint kicked his arm again just as he pulled the trigger and redirected the gun barrel.

The gunshot entered the man's head below the chin.

The side of his skull splattered across the white snow like strange red, gray, and beige pop art. His lifeless arm flopped onto his chest, the Glock still gripped in his gloved hand.

Flint glanced around the neighborhood but saw no one running out toward the noise.

The suppressor, and the close proximity of the gun to the guy's body when it fired, muffled the shot, but it hadn't been quiet enough to go unnoticed.

He quickly patted the guy down and found his burner phone.

No time to look at it now.

He shoved the phone into his pocket.

He snapped a couple of quick photos of the guy, even though less than half of his face would be recognizable to anyone now.

Flint heard sirens in the distance. He took four steps toward Sally, grabbed her arm, and pulled her away.

They ran to the corner and back through the residential streets until they reached the stolen SUV.

Flint opened the passenger door and pushed Sally inside. He hopped into the driver's seat, started the engine, swiped at the frosty windshield with his palm to clear a small field of vision, and pulled away from the curb.

He saw the red-and-blue flashing lights behind them in the rearview mirror, but he kept his foot on the gas and the SUV pointed toward the Pilatus.

Flint had removed Paxton and Trevor from play back in Charlestown. But Crane was sure to have been tethered to them in some way.

Crane must have sent the second team to finish the job his first stringers failed to complete. Or maybe these three had been following behind Paxton and Trevor all along.

The timing was crucial.

If Laura Oakwood had signed that consent before she died, Crane's claim to the Juan Garcia Field would have been lost. The matter would have been settled in Shaw's favor, not Crane's.

But Laura hadn't had time to sign.

And the question in Flint's mind right now was whether or not Crane knew that.

Flint's quick assessment of the dead operatives hadn't located body cams. But they might have had exterior surveillance trained on the house giving them audio, or even video, of the events inside.

Maybe they saw and heard Flint's discussion with Laura and her daughter, and that's why they burst into the house when they did.

Because they knew Laura hadn't executed the documents yet and they wanted to make sure she didn't. That set of facts tracked and made sense.

With Laura Oakwood out of the way, Crane would win Juan Garcia Field.

If Crane knew she was dead, he'd be feeling complacent and pleased, to say the least.

But if he knew about Laura's daughter, the situation would become a lot more complicated.

Either way, leaving Sally Owen in that house was not an option. At the very least, she'd have been able to answer questions from Canadian authorities about Flint that he didn't want answered. Bringing her along was the only choice he could make.

He drove the reverse route to the airfield, where Drake waited with the Pilatus fueled up and ready for takeoff.

Sally sat still and quiet in the passenger seat. Almost catatonic. She'd shrugged out of the parka and her clothes were caked with her mother's blood. She had to be cold, even though Flint ran the heat in the 4Runner at full blast.

He parked the SUV in the corner of the lot where he'd found it. He got out, ran around to the other side, opened the passenger door, and pulled Sally outside.

The cold wind blasted her body and seemed to revive her. He grabbed the parka and the purse containing her medical supplies.

She shouted to be heard over the jet's engines. "Where are we going?"

"I'm not sure yet." He led her to the Pilatus and pushed her ahead of him as they both climbed aboard.

Flint pulled up the flight steps and closed and locked the exit door. Drake was ready in the cockpit. "Let's get out of here while we still can."

"Roger that." Drake completed the preflight check as Flint took the copilot's seat. "Where to?"

"Montana. I'll get coordinates, but let's head in that direction." Flint turned to Sally. "Buckle up, okay? We'll be airborne in a few minutes and then we can talk."

She nodded, and her fumbling, blood-covered fingers followed his direction.

Flint fished the third guy's burner phone out of his pocket and punched up the call log.

Four calls. All the same number. Two outgoing, two incoming.

The last one was an hour before the three gunmen broke into the Saint Leo house. It was the same number he'd seen on the others.

Three gunmen. Three phones. All contact directed to a single phone number.

Flint pressed the redial. He heard the phone ring three times at the other end.

"Is it done?" It was a man's voice. One Flint recognized.

"Yes."

"She's dead?"

"Yes."

"Good." He disconnected.

Flint looked down at the phone for a moment. He pressed the button to end the call. He dropped the phone into his pocket.

Drake glanced toward the back of the plane at Sally. "Laura Oakwood?"

"Sally Owen." Flint put his headset on and fastened his harness. "I'll explain later. VFR. No transponder. And let's hustle, okay?"

"Moving as fast as I can here," Drake said, but Flint, scanning for red-and-blue flashing lights and sirens coming toward the Pilatus, barely heard him.

CHAPTER FORTY

SCARLETT HAD SAID THAT Shaw and Crane were meeting at The Peak Club in Montana. Flint had been there before.

It was the kind of secret hideaway he avoided whenever possible because exclusive places peopled by the astonishingly rich were usually pretentious and boring.

He was from Texas, where money ebbed and flowed with the oil business, and which meant he was completely comfortable among the merely wealthy.

Triple-digit millionaires had hired him to hunt one person or another for various reasons, and he preferred to work for them. The stakes were higher, the challenges greater, and the rewards more substantial.

But The Peak Club was in a totally different league. A private ski resort so exclusive that most people, even the ridiculously wealthy ones, had never heard of it.

It was the perfect spot for Shaw and Crane to conclude their final affair away from prying eyes of the merely curious and in front of everyone who might actually care whether one of them bested the other.

The Peak, as it was affectionately called by those few who owned it, was a place where the beyond-imagination rich could ski and mingle with their own kind amid two things they couldn't find anywhere else.

Complete security without the constant presence of bodyguards. Which also guaranteed total privacy without paparazzi.

Security for winter sports on the private powder was provided by former Secret Service agents, as was security for all aspects of the private casino, nightclubs, lodges, and residences.

Every security agent had been vetted by the best security analysts in the world.

The rich loved nothing more than their secrets and would go to great lengths to protect them, as Flint knew only too well.

Membership was bequeathed to one's heirs. When a spot opened up, which had happened rarely in the resort's history, application criteria for replacement members were rigidly enforced. Background checks were updated annually and rivaled those for a commoner seeking to marry an emperor when she is despised by his mother.

The Peak owned its mountain and all facilities.

A limited number of billionaire members were allowed a hundred-year lease for the private residences on its property.

Restaurants were staffed with the world's best culinary artists on a rotating basis. The chefs applied for the opportunity to set the menus for each season.

The on-site medical facilities were operated by a team of well-qualified professionals.

The resort was accessible only by private jet or private helicopter. Which meant the Pilatus was the perfect vehicle for inbound transport.

All of which made it the perfect location for what Flint had in mind. The only thing he needed now was a place to sequester Sally Owen until the right moment.

Flint contacted a former Secret Service agent connected to a recent presidential candidate they'd both served.

Ten minutes later, he received permission to land on the private runway owned by one of the world's reigning monarchs. The monarch's residence had also been made available for Flint and his companions.

Flint's contact provided the landing coordinates, and he passed them along to his pilot.

Drake raised his eyebrows. "Not an easy fly in or out with those mountains this time of year. Lots of snow up there. We should land somewhere else and grab the right helicopter."

Flint stretched his arms straight out, fingers laced together, and rolled his shoulders to ease the cramped muscles. He needed to ice his shoulder, too. "Can you set this jet down on that runway or not?"

"Maybe. Landing at these mountain resorts is always tricky under the best conditions. Depends on weather. Winds are up. It's snowing pretty hard. Forecast is twelve more inches overnight." Drake looked at his charts again for a good long while, thinking things through. "The runway's long enough. We'll need help from the ground."

"Let's do that." Flint noticed the concerned look on Drake's face. "We've got plenty of fuel for an approach. When we get there, if we can't land, I'll come up with a plan B."

Drake nodded.

Flint unlatched his harness and made his way to the back of the Pilatus, where Sally was seated.

She looked a mess. Her clothes were covered in blood. Her brown hair hung in strings. She'd cried away her makeup and smeared the tears around. She'd chewed her lips until they bled, adding to the overall horror show that was her face.

"Sally," he said gently as he knelt in front of her. He placed a calming hand on her forearm. "Are you okay?"

She shook her head. The tears started again. She made little whimpering sounds and twisted her fingers together.

He went back to the head and ran some hot water over a paper towel and collected a fresh hand towel. He grabbed three bottles of water from the galley fridge on the way back.

When he squatted down near her again, he offered her the paper towel. She didn't reach for it, so he used it to clean up her face and remove the dried blood from her hands.

She was still crying, but at least the black mascara streaks and lipstick blobs were gone now. Without makeup, she looked like a teenager.

He opened one of the water bottles and handed it to her.

"Take a sip of this."

She looked at the bottle.

He pressed it into her hand and lifted it to her mouth. "You know you need to stay hydrated. Come on."

He'd already thought of a thousand problems caused by having her on board. Managing her sickle cell disease was only one of them.

But he couldn't fix anything until they landed.

She was mired in confusion and shock. She'd be of little help until she could muster some healthy anger, and she had plenty to be angry about.

He left her with the water and another damp paper towel and returned to the cockpit.

"How long before we get there?" He held out a water bottle to Drake, who took it and drained it greedily.

"Three hours, give or take." Drake tossed the empty plastic bottle aside. "The snow's getting heavier. If we don't land the Pilatus, we won't be able to do this tonight. And no way we'll get a helicopter up to The Peak in this storm. We're gonna need a hotel somewhere. We can try again tomorrow after the weather clears."

"Understood."

Flint had no intention of waiting. Tomorrow would be too late.

It was a paradox of aviation history that a strong desire to reach one's destination could mean never arriving at all. Pushing the safety envelope was not a life-prolonging activity.

Yet arrive tonight they would.

He pulled out his laptop. "I'll figure it out. Let me know if you need assistance."

Two hours and fifty-six minutes later, after a harrowing fight with wind shear and a missed first approach, the Pilatus was safely on the ground.

Drake looked like he'd wrestled a big bull alligator and lost the fight. "I need a drink."

"The house is well stocked. You've earned it. Nice work." Flint lowered the flight stairs.

Wind gusts blew snow and frigid air into the cabin. Sally Owen barely seemed to notice.

He bundled her into the parka, picked her up, and carried her to the courtesy limo waiting on the ground. Drake collected everything else.

They didn't speak during the drive.

The limo pulled up in the driveway at the Fairview Estate on the south edge of The Peak Club property. Drake looked from side to side at the ten-thousand-square-foot home, straining to take it all in.

Three levels, six bedrooms, a bunk room, seven full baths, dining room, ski room, two great rooms—one on the first floor and one on the second—and a kitchen that rivaled a palace.

"What a pleasant little weekend cottage," Drake said drily.

Flint grinned. He had picked Sally up and carried her from the limo to the front door.

Drake punched in the pass code Flint gave him and the door opened after a solid click. They walked inside and Flint put Sally down on the first upholstered seat he saw.

The house was vacant but well lit, warm, and inviting. A fire burned in the monstrous fireplace. Windows filled every wall and provided majestic views of the mountains, even in the dark.

"Does this place come with servants?" Drake's amazement was comical.

He craned his neck to see the almost 360-degree view of the snow-covered mountains that made you feel as if you were standing in the middle of it all instead of warmly cocooned inside.

"Self-service only tonight, I'm afraid. But the bar's over here. Let's get that drink." Flint turned to Sally. "You're welcome to come with us, but you'll need to walk."

She followed behind, still not speaking, seeming almost unaware of her magnificent surroundings.

Flint poured drinks and raised a silent toast to their bumpy but successful landing. As they sipped, in quiet tones he quickly filled Drake in on the attack by the three men at the Owen house.

Drake listened without comment. "Locals are going to figure out soon enough that someone else was there."

Flint nodded. "They won't notice right away, if we're lucky. We might have as much as a couple of days before someone comes knocking."

"Safer to assume they'll find out sooner and get it taken care of." Drake refilled his glass and stood looking at the dramatic snowy mountain view through the ten-foot windows lining the back of the room.

"I'll make the call." Flint nodded and turned to Sally. "We can take you back home tomorrow, if you want to go. But there's nothing you can do for your mom now. And going back will only cause problems for you, both with the police and with the man who employed those guys to kill her."

Her sharp intake of breath surprised him.

"Sally, how much did you know about your mother's past before tonight?"

"Most of it."

It was the first time she'd focused on conversation since the shooting. The scotch was warming her up. Maybe it would cause no harm.

"I know I was born in Texas. My father died during a robbery. My parents needed money to get away from a guy who'd tried to rape Mom." She paused and cleared her throat. "She ran to Canada to protect me. So I could grow up near family and good doctors. You know I have sickle cell disease so I've been sick a lot. That's why Mom became a nurse. So she could take care of me."

Flint nodded. Laura had been fairly honest with her daughter. She'd left out the criminal history and the sordid parts, but maybe a mom couldn't be faulted for that.

"Have you ever been back to Texas? Met your father's family?"

"Mom gave up everything to make sure I had a safe life. A better life than she had." Sally's tears started again. She hung her head and the salty drops landed on her bloody dress. "I would never have jeopardized that."

That version was well framed so that a young girl would feel cherished but was not even close to true.

What Laura Oakwood gave up in Texas was pretty easy to walk away from.

She'd have been tried and convicted and probably executed. But even if her life had been spared, a sentence of life without parole wasn't very appealing either.

Sally would have been an orphan at a much younger age than the orphan she'd become tonight.

Flint kept his tone quiet. "Your mom had a loaded gun in the kitchen of your home. She must have been worried about something."

Sally nodded, head down, rapidly falling tears spotting her dress.

"She worried about everything."

"Then you knew she was a fugitive?" Flint asked.

"She never said that to me, but I figured it must have been something like that."

"Do you want to know what I've found out about her since I took on this case?"

"I'm tired." Sally closed her eyes and took a couple of deep breaths. She didn't say anything for a while. She sipped her drink. "I think I'll get some rest. Maybe you can tell me about it in the morning."

"Whenever you're ready." Flint squeezed her hand.

Sally squeezed back, which he took as a good sign.

He located a guest room with a private bath for her on the west side of the house across from the rooms he and Drake would sleep in.

She went inside and closed the door.

When he returned, Drake had leaned back in one of the club chairs and propped his feet on the coffee table. "You can tell me about her mother, if you want."

Flint grinned. "You've got no need to know."

"Apparently she doesn't either." Drake lifted his drink in Sally's direction.

"They sent over some prepared food and groceries from The Lodge for us. I've got to make a call and get a shower. Then we'll grill a steak," Flint replied.

Drake said, "Good plan. I'm starving."

"Your room is all set up. Second door on the right down that hallway. Make yourself comfortable."

Flint went into his room and closed the door. He pulled out one of the disposable phones he hadn't already used and dialed.

"Scarlett Investigations," she said, distracted as always.

"We've run into a problem."

"Another one?"

"A problem we can't fix."

"What's that?"

"Laura Oakwood is dead." He paused to give her a chance to focus. "And she didn't sign the consent form. She didn't sell her mineral rights to Shaw before she died."

Scarlett didn't say anything for a long time.

He knew she was stunned. He was stunned, too.

Flint had boasted he could find anyone, anywhere. Which had always been true before. He hadn't failed yet.

Never.

And, strictly speaking, he hadn't failed this time either.

He had found Laura Oakwood.

But he hadn't kept her alive.

Not that he'd ever claimed he could prevent murder.

But in this case, the promise was implied, surely.

He'd failed the mission. No question. No point in splitting hairs about how big a failure it was.

"Looks like Crane is the big winner here then. We backed the wrong horse." Scarlett's voice trailed off, weary.

"Not a chance." Flint waited a beat to be sure Scarlett was paying close attention. "Two well-trained operatives took her out. She killed them both before she died. But make no mistake. Crane killed Laura Oakwood *for a business deal*. How depraved is that? Crane did this. And he'll pay for it."

She groaned. "What do you want me to do?"

"Did you find the original option agreement? The one that gives Shaw the field if and when he acquires Oakwood's rights?"

"Not exactly."

"Meaning what?"

"These are private deals, Flint. It's not like I can go down to the registrar and pull up the documents. Shaw never gave me the paperwork. He hired me to find Oakwood and get her consent. That's the job." She paused and softened her tone a bit. "I don't see what relevance any of that has now that she's dead."

Truth was, he didn't know why or if it was relevant.

The option contract was a loose end. It dangled out there like a dynamite fuse.

He had an idea about how to salvage the entire mess, but he didn't want it to blow up in his face, which it might still do.

"Under Texas law, what would happen to Laura Oakwood's rights after death?"

"Depends on a lot of variables. You know that." Scarlett took a breath. "Did she have any rights to begin with? Did she have a will? Did she leave the rights to anybody in her will?"

"We have to assume Laura had rights in that field, since we can't see the option contract. Otherwise, neither Shaw nor Crane would want to find her badly enough to pay my exorbitant fees." He grinned and he thought maybe she did, too. "I don't know if she had a will. I guess we can find that out. But what I believe is that Oakwood's daughter is her only heir. Which should mean she owns Laura's entire interest in the Juan Garcia Field now."

Scarlett's response came slower than he expected. "Maybe."

"I don't think she would have disposed of her mineral rights, because Laura seemed genuinely surprised to hear about the field," Flint said. "She wouldn't have sold or given away something she didn't even know she owned."

"Sometimes people don't know what they're signing away." Scarlett's breath was audible through the cheap phone. She'd been thinking the question through, though. "And you'd have to find the daughter. And get new paperwork and persuade her to sign the rights over. And you've got less than nine hours to do all that. Which is a stretch, Flint. Even for you."

"I'll work on all that. But I need the paperwork for Selma Oakwood Prieto to sign pronto," Flint said. "Can you get the lawyers to whip up whatever magic words we need and deposit new paperwork in my secure server within the next couple of hours?"

"It's late. I'm tired."

"Come on, Scarlett. You're an orphan, just like I am. We know what it's like to have no family, to belong nowhere. And we're both healthy. Imagine if we weren't." He ran his fingers through his hair and closed his eyes a moment. "We can't bring Sally's parents back to life, but that money would make the rest of her life a hell of a lot more comfortable."

"I don't see it working, that's all. Could be time to let this one go." She sounded defeated, which was unusual for Scarlett.

Made Flint wonder what else was going on with her that he didn't know about.

She let out a long breath. "Look, Flint, we've been going balls out on this project since we took it on and we're nowhere. What are you going to do now that's different?"

He felt the heat rising in his face.

"Crane doesn't get to cheat this kid out of her money after killing her mother. Not on my watch." He didn't wait for another objection. He was doing this, with or without Scarlett on board. "Tell me what you've learned about Jeremy Reed. It might impact my plan here."

"Jeremy Reed?" Scarlett paused, as if she was preoccupied with something else, but in a couple of seconds she recovered the fumble. "Right. The squatter."

"Does he have a colorable claim to the Oakwood ranch surface land or not?" Flint held his palm over his eyes to reduce the burning of fatigue.

"Well, first I checked the bio data you gathered. A lot of it was contaminated, but it doesn't take much for analysis." Scarlett began to read off a report of some kind. "Petty crimes as a kid. Mostly unemployed for the past ten years or so. Couple of hospital admissions for substance abuse. Seems like Jeremy Reed is who he claims to be."

"Too bad for him, I guess." Flint sighed. "But good for us. At least he's not one of Crane's kids or someone looking for another way to cash in on Laura's claims. I guess you can send him home. What else?"

"In Texas, as you know, he's got to satisfy the adverse possession statutes to acquire ownership to the ranch land. Those rules are tough." A spot of humor entered her tone. "We have a lot of respect for property ownership out here in the Wild West, Flint."

"Yeah, yeah. And?"

He stood and rolled his shoulders and stretched his cramped muscles, one group at a time. Too much sitting time today on top of the physical exertion. He needed a long, hot shower to loosen up the knots.

"And it looks like Jeremy Reed is no lawyer. He's missed a couple of important steps and he hasn't been squatting long enough. So Oakwood's daughter could kick him out now and she'd be okay, assuming she is her mother's sole heir."

Scarlett paused briefly and he heard her drinking something. Booze, probably. It was that time of night in Houston, too.

"She should do it soon, though. If he doesn't go voluntarily, the back and forth can take a while to get him evicted. It's all the usual legal crap," Scarlett said.

"Got it." He was ready to get moving, but he could feel some sort of vibe coming from her that needed immediate attention. "What else is worrying you?"

Keyboard keys clacked rapidly on her end. "Tell me more about the two men who killed Oakwood."

"Two professionals burst into the house and a third one was waiting outside. The first two shot Laura Oakwood point-blank. She returned the favor." He continued stretching, one muscle at a time now, before he froze up completely. "They're dead and I took care of the third guy. It's a short story."

"The house in Saint Leo, Manitoba. Send me the photos." Her voice was steely now. The tone he recognized from childhood.

The one that meant she wouldn't back down, no matter what he said or did.

"Roger that." He didn't have the extra energy to fight with her tonight, anyway. Save that fight for tomorrow. "You get me the documents for the daughter. I'll send the photos. We'll get this one wrapped up in the morning. I'll be back in Houston by tonight."

Scarlett didn't reply. She was already immersed in something else.

He called his FBI source again and tasked him with taking care of the mess at the Saint Leo house and a few other matters and dropped the cell phone on the bed.

CHAPTER FORTY-ONE

FLINT TURNED ON THE shower and stood under the hot water to ease his exhaustion. He dipped his neck into the heat for at least thirty minutes.

After the shower, he pawed through the owner's fully stocked closet to find après-ski leisurewear he wouldn't be embarrassed to be caught dead in.

He settled for a pair of cords and a sweater owned by a man with deplorable fashion sense but close to Flint's size. He slipped his feet into the guy's lambskin flats and headed for the kitchen.

Drake had also showered and changed. He'd unpacked the food.

Flint fired up the grill and seared two steaks. The meal was ready in fifteen minutes. He opened a bottle of red wine and they carried plates to seats near the fireplace and tucked in.

Drake was as hungry as Flint. They wolfed the food without conversation.

When Flint's plate was clean, he refilled his wineglass and moved to a chair closer to the fire. He leaned back.

A full stomach and a couple of drinks, on top of the hot shower and the long day, relaxed him. He felt his eyelids drooping. His chin dropped to his chest. He floated to the edge of sleep and stayed there awhile.

Until a voice interrupted. He raised his eyelids halfway.

The voice belonged to a visitor, casually dressed in appropriately high-end ski resort wear, including a parka with a Peak Security logo patch on the left sleeve. He was warming his hands by the fire.

Flint didn't know him but recognized the evidence of his Secret Service background.

Drake approached with three crystal snifters filled with warm brandy. Flint opened his eyes and accepted the offering.

"Flint?" The visitor extended his hand. "Kevin Elliott. Sorry I didn't get here sooner. We've got a private party going on up at The Lodge, and this was the first chance I had to get away. Bunch of guys here for their annual strut-your-man-stuff week, you know?"

Elliott shook his head and Flint nodded forgiveness.

Elliott continued, "Anyway, we're notified of arrivals and departures through our air space, and whenever one of the residences is opened, security's supposed to check in with guests. Everything okay here?"

"All good, thanks." Flint nodded again, but he didn't get up. "We've just settled in and had a bite to eat. Anything we should be aware of?"

"Snow's supposed to stop before morning. We've had more than twelve inches in the last twenty-four hours and some iffy weather lately affecting the snowpack. Which means keep an eye out if you're planning any backcountry skiing, snowboarding, or whatever." Elliott sipped the brandy.

Flint pretended not to notice he was drinking on duty.

Elliot said, "Officially, the avalanche condition level is moderate. People don't come to The Peak to stay inside by the fire, so we do what we can to keep the groomed slopes free of hazards. We can't do as much for backcountry. Too much land out there."

Flint nodded again. "Understood."

He didn't expect to be engaging in winter sports. His plan was to get in, get the job done, and get out.

"I have a message for you from one of our members." Elliott shot a questioning gaze from Drake back to Flint, who shrugged.

He knew and trusted Drake. He'd met Elliott three minutes ago. Whatever Elliott had to say, Drake could hear.

Elliott said, "Sebastian Shaw will meet with you tomorrow morning at ten o'clock in The Grille at The Lodge."

The Grille was the private dining room in The Peak Lodge reserved primarily for sensitive business matters. Flint had been there before. Clients generally wanted to book at least one business meeting in The Grille to justify expenses to various tax authorities.

Flint nodded and raised his glass but still didn't drink the brandy.

"Is he expecting you to deliver my reply tonight?"

"Reply? What reply?" Elliott grinned. "He's expecting you to show up."

"Of course he is." Flint curled his lip and Elliott laughed. "You're familiar with him, then."

"You bet." Elliott nodded. "He's got a group going out to the backcountry right after. Snowmobiles and a few snow bikes and skiers in the group, too, I think. So he won't keep you overlong."

"I guess that's something." Flint felt his eyelids scraping his corneas and forced them open.

Elliott drained his glass and set it on the bar. "Anything you need, just give us a call. Security is number one on the speed dial on all the house phones."

Drake said, "I'll walk you out."

Elliott's boots echoed on the slate floors all the way to the front door.

After Drake locked up, he returned to the fire. "Anything I can do to help?"

"Can you watch Sally in the morning until I get back?" Flint said. "Keep her inside the house. If the wrong people find out she's here, things could get ugly."

"I can do that. Tell me what I'm watching for."

"Anybody trying to kill her, mostly."

Drake nodded. "Yeah, that's what I figured."

"This place has a massive garage. Let's see what kind of transportation we've got available." Flint pushed himself out of the deep, comfortable chair.

They found the garage at the opposite side of the house from the covered outdoor deck that flanked the kitchen.

He flipped the lights on inside the cavernous space. He'd seen three roll-up garage doors, two double and one single, when they'd arrived earlier. From the interior, the storage options were more generous than the five-door setup suggested.

Two full-size all-wheel-drive SUVs were parked closest to the entryway. Their candy-apple-red metallic paint sparkled. They'd be blindingly obvious in the snow, which was probably the point.

But most of the roads here were not plowed for driving in the winter.

Beyond the SUVs, winter transportation sat ready to ride. A lineup of six highly polished snowmobiles gleamed. Next to them was a group of motorized snow bikes.

"Nice machines," Drake said in the way a man might admire an attractive woman. "I've read about them, but these are the first dirt-bike-to-snow-bike conversions I've seen. Strange-looking creatures, but I'll bet these puppies scream."

"When I get back in the morning, you should take one out. Give it a go." Flint shrugged. "We'll need to fly out by two, but you'd have time for a quick ride."

"Is it similar to mountain snowmobiles? Or more like a dirt bike? I've ridden plenty of both." Drake was an excellent pilot. Of course he'd be interested in anything with a motor on it.

Flint nodded. "They'll surprise you. They're light and nimble. Agile. More capable than you think for such a small motor, even on fresh powder."

Drake had knelt down to get a better look at the undersides. "This looks like essentially a motorized mountain bike, converted to use for snow, with a track system instead of wheels, right?"

"Pretty much." Flint nodded again. "Be careful, though. They go places many snowmobiles can't and you can get into trouble really fast. You can take them into extreme terrain without even realizing it."

"Got it." Drake stood and dusted his palms together.

He looked beyond the snow bikes deeper into the garage and simply stared.

Flint followed his gaze.

Against the far wall was displayed the equivalent of an entire sporting goods store's snow season inventory. At a quick glance, he noticed several pairs of skis, poles, boots, and outerwear. Snowboards, ice skates, sleds, and various sized hockey sticks.

Cabinetry lined the walls, probably to store more winter sports and safety equipment.

At one end was a set of lockers and benches to use when dressing in the bulkier gear.

"Looks like we can find just about anything we want here." Drake laughed.

Flint merely nodded again. The right equipment was essential in terrain like this. Good to know he had viable options, if he needed any of it.

"I'm turning in, man. I'm dead on my feet. Another long day tomorrow." Flint nodded and threaded his way through the garage toward the house.

"You go ahead." Drake had moved for a closer look at the snow bikes. "I got good shut-eye today while I was waiting around for you."

Flint kept moving until he reached his bed. He fell onto it and didn't stir until seven o'clock.

When he opened his eyes, he had three hours before his meeting with Shaw to get the new documents Scarlett had sent to his secure server, and prepare Sally Owen to execute them.

After that, he'd deal with Crane.

CHAPTER FORTY-TWO

SUNRISE IN THE MOUNTAINS was spectacular during snow season.

Standing by the windows with a steaming mug of coffee, Flint saw the moon in the pale morning sky nestled between the peaks while the highest of nature's skyscrapers was bathed in pink sunlight like a swipe of color applied by an artist's brush.

Fairview Estate had a fully equipped office, too.

He located the new documents on his server, downloaded, printed, and prepared them for Sally's signature.

When he returned to the kitchen, she was already there. She'd showered and pulled her hair back in a ponytail. The clothes she'd picked out made her look elegant.

Flint set up a video recording as Sally identified herself and signed the documents. Flint scanned them and uploaded everything to his secure server and sent a note to Scarlett.

All the paperwork was completed by 9:30 a.m., Houston time. Well before the 11:00 a.m. deadline.

"Do you really think I'll collect fifty million dollars? It seems unbelievable to me that Mom could have been that wealthy all these years. We ate a lot of mac and cheese at our house." Sally had poured more coffee and found eggs in the kitchen.

Flint considered her appetite to be a good sign.

"It's not a sure thing, Sally. Your claim will probably be disputed." She poured another cup of coffee for him, but he felt like he was swimming in caffeine already, so he pushed it aside. "But I'll do everything I can to make sure you get what's rightfully yours."

She patted his shoulder but said nothing more.

He glanced at the clock. Time to meet Shaw.

He bundled into a snowmobile suit, headgear, face mask and eye protection, socks, boots, gloves, and oversize mittens.

He felt like a neon-green *Star Wars* Storm Trooper in the getup, particularly for such a short ride. The gear would keep warm enough for the subzero morning temps, and his quick search through the estate's clothing selection had failed to uncover anything else as effective and less garish.

He raised the smallest of the garage doors and pushed one of the snow bikes outside before starting it up. The engine noise revved through the quiet snow-covered morning like a chainsaw.

At the end of the driveway, he glanced over his shoulder at Fairview Estate now that he could see it in the daylight.

The home's name, unlike everything else about the place, was woefully understated. The views were well beyond fair. Words like *magnificent* and *breathtaking* were inadequate to describe the vista in every direction.

Flint had traveled extensively since he left Bette Maxwell's grubby boarding school in West Texas all those years ago. He'd seen both horrifying and amazing places.

But The Peak occupied one of the most majestic landscapes on the planet. Maybe money couldn't buy love or health or happiness. But it surely could buy access to beautiful places.

He revved the snow bike's engine again and slipped it into gear. The Peak Lodge was only two miles west of Fairview Estate, around a few curves and up the mountainside. The snow bike quickly covered the distance.

When he came around the last corner, The Peak Lodge revealed itself to be a larger and more astonishing version of Fairview Estate. Similar fieldstone-and-timber façades, expansive windows, and a uniquely perfect setting.

The Lodge housed amenities and guest suites, as well as apartments for those members who preferred not to own individual estates.

One lane of the long driveway approaching The Lodge had been plowed for road vehicles. Two lanes were groomed but unplowed, allowing for the use of normal winter daily transportation like snowmobiles and snow bikes.

Flint rode the groomed lane and parked near the entrance, where at least two dozen snow bikes and snowmobiles were already parked.

He made his way into The Lodge and trudged through the open interior toward the private elevator nestled in the stones to the left of the five-story central fireplace.

The lobby bustled with early risers already back from the slopes. Many were dressed in similar Storm Trooper attire.

A party of thirty or so rowdy men was having breakfast in the Elkhorn Cafe. Their raucous voices invaded the lobby, even penetrating the closed elevator until it reached the third floor, where the noise receded.

The Grille was on the fifth floor.

Baz Shaw was waiting at a table by the window wall that overlooked one of the stunning ski slopes.

He was the very picture of a model for an expensive winter vacation catalog for active seniors. His dark hair and darker tan contrasted perfectly with the turquoise shirt that hugged his fit body.

A pot of coffee and two cups rested on the table.

When Flint approached, Shaw did not stand up.

Flint placed his helmet onto a side chair and seated himself across from the magnate. He poured coffee into his cup and took a sip. Good coffee. He'd already consumed two pots this morning. But he'd been summoned here, and he'd be damned if he'd talk first.

He shook his head.

Baz Shaw was a piece of work.

Five full minutes passed before a word was spoken, and it was the waiter who broke the silence.

"Are you gentlemen having breakfast this morning?" He looked first to Shaw, of course.

"I'll have my usual order, Brian. Thanks."

Brian looked at Flint.

"Make that two," Flint said, simply to avoid prolonged discussion.

"Very well, sir."

When the waiter left, Shaw leaned forward, placing both forearms on the table. "Why are you here at The Peak, Flint?"

"I found Laura Oakwood." Flint watched Shaw for his reaction.

He'd told Scarlett that it was Crane's men who killed Laura Oakwood, but he had no reason to share that information with Shaw. *Let him sweat.*

Shaw's eyebrows shot up and his eyes widened. "Is that so?"

"It is."

Truth was, Crane was ruthless and so was Shaw.

Crane would kill to get what he wanted. So would Shaw.

Flint didn't trust either of them.

"Excellent," Shaw said. An expression Flint interpreted as pleasure occupied Shaw's face. "You have her signed consent to sell me the mineral rights, then?"

Flint didn't know what games Crane and Shaw were playing. But he did know they both had hidden agendas. "No. Unfortunately, I don't."

The delight ran away from Shaw's face, leaving no trace. "Katie Scarlett has less than one hour left to deliver what she promised when I gave her this job. She relied on you."

Shaw's tone was as hard as those granite mountains soaring outside and twice as lethal. "If Crane wins the right to buy Garcia Field, I'll ruin you both. Make no mistake, Flint. I'm not gracious in defeat."

Flint smirked. *What a shock.*

He cocked his head and narrowed his gaze.

He had delivered bad news to powerful men before. Some reacted better than others.

Here in The Grille, and in all of The Peak, Baz Shaw was well known and at least feared, if not respected or beloved.

Which meant he was unlikely to have a full-on hissy fit right at the moment.

Flint believed Shaw had been happy to know that he'd found Oakwood. He was pissed now, too.

He'd have had neither reaction if he'd already known that Oakwood was dead.

Maybe Flint and Scarlett were on the right side of this particular fight after all.

The waiter arrived with their two plates. "Anything else I can bring you?"

Shaw cleared his throat, but he kept his glare aimed at Flint. "Thank you, no."

"I'll leave you to it, then. Bon appétit." The waiter withdrew.

Flint pulled out his digital camera, turned it on, and laid it flat in front of Shaw. The photo showed Laura Oakwood, wounded and dying in her kitchen, held in her daughter's arms.

Shaw glanced at the photo. If he knew or cared what it was, he gave no visible sign. He noticed the time and date stamp on the photo and zoomed to read it.

Flint pointed his chin at the photo. "That's Laura Oakwood. She was killed before she could sign over her rights to you. She wanted to sell. She simply didn't have the chance."

Flint picked up his fork and cut off a piece of the Denver omelet and ate it. The food was amazing here. And he was hungry.

Shaw looked at the photo again, then handed the camera back.

Flint flipped to the next photo and slid it across the table.

Shaw glanced at the two dead shooters. "Who are these guys?"

Flint swallowed another bite of omelet and said, "You tell me."

Shaw scowled. "How the hell would I know?"

"Never seen them before?"

"Never." Shaw shoved the camera toward Flint.

Flint swallowed another couple of bites while he let Shaw's curiosity simmer. "That's what I thought."

He didn't show Shaw the third man's photo. Laura Oakwood had killed the two men, but the third death was on Flint. He needed to clean that situation up, not splash the evidence around.

He found one more photo and showed it to Shaw. The photo he took while he was in the Barnett house of Sally Oakwood and her mom on Sally's eighteenth birthday.

"That's Laura Oakwood and her daughter."

Shaw had seen the age-progressed images of Laura Oakwood, and the images of these two women were very close to the computerized versions.

He seemed to understand where Flint was going with this and nodded.

Shaw's features softened a bit. "Can we prove the relationship between them?"

"If we need to." Flint polished off the omelet and lifted a piece of toast with his fingers. "We have DNA. From both parents and from the girl. But there's no question of her status."

"Does Crane know about this?" Shaw continued to look at the photo as if he were mesmerized by something.

"Possibly." Flint wiped the toast crumbs off his mouth with his finger and poured more coffee. "Crane's been spying on Scarlett and me. You, too, probably. We've taken precautions. Eliminated the two land men we knew about. But I didn't know these two were right behind me when I found Oakwood at the Saint Leo house. So we're not sure how much Crane knows or how he's getting his information."

Shaw looked up from the photo. "The Saint Leo house?"

"Long story. And not important right now. I'll deal with Crane." Flint finished chewing the toast. He swallowed it with more coffee. "What I propose is that you accept the daughter's signature on the consent form instead of Laura Oakwood's. We altered the form to show the daughter as the real heir to Garcia Field's mineral rights. She's executed it well within your deadline. And I have the video of her signing the consent. You've got DNA to prove she's Oakwood's kid. You should be good to go."

"Crane won't accept that," Shaw said, shaking his head. "He'll insist the daughter's consent is not sufficient."

"Maybe it is, maybe it isn't." Flint shrugged. "Either way, give her the money and let her move on. Then you two can fight it out."

Shaw frowned. "The legal war will go on forever."

"Highly likely. Like I said, I'll deal with Crane. Our facts are solid and he's the one responsible for killing Laura Oakwood. You'd have her signature on that consent if he'd left her alive. The courts won't let him profit from her murder."

Which could all be true.

Or not.

The final outcome *should* be in Shaw's favor, even if it took a couple of decades to get there.

Flint lowered his voice and Shaw leaned in to hear. "This girl lost her mother because of you and Crane. Her father was already dead. Consider it a test of your character. That amount of money means nothing to you, but it would help her more than you can imagine. Do the right thing here, Shaw."

At last, Shaw began to eat his breakfast, still looking at Sally Oakwood's eighteenth-birthday photo. "Let me run it past my lawyers. I'll let you know."

"And pay Scarlett now. She's worked this thing hard for you. She deserves her fee." Flint collected his camera and pushed away from the table.

He thought for a moment about what he'd do next. Ginger deserved his attention. And the French woman had been more than patient about her painting.

He had one more thing to take care of first. "Where is Crane?"

Shaw looked up briefly before returning to his meal, shoveling it in like a man fueling a coal furnace. "Guys are meeting downstairs in about ten minutes for the annual jackalope hunt."

"Jackalopes?" Flint's eyebrows arched. "Aren't mythical vicious horned rabbits a Wyoming thing?"

"You've got a snow bike, right?" Shaw pushed his chair back and tossed his napkin on the table. He took a last swig of coffee and grinned. "Join us. You'll see how real men hunt jackalopes. Those suckers can weigh up to a hundred and fifty pounds."

Flint frowned but not because of the jackalope crap, which was nothing more than an excuse for a bunch of jackasses to race around in the snow on their big toys making fools of themselves.

The waiter came over with a silver pocket flask and handed it to Shaw. "Bring one for my friend here. Whiskey is the perfect jackalope bait, Flint. Just open the cap and swig and they'll come running at you. Then you shoot them."

Oh, brother.

What Flint preferred was to face Crane privately back in Houston, with law enforcement standing by in the next room.

But he might have a better chance of cornering Crane here.

He waited for the waiter to bring the pocket flask. He slipped it into one of the zippered pockets on his neon-green snowmobile suit.

He collected his helmet and followed Shaw to the hunt.

CHAPTER FORTY-THREE

THE GROUP OF MEN who'd been having breakfast in the Elkhorn Cafe were now milling around the snow machines parked outside.

Snowmobile suits only came in so many color combinations, which meant several of the suits were duplicates. With their full-face helmets on, the individual members of the group were unidentifiable.

The security staff mingled among the members. Elliott noticed him and nodded in Flint's direction.

Shaw slapped him on the back. "My machine is over here. You can follow me out if you want."

He pointed to a gleaming black monster with red-and-yellow accent paint. Shaw's suit and helmet had been designed to match.

The getup reminded Flint of the coral snake Scarlett had executed so long ago.

Flint squinted into the full sunlight. "What's the point of this? It's a snow cross? A race? What?"

"I told you. It's a jackalope hunt. We'll be running together until we get to the clearing around the bend over there on the west side of the ski lifts." He pointed and Flint followed his gaze.

"After that, we'll break up into small groups. It's better not to ride alone through the backcountry. Too many hazards. You need someone to call in your body when you fail, right?" He slapped Flint on the back again and guffawed.

Shaw was cheerful in victory.

Flint wondered how Crane would deal with defeat.

Shaw said, "We're free to hunt for the jackalopes wherever we think they might be. They're vicious creatures. If you see one, shoot it. No questions asked. And we meet up right here after two hours and count our kills for the trophies."

Flint was about to beg off and head back to the Fairview Estate when he saw Felix Crane standing in a group of three at the opposite end of the line of parked snow machines.

One of the men with him was younger and taller. Maybe another member of the security staff or a guide. The third man was the same vintage as Crane and Shaw, so probably another jackalope hunter.

The younger man moved on to the next pair of hunters and kept moving down the line, passing along to the next. He looked to be checking off names. After he finished with each pair, they donned their helmets and mounted the machines to head out.

Flint saw a few of the shiny pocket flasks glinting in the sunlight as the riders started the morning with swigs of whiskey.

"I see Crane over there." He kneaded the back of his neck with his hand.

"Watch yourself." Shaw laid a restraining hand on Flint's shoulder. "Crane's a street fighter. Mean as a grizzly bear. If you corner him, he'll come out swinging."

"Good to know." Flint nodded but kept his gaze on Crane. He'd be easy to lose amid the crowd once they were on the hunt.

Shaw moved toward his own machine, speaking to his friends and slapping backs and waiting to talk to the guide before he mounted and started his engine.

Flint had taken a few steps in Crane's direction when the riders behind him began revving up their engines.

From the other end of the line, Crane turned toward The Lodge. He saw Flint. His steely gaze met Flint's and held. Neither man smiled.

Neither looked away.

Flint threaded his way through the throng toward Crane's position.

When Flint was a dozen machines away, Crane patted his snowmobile suit as if to reassure himself that he'd packed correctly. He slipped into his royal-blue helmet before he turned away and settled himself on his snowmobile. He started the engine.

If Flint kept walking, he wouldn't reach Crane before he took off. Crane would leave him standing in the cold, empty air. He turned instead and hustled back through the crowd.

Flint slipped on his face mask and sunglasses, settled his neon green helmet, and strapped it on. He jumped onto his snow bike.

The younger guy who had been talking to each of the riders never made it all the way back to Flint before he throttled up and moved out.

With some maneuvering, he managed to pull into the shifting lineup six or eight machines behind Crane.

Flint followed the machines in front of him as the orderly pack thundered across the open area to the west, inching closer to Crane's machine whenever he had a chance.

Crane's snowmobile was a bigger, faster, heavier machine than Flint's snow bike. Once they left the groomed ski slope area, Crane revved his engine and broke out of the pack, gaining ground faster than Flint could cover.

He looked back to be sure Flint was following. Crane opened the throttle and lurched ahead again.

Flint saw the clearing where the riders planned to gather before the start of the hunt. Four or five snow bikes and snowmobiles were already there.

Flint slowed as he approached the meeting spot.

Crane blew right past the clearing and raced ahead. He ran full out along a flat valley between two soaring mountains, which was probably a shallow riverbed in summertime. Now the water was frozen and several feet of snow covered the path. It looked like a pristine white ribbon flowing between the peaks.

Crane kept going. The gap between Crane and the others widened.

What the hell was he doing?

Twenty-eight machines had begun this trip back at The Lodge. The drivers were competitors in business and in the hunt. Crane's behavior seemed to spur them to recklessness.

Two machines peeled off and headed up the right slope. Two machines peeled off to the left and headed up the slope on the other side of the valley. Two more throttled up and closed the gap behind Flint.

As the late starters at the end of the line came around the bend and saw the clearing empty of machines, they peeled off in all directions, racing to catch the early riders who jumped the start.

Whatever the prizes were for winning this crazy jackalope hunt, they were desirable enough to launch a dangerous race to the finish.

Crane stayed in the lead.

He'd been the first to break away from the pack and he held the pole position.

Flint leaned in to reduce wind resistance as much as possible and followed, both hands on the handlebars, weaving through the hazards.

At the beginning, when all the machines had been traveling together, their roaring engines had surrounded the pack like a prison of vibrating cacophony.

The only engine Flint felt now was his own smaller one. His snow bike weighed probably three hundred pounds. But it was puny in comparison to Crane's, which was at least twice as heavy and three times as powerful.

Flint's snow bike was nimble, agile. He could run through terrain too rough for the bigger snowmobiles, closing the distance to Crane and leaving the others behind.

But travel speeds were uneven. Flint burst through the powder, throwing snow wash on either side of his bike like giant white waves. The engine bogged and lurched repeatedly. His forearms and biceps were already feeling the fatigue and his sore shoulder was complaining.

Crane's snowmobile reached a long, flat stretch. He opened the throttle again and vaulted ahead.

Flint followed behind him, moving faster and faster, deeper into the bitterly cold, majestic backcountry.

Flint looked down at the GPS on his customized instrument panel. He'd lost the starting point beacon. He quickly took stock of his surroundings.

He'd been traveling due west along the winding riverbed. The Peak was behind him somewhere. East.

But how far? He hadn't checked the starting odometer.

He didn't have a satellite phone or radio with him to call for help if he needed it.

It was cold as hell out here.

Continuing to chase Crane might be an error in judgment.

He slowed his snow bike to a crawl.

He didn't have to keep going. He could find Crane again. He could find anybody.

At first, Crane kept going full throttle into the wind. But Flint expected him to circle back, and after a few minutes, he did.

Crane pulled his huge snowmobile within twenty feet of Flint's snow bike and shut off the engine. Flint shut his down, too.

Crane removed his helmet. Flint did the same.

The first sensation Flint noticed was the bitter cold wind against the slivers of skin exposed by his face mask and goggles.

The second thing he noticed was the quiet. Without the revving engines, the sun-drenched, snow-covered world was like a vibrantly beautiful silent film.

He heard no running water, of course. Everything was frozen solid.

No birdcalls or human noises of any kind reached his ears at first.

The two men were totally alone.

"Can't keep up, Flint? Is that the problem?" Crane wore a face mask and sunglasses, too. Only his voice identified him in that suit. "Trying to join in with the big boys and falling short? How many jackalopes have you bagged today?"

"None yet," Flint answered, keeping his gaze steady. "But the day is young."

Crane's face mask revealed only his mouth and nose. Every remaining inch of him was covered by gear.

He threw his leg over the snowmobile and walked a couple of feet and glanced up at the sky. "Where is the Oakwood consent form?"

"You know I don't have it."

Crane smiled. "You know what time it is?"

Flint glanced down at the custom instrument panel on the snow bike: 12:45, mountain time. Quarter to two in the afternoon in Houston.

"You're done, Flint. You're out of time. You've failed." Crane pulled off his heavy mittens, revealing two gloved hands.

He reached into one of his pockets and pulled out a lighter and a cigar he'd been puffing on earlier in the day. After a couple of puffs, he had the cigar going well enough. "I knew you couldn't do it."

"You weren't *that* confident." Flint heard the roaring engines of snow machines on the slopes above and to his right.

The noise assuaged his concerns about being lost. He could follow the noise and find the others if he couldn't find his way out.

Flint said, "If you had been, you wouldn't have sent those guys to kill Laura Oakwood."

"Every good businessman carries insurance." Crane grinned and lifted his shoulders in what might have been a shrug if he weren't so heavily weighted down by the suit.

"You know I can't let that go, Crane."

Flint had moved his Glock into the small storage compartment of the snow bike. He could reach it easily enough. The extreme cold shouldn't impact its stopping power as long as he kept it dry.

"The FBI is on the way to pick you up when we get back to The Lodge. You're the one who's out of time."

Crane's tone was dismissive. "What exactly do you think you can do? You've got no proof. Nor will you ever have."

Gone was the friendly fellow who offered to pay Flint to stand down and let him run out Shaw's time clock on the Juan Garcia Field.

"I was right here yesterday when Oakwood was killed. I've got dozens of witnesses. Case closed," Crane said, with the sort of finality he used to win every day.

"You should have thought of that before you answered that burner phone last night," Flint said, even though Crane might be right.

He'd recognized Crane's voice when he called the number on the burner phone. But he couldn't testify without explaining where he got the phone and how that third guy ended up dead.

The FBI would need solid evidence tying Crane to the killers, and Flint didn't have it. Not yet.

Crane's eyes were hidden behind the sunglasses. If he was bothered about the burner phone, he didn't show it.

"I'm leaving the country for a while. Now that Garcia Field is mine, I've no need to stay here. My helicopter is picking me up at the flat spot around that next bend." Crane pointed the stogie farther west on the riverbed trail. "I won't be going back to The Peak today. If you keep following me, you'll run out of gas in that little tank and you'll freeze to death out here. Turn back now while you still can."

The snowmobiles running higher up the left slope were louder now. Maybe a dozen or more seemed to be running in circles or something.

Flint heard rhythmic gunshots, like target practice.

Had they found the jackalopes? And what the hell were jackalopes, anyway?

"Don't worry, Flint." Crane pulled an H&K pistol from one of his pockets and shot twice into the air. Two quick shots sounded from above on the right, followed by two quick shots from the left slopes.

The jackalope hunters were responding to each other.

Crane grinned. "Gunshots don't really start avalanches except in the movies. They're good for fixing our locations, though."

"Laura Oakwood and Leo Prieto had a daughter, Crane. She's her mother's sole heir. Whatever rights Laura had to Juan Garcia Field now rest with the girl."

Crane showed no surprise about the daughter. "Doesn't matter. It's over. The field is mine."

"That will be for a court to decide. Maybe it'll get worked out sometime before the next oil boom. If you're lucky."

Crane walked back to his snowmobile and lifted his helmet. He looked directly into Flint's eyes. "Back off, Flint. This is the last time I'll give you a pass."

Flint moved to open the storage box. He saw his Glock resting there, but he couldn't pick it up wearing the heavy mittens and Crane could easily shoot him before he pulled the mittens off.

The unmistakable sound of helicopter blades filled the valley. A Sikorsky, probably. Arriving from the south. Headed toward Crane's pickup area.

"Why didn't you kill me already? You've had several chances," Flint said.

He had been curious about this from the beginning. From the very first day, when Paxton and Trevor didn't simply shoot him and get him out of the way when they had every chance to do so.

"Why not do things the easy way, Crane? Why put us through all of this?"

Crane took a few more puffs on the cigar until glowing red embers traveled up the brown tobacco. Then he spiked the cigar aside, hot embers down. It melted the fluffy white powder and slid about two inches deep before it stopped, a turd in the snow.

"I didn't kill you because I knew your mother," Crane said.

Flint frowned, confused. He heard more snow machines running in the background. Above, below, and behind. "What does Bette Maxwell have to do with this?"

"Your real mother." Crane shook his head as if Flint's ignorance were beyond his ken.

He put the gun down and used both hands to cover his full head and face with the helmet again.

Flint used the moment to slip his mittens off and grab the Glock.

Crane's helmet restricted his vision. When he moved his head to collect his mittens, he saw the Glock pointed straight at him. He barely paused. He lifted his H&K, aimed, and fired all in one fluid motion.

The shot was awkward. It ran high and wide.

Reflexively, Flint shot back. The round penetrated Crane's snowmobile suit in the area of his right torso, but Crane barely flinched.

Instead, he mounted the snowmobile and started the engine. He raised the pistol and aimed. Flint ducked as Crane shot again. Flint returned fire. His second shot hit Crane in the back but didn't stop him.

Crane slumped to the left in his seat. He revved the throttle and the powerful snowmobile jumped away, traveling hard in the direction they'd been heading before. Toward the Sikorsky's landing spot. The distance between them widened.

He knew my mother?

Flint dropped the Glock into the box and latched it. He strapped his helmet in place and pulled on his mitten. He watched Crane's retreating back as he rapidly restarted his snow bike.

Flint heard a massive *whumpfh*!

Was that Crane's engine acting up?

Had Flint caught a break here?

He listened again.

Everything paused. Even the cold wind, ever present since he'd arrived at the airport last night, seemed to inhale.

After that, everything happened way too fast.

He felt a giant, percussive shake followed by a roaring rumble.

Flint looked far up the mountain. All he could see was a wall of snow tumbling down the mountainside, gaining ground, growing larger, consuming the entire slope, running toward Crane, toward Flint with ever-increasing, overwhelming, frightening speed.

He screamed, "Avalanche!"

But he couldn't even hear himself.

No one else would hear him either.

He goosed the snow bike's throttle.

He held his breath as he turned 180 degrees, throwing up a rooster tail of snow, and headed back the way he'd come.

He traveled along the riverbed with the throttle wide open, moving toward the east side of the massive avalanche.

The wall of snow rushed faster, wider, picking up speed and volume and noise loud enough to penetrate his helmet and louder than the straining engine.

He'd traveled less than fifty feet before the avalanche overcame him.

He released his grip on the snow bike and started battling in a convulsive, thrashing way, swimming upward through the rushing snow and debris.

He paddled a frantic backstroke, trying to move the bulky snowmobile suit up through the heavy, rapidly tumbling wall of snow.

He kept swinging his arms, kicking his feet.

The heavy suit surrounded him.

What had been fresh powder snow now felt like concrete, and he was flailing through it.

He inhaled and held a deep breath and pushed one arm above his head and kept the other near his face and flailed as hard as he could.

His struggle was all for naught.

In moments, he was surrounded on all sides by dense, hard-packed snow debris.

Buried alive.

The energy of the avalanche caused the powder to melt, and it refroze again the instant the avalanche stopped.

He couldn't move.

Inside his helmet, he somehow had a pocket of air. He was lucky. He could breathe. At least for a while.

He didn't know how deeply he'd been buried. He could see daylight through the snow, which meant he wasn't more than about six feet from the surface, he guessed.

He heard nothing but silence, which could mean that he was buried too deep to hear anything inside his face mask and helmet.

Or it could simply mean there was no sound to hear.

The snowmobile suit might save him.

The suit should keep him warm enough to prevent a quick death by hypothermia, which was good.

Even better, his avalanche beacon and Recco transponder were nestled in a special pocket of his suit.

He'd seen them there when he dressed this morning. He remembered thinking he wouldn't need them for a quick run to The Lodge and back, but they were part of the borrowed gear.

He should have grabbed the Avalung when he was collecting gear this morning. But he hadn't.

Without the Avalung device, which he might not have been wearing anyway, all he had was an air pocket.

His breathing would fill the pocket with carbon dioxide soon enough.

As his oxygen supply dwindled, he'd become confused and then lose consciousness.

Under the circumstances, he figured rescuers had about thirty minutes, thirty-five max, to find him and dig him out before he suffocated.

What about Crane?

His machine was bigger, heavier, faster than Flint's snow bike

He might have made it all the way to the western edge of the avalanche and escaped. He might have reached the Sikorsky. He could be flying overhead now, puffing a new cigar, having the last laugh.

If he made it out, Flint would find Crane again. Make him pay for killing Laura Oakwood.

Flint could find anyone. Anywhere. No one could disappear forever.

To pass the time, he focused on shallow breathing and thought about how he'd find Crane. Where he'd look. What might entice Crane to return to FBI jurisdiction.

He thought about the French woman and her painting. He'd told her where the painting was hidden. Scotland. If he didn't make it back, she could ask Scarlett to collect it.

Ginger. He didn't allow his mind to go there. Mainly because Ginger wouldn't miss him much. She was a good woman and he liked her. But he didn't imagine that she felt any more for him than he felt for her.

He thought about Maddy Scarlett's sixth birthday party on Saturday. She'd pulled his thumb back and held it painfully against his wrist until he'd promised to come. Until he'd also promised her a special present. Maybe her mom would cover his butt on that one, too, if he missed the party.

He grinned. The kid was adorable, exactly like her mother. He saw her wild black hair and her freckled face and those flashing eyes.

Exactly the way he remembered Katie Scarlett the first time he'd seen her in Bette Maxwell's dusty schoolyard. If he missed Maddy's party or failed to deliver the awesome present, she'd hold that grudge forever.

He felt tired. He closed his eyes.

How long had he been buried? Too long, surely.

Despite the likelihood that he would die here, entombed by the snow, what kept running through his mind until he passed out, like a ticker on the bottom of a television screen, was Crane's final taunt.

I knew your mother.

CHAPTER FORTY-FOUR

Houston, Texas
Four days later

BY THE TIME FLINT arrived at Maddy's birthday party, the event was in full swing. Thirty screaming kids and their parents were scattered around the house and grounds. It was a perfect spring afternoon in Houston.

Not too hot.

Blessedly, no snow. Flint didn't want to see so much as a snowy Christmas card again for at least a decade.

He was sore all over, but the neon snowsuit had operated as designed and protected him from serious injury during the avalanche.

Bottom line: his body had felt worse, but not in a very long time.

He made his way through the throng inside the house, snagged a beer in the kitchen, and joined the group on the patio.

Drake raised his soda bottle in a silent toast from the far corner. Flint nodded.

Maddy had invited Sebastian Shaw because she'd invited everyone she had ever met, even strangers in the grocery store.

Shaw didn't attend, but he sent a magician. The next David Copperfield everyone said, straight from one of the Las Vegas hotels, who currently held the entire party crowd enthralled.

The guest of honor had a front-row seat and she watched with eyes as big as her party balloons.

Scarlett joined Flint in the back of the room. They stood watching the magician create a rose from a handkerchief then turn it into a napkin and set it on fire. As the fire burned down from the top to the magician's hand and ended in a poof of smoke, a real red rose, live and beautiful, magically appeared in the empty air and everyone applauded.

"He's sexy as hell, too, don't you think?" Scarlett said.

Flint shrugged. "Not my type, thanks."

She grinned. "Where is Ginger, anyway?"

"Meeting me in Edinburgh tomorrow, actually. So I can't stay long." He sipped the beer.

He planned to end things with Ginger, but he didn't tell Scarlett that. He didn't want to listen to any speeches.

Flint asked, "Have you had a chance to handle the cleanup we discussed?"

"We returned Sally Owen to her Aunt Melanie's home in Charlestown, along with a sizable bank balance, yes. She didn't want to go back to her mother's house, and I don't blame her."

"Did you find out who those three men were?"

"Yes, well, about that." Scarlett cleared her throat. Her gaze stayed on the magician. "I already knew who they were. They were freelance guys on my team, unfortunately. I sent them up there when we were still tracking down the hospital connections. What I didn't count on was Crane intercepting and buying them out from under me."

Flint frowned. "There seems to have been too much of that going on in this case, Scarlett."

"Point taken." She closed her eyes for a moment. "I'd known those guys awhile. They'd worked with me before. But Crane offered them five million each for a single day's work. All they were supposed to do was stop you from getting Oakwood's signature, and I guess the immediate cash in hand was more than they could resist."

They stood quietly for a moment.

She watched the magician perform a card trick that delighted the children. "I don't think they would have killed her if she hadn't shot first, though."

What she meant, of course, was that she hoped she hadn't misjudged them so badly. She'd been wrong. A bitter pill for Scarlett to swallow.

Flint preferred to work alone. The betrayals by four different operatives handpicked by both Drake and Scarlett in this case were only four of the reasons why.

"We still need to staff up, so we have a deeper bench. You know that's why I added Carlos Gaspar to our team," Scarlett said. "Gaspar's one of the best operatives we have on the payroll now. You've worked with him. I'm sure you agree."

"I do, actually. Solid decision," Flint nodded. "His former partner, Kim Otto, isn't all that thrilled that we hired him away from her, though."

Scarlett shrugged. "The FBI has plenty of agents. They'll give her a solid replacement. Eventually. Until they do, Gaspar's still consulting with her."

Flint changed the subject. "Any trouble getting Jeremy Reed evicted from the Oakwood ranch?"

"We're working on it." She paused again. "And before you ask, we followed up on that truck driver, Manning. He's exactly what he claimed to be. Shaw made a contribution to his Road Warriors, as you promised."

"Good to know." Flint finished off his beer and tossed the empty bottle in the closest trash can. "Tell Maddy happy birthday for me. Her present is inside with the others. I'll stop in to see her one day soon when things are a little less hectic. Right now, I've got a painting to retrieve, and Ginger's waiting."

"I'll tell her, but she'll be annoyed with you. What's the present?"

"That's between Maddy and me." He grinned.

Maddy had asked for a puppy. He'd planned to clear it with her mother first before he bought the little schnauzer she'd picked out.

Until he'd spent twenty-seven minutes buried alive and decided that making a six-year-old happy was more important than keeping her mother off the ceiling.

"You don't want to leave her gift inside too long."

Scarlett frowned, but she didn't push. "Shaw has deposited our fee in my account. Shall I transfer your share to the Caymans as usual?"

"Works for me. As soon as I finish with the French woman's painting, I may take a little vacation."

"You always were lazy, Flint," Scarlett said. But her smile softened the insult, and he gave her a hug before he left.

He nodded toward Drake, who followed him out to the SUV at the curb.

Drake drove the Navigator to the private airport and spooled up a newer Sikorsky than the one Phillips had crashed in the middle of that Texas field.

Not quite as new as the one that had airlifted Flint and twenty-six other survivors out of the Montana mountains after the avalanche, though. Their snowsuits had beacons in them.

Almost everyone was located and rescued, including Flint. He'd been floating toward unconsciousness when they dug him out and revived him.

He preferred not to think about how close he'd come to death that day.

Indeed, there had been only one casualty, after all. Which was something close to a miracle, they said.

Flint sat alone with his thoughts during the short flight.

They still hadn't found Felix Crane's body, and they probably wouldn't until the snow melted.

Crane had been hit by the middle of the avalanche while he was riding along the riverbed. An avalanche is always strongest in the middle. That's where the most and the heaviest snow debris falls.

The rescue teams found Crane's beacon inside his snowmobile instead of his suit. Friends said he always removed it to make room for his cigars.

But after digging for more than four hours, and darkness falling all around, they had no choice but to give up that night. They'd been back twice more but hadn't found so much as a mitten so far.

When authorities found Crane's body when the snow melted, would his cause of death be suffocation or gunshot wound? Would manner of death be ruled accidental or homicide?

Flint had shot Crane twice. Maybe one of those wounds had prevented him from escaping the avalanche.

Or maybe, when the avalanche hit him, he was already dead.

With Crane out of the way and the Juan Garcia Field within his command, Sebastian Shaw was now the undisputed king of Texas oil. The richest and most powerful man in Texas.

Crane had been his only serious competition, the one person who kept him in check.

With Crane gone, Shaw was now free to flex his muscles in all sorts of unsavory ways. Even Texas wouldn't be big enough for his megalomania.

With any luck, Flint would never see him again.

CHAPTER FORTY-FIVE

DRAKE FLEW THE SIKORSKY expertly. Flint watched the dry Texas cattle country spread out below.

The flight to Bette Maxwell's Lazy M Ranch was short. They passed over the truck stop at Mildred's Corner, which was busy as usual. Flint hoped Steve Tuttle was fully recovered and back to work.

Bette had left him a voicemail message Monday night, while he was flying from Saint Leo to The Peak. She wanted to see him. She'd found out something more about his mother. Something odd and important, she said. She wanted to tell him about it in person.

Bette asked him to come out today.

But he hadn't retrieved the message until yesterday.

If not for Crane's cryptic comment about knowing Flint's mother, he might have put off the visit until he returned from Scotland. Crane had made him more curious about his mother than he had been before.

And Bette wanted him to know something she felt was important. He altered his plans. He'd check in with Bette now and deal with whatever needed to be handled when he came back.

A few minutes more and the Lazy M's rusty archway came into view. The ranch seemed as dreary and decrepit as it had when he was here last week. He didn't want to make a habit of visiting this place too often.

Drake set the Sikorsky down in the front yard. "Shut her down?"

"We won't be here that long. I've got a plane to catch." Flint unfastened his harness and climbed out. The noise of the Sikorsky's rotor wash surrounded him and the entire building.

Bette was not seated on the porch, drinking sweet tea, shelling more peas. Flint hopped up the steps, crossed the porch, and knocked hard on the crooked screen door.

He reset the screen on its hinges and turned the knob to open the entry door and walked inside, calling, "Bette? It's Michael." No response.

He walked farther into the house. The air inside was warm and stale.

"Bette? It's Michael. Where are you?"

He called out as he walked down the hallway in the direction he remembered toward her bedroom. The doors on either side of the corridor were open and the furnished rooms were unoccupied.

When he reached the door to the last bedroom on the right, he walked through.

Bette's bedroom was vacant, like all the others. Her bed was made. Her bathroom was clean.

He walked back to the kitchen. The room was tidy. No signs of any activity going on here today. No tea, no cookies, nothing in the sink. The violets in their pots on the windowsill looked wilted, as if they hadn't been watered in a few days.

Why would Bette ask him to come here and then not be home? He shook his head. He looked around the room one more time.

He noticed a folded newspaper on the table.

He picked up the newspaper and read the death notice beside a small black-and-white photo of Bette.

MAXWELL, Bette Anne died Tuesday. She was born at the Lazy M Ranch on August 7, 1949. Visitation on Thursday from 5–6:30 and funeral following at Texas Memorial Gardens.

Flint read the notice three times. Nothing about cause or manner of death. No next of kin. Nothing about her many years of helping children here at the Lazy M boarding school. A short, unadorned statement of plain facts.

Bette would have appreciated that. He wondered if she'd written the obituary herself.

He stared at the notice a bit longer. The funeral was two days ago.

There was nothing more he could do here.

"Rest in peace, Bette. I love you and I'm a better man today because of you," Flint said aloud to the empty home.

He put his sunglasses on and walked back to the Sikorsky.

He looked around one last time at the only childhood home he'd ever known. Because heir hunting was his business, he wondered briefly who would inherit Bette's property.

He climbed aboard and fastened his harness in the copilot's seat. The big Sikorsky lifted off.

When they set down on the helipad at George Bush Intercontinental Airport, Drake said, "Let me know when you're coming back from Edinburgh. I'll be here."

Flint climbed out of the copilot's seat and clasped his palm on Drake's shoulder. "Will do."

He left the Sikorsky and headed into the terminal.

AUTHOR'S NOTE

EVERY NEW BOOK BEGINS with a spark that leads to an idea I can turn into an exciting story. In the case of *Blood Trails*, the idea was sparked by a friend's real-life experience.

Who doesn't dream of receiving a windfall from out of the blue? Well, that's what happened to my friend a few years ago.

She'd been contacted by a land man whose job was to locate heirs to certain Oklahoma mineral rights. A legitimate land man is usually an independent contractor who bridges the gap between people who own oil and gas rights and oil companies who want to buy them. My friend said she had never lived in Oklahoma, owned property there, or been related to anyone who did. The land man assured her otherwise.

Frankly, she thought the whole thing was a scam.

She was wrong.

It turned out that her long-deceased grandfather, a man she'd never met, had owned what were worthless mineral rights sixty years ago. With the advent of new mining technologies and changes to drilling laws, the mineral rights became valuable. But the rights had become fragmented over time and his heirs had "disappeared" from the property indexes and scattered across the country. The land man located the heirs and facilitated the transfer of mineral rights to an oil company.

Eventually, substantial royalties that had been accumulating were paid out to my friend, her sister, and her son. They will continue to receive royalties for years into the future. What a happy ending!

Thus my research for *Blood Trails* began. What I learned along the way forms the foundation for this story and my new series featuring Michael Flint.

A real-life heir hunter is a forensic genealogist, someone who researches ancestry by means of standard records and more, for profit. It was the "and more, for profit" piece that I've used to create the Michael Flint novels. The "and more, for profit" opens all sorts of story possibilities, doesn't it? My writer's mind went to work, furiously plotting.

For *Blood Trails*, my research revealed that billions of dollars in unpaid oil and gas royalties rest in state coffers. That money will become the property of the states if the rightful owners do not claim it. Those rightful owners often don't know the money exists. Many states have dormant mineral rights laws that provide a process for finding missing heirs and settling their claims. Land men attempt to find those owners and collect a finder's fee when they succeed.

Like my friend, we could all be unlocated heirs. Who knew?

ACKNOWLEDGMENTS

EVERY BOOK IS CREATED with the help of experts, readers, editors, and friends. This one is no exception. My undying appreciation goes to readers who believed in this project and helped me bring it to you.

Michael Flint would not exist in his current form without the support of my friends who call themselves Capristers. For weeks, they helped me search for precisely the right name and had a lot of fun doing it. Capristers are the best readers in the world. I love you guys!

—Diane Capri

ABOUT THE AUTHOR

Diane Capri is an award-winning *New York Times*, *USA Today*, and worldwide bestselling author. She's a recovering lawyer and snowbird who divides her time between Florida and Michigan. An active member of Mystery Writers of America, Author's Guild, International Thriller Writers, Alliance of Independent Authors, Novelists, Inc., and Sisters in Crime, she loves to hear from readers. She is hard at work on her next novel.

Please connect with her online:
http://www.DianeCapri.com
Twitter: http://twitter.com/@DianeCapri
Facebook: http://www.facebook.com/Diane.Capri1
http://www.facebook.com/DianeCapriBooks

Made in the USA
Las Vegas, NV
12 June 2022

50112514R00198